CHANGING THE ODDS

A JACK SHEPHERD THRILLER

Jeff Dowson

Published in 2015 by
Oak Tree Press
www.oaktreepress.co.uk

Oak Tree Press is an imprint of
Andrews UK Limited
www.andrewsuk.com

Cover Design by Fenris Oswin

For Mary... always

Thanks to…

All the Staff and Volunteers in Bristol Night Shelters and Drop In Centres, for the unsung work they do and for their advice on making this story truthful.

Doctor Bob Price, for his medical guidance and for being a friend for more years than either of us wish to count.

Alan Brown, for leading me through the Mendip woods and for valuable lessons on how to treat the power of guns.

Caroline Montgomery and everyone at Rupert Crew who told me when my story-telling was foundering, and who gave me encouragement when it was working.

CHANGING THE ODDS

A JACK SHEPHERD THRILLER

Chapter One

The woman I hit turning the car into the lane behind my house, died three quarters of an hour into April Fools' Day.

"Mr Shepherd..."

I was leaning forwards in the blue plastic chair, elbows on my knees, staring down at the threadbare carpet in the A&E waiting room. I sat up straight, lifted my head and looked into the face of the man standing in front of me.

"I'm David Young," he said. He stretched out his right arm. I stood up and shook his hand. "Supervising doctor this evening." He looked at his watch. "Actually, this morning."

I checked my watch, too.

"I understand you rode here in the ambulance with the lady."

"Yes."

"We have had to inform the police, obviously, and there is a Detective Constable on his way here to talk to you. He asked if you would wait." He pointed to his left. "Consulting Room 4 is free. You can talk there."

DC Reynolds arrived ten minutes later. A straight forward sort of copper; brisk and efficient. He asked if I had been drinking. I told him I hadn't but blew into his breathalyser anyway. He looked at the read-out.

"Well that's okay then," he said.

I had spent the last six days checking beaches on the Cornish coast, trying to find a client's seventeen year old surfer daughter. Without much success. I did meet a couple of dedicated water dudes in wet suits, who recognised her from the photograph I showed them. They said that they hadn't seen her so far this year. I decided not to spend another night in another cheap hotel and left Newquay to drive home. The traffic came to a standstill on Bodmin Moor. Up ahead, there was some commotion I couldn't see. I managed to get off the A30, threaded my way through a tangle of B roads to Jamaica Inn, and sat in the Smugglers Bar for an hour and a quarter drinking orange juice. At half nine, a uniformed PC in bike leathers came into the bar and announced that the road to Launceston was now clear.

It was five minutes to midnight when I swung the Healey into the lane leading to my garage. The headlights panned across the woman a nano-second before she was felled by the front bumper. I got out of the car. She was unconscious and bleeding from a deep cut in her forehead. Her shoulders were corkscrewed to the right and she seemed to be imprisoned under the chassis. Rather than reverse the Healey and risk inflicting more damage, I decided to leave the next few minutes to fortune, dug my mobile from the pocket in the driver's door and called an ambulance.

The medics said I had been right not to move the woman. However, as they couldn't work on her where she was, reversing the car clear of her body was actually the thing to do. I did so. The medic kneeling down, looking under the car and lit by the headlights, grimaced.

I took a long look at the woman during the ambulance ride to Southmead Hospital. Mid 50s maybe, her face tired, creased and beaten. She was wearing a long, black woollen coat which looked as worn out as she did. She survived the journey, but died in A&E with multiple fractures and a ruptured spleen.

DC Reynolds apologised for detaining me, and gave me a ride home. He examined the scene of the accident while I stowed the Healey in my garage. He said I should go to the nearest police station when I got up the next morning and make a statement for the record. We shook hands. He watched as I crossed the garden and went into the house via the back door.

The number of accidents I'd been involved in previously could be counted on the fingers of one hand. Two rear-enders courtesy of other drivers, a skid into a telegraph pole in the snow, and an unpleasantness when reversing out of a space in a multi-storey car park. All four in eighteen months, when I was a young DC. The rear-enders were right-offs, the skid necessitated two days in a body shop. My insurance company paid for the car park incident, and I was rewarded with a huge hike in payments next time around. Unnecessary moments all of them. Annoying, frustrating, and in the case of the multi-storey car park, an angry exchange of views. But no more than that. There were no injuries. No grisly, late night carelessness. And no deaths.

I didn't sleep. Or rather, I had short, fractured bouts of sleep, and re-runs of the accident while awake.

After breakfast I walked the few hundred yards from my house to Redland Police Station and explained all to PC Knowles. He gave me my statement to check, and asked me to sign it. He told me to expect an interview with the Coroner sometime soon, once an autopsy had been done.

I spent the rest of the day trying to concentrate on the surfer daughter case, without coming to any helpful conclusion. I called my clients, carefully suggesting there was no point spending more money. They thanked me for being courteous – I thought I was stumbling a bit – and told me to send them a bill. They were a gracious and gentle middle-aged couple, baffled by the situation they found themselves in, but trying to look ahead in expectation rather than hope. I always feel I'm selling cheap tickets at an inflated price at times like these. Mr and Mrs Edwards had given me a retainer up front to cover five days' work. I mailed them the Cornish hotel and petrol receipts.

* * *

DC Reynolds rang the following morning.

"Just a courtesy call, Mr Shepherd," he said. "Apparently, the lady you knocked down was called Lily. She had a silver-plated name tag chain around her neck. The sort of trinket you can buy in any souvenir shop on the sea front at Weston. I thought you might want to know."

"Why was she wandering around Redland at midnight?" I asked.

"No explanations yet. The pervading theory is that she was homeless. The case has been passed to Missing Persons. It's no longer the concern of Traffic. But in matters like this, I try to wrap things up as best I can."

Not much of a job, a DC in Traffic. More administration than investigation, which was probably a pity, because Reynold's bedside manner was good. He seemed like the sort of copper who should be on the front line not back in the office. He apologised for troubling me and then remembered something else.

"Oh yes. The lady was missing a kidney."

* * *

Two days later, I had my date with the Coroner. She mentioned the kidney too. The Forensic Pathologist said the extraction had been a skilful piece of surgery. The Coroner's Court recorded a verdict of 'Death by Misadventure'.

The only detective I knew in Missing Persons, was a dedicated misogynist called Hitchens. We had growled at each other a couple of times. He was where he was because he couldn't hack it in any other department. And he wasn't helpful – but then he didn't like me very much, so that was to be expected. He did confirm that Lily was a vagrant of no fixed abode. Not much detective work needed for that analysis.

So I called somebody who knew a lot more about street people than both Hitchens and me.

May Marsh was in her mid-60s and a force of nature. I'd known her husband Bill a long time. May was the patron of several local charities, a thorn in the flesh of committee members, town councillors, desk jockeys, time servers, the faint hearted and the poor in spirit. A constant lobbyist on behalf of the homeless and the forgotten. She ran a second hand furniture shop and a Drop In Centre in east Bedminster.

A week ago, she had been on *Points West* mixing it with a property developer who wanted to pull down an empty block of flats over a boarded up pub. The developer insisted that part of town needed a mini shopping mall. May maintained that a community centre and a children's playground was a much better idea. The developer said this was a great opportunity to earn much needed revenue. May asked for whom? The developer side-stepped that and said the site was an eyesore. May agreed, and said that a community centre with a garden on the roof and a playground built out of user friendly materials would solve that issue. The developer said she was talking nonsense. May asked him if he intended to shop in this proposed mini-mall of his. The developer said he didn't live in the area. May suggested that his only intention was to line his pockets. The developer was outraged at the idea and began to bluster. The beaming news presenter ended the conversation there and handed over to his colleague, who led into the next item.

Two days after the confrontation, the BBC asked May if she'd be the subject of a local documentary. She said no. The astonished twenty-two year old researcher asked why. May's response was typically forthright. Not the thing to do. The researcher should have left it at that, but instead suggested that the 'homeless issue' needed to be aired. May said no, it needed to be dealt with – which wasn't the same thing.

"Our visitors trust us to keep them away from journalists," she said. "The last thing they and the volunteers who work in the Drop In Centre desire is a TV crew following them around."

The depressed researcher went back to her desk to think up another 'appointment to view' TV idea.

I told May about Lily. She shared the information with the Drop In Centre volunteers. None of them knew her, or had heard anything about her.

"Not even Harry," May said. "And he recalls people and faces like no one else in the place. If Lily was, or had been, one of our visitors, he would know."

She suggested a couple of other places to try and wished me the best of luck.

Annie, the administrator of a Night Shelter in St Werburgh's, greeted me affably enough, but had some questions to ask. On hearing the answers, she phoned May. She sat with the receiver at her ear for a minute or so, then scrutinised me from across her desk.

"Around six feet, I estimate," she said.

"Five eleven," I said.

"Grey eyes, dark hair," she went on.

I helped out. "Forty-seven years old, just under twelve stone, collar size—"

Annie raised her hand and went on. "Light brown blouson jacket, dark trousers, pale blue shirt, no tie."

She listened to the response, thanked May, put the phone receiver back in its base, and smiled at me. It was a great smile and genuinely offered.

"You may not be on the side of the angels, but May says you're alright."

Good to hear, although the rest of the story wasn't. Lily had been a regular visitor to the Night Shelter until four weeks ago. None of the volunteers had seen her since early March. No one could say where she had gone.

Annie looked at me, dead centre. "Why are you doing this, Jack?"

"Because I killed her," I said.

She nodded at the phone. "That's not the way I heard it."

"That's the way it was."

"It was an accident," she said.

I was the last person to slip into Lily's broken down world. Tired and short on concentration. Less than a hundred yards from my garage and counting the seconds to home.

"My job is finding missing people," I said. "Not running them over."

"I'm sorry I can't help you more," Annie said. "The Salvation Army might be able to."

I paid a visit to the East City Corps and talked with Captain Rachel Maitland. She listened to the story.

"I know the work you do with street people," I said. "Can you help me with this?"

"We'll do our best."

I thanked her.

"You seem to be on something of a mission," she said.

"It appears to be that way."

"Do you get sentimental, Jack?" she asked.

I shook my head. "I get involved in stuff. I get frustrated when I can't make sense of what I'm trying to do. My daughter says I get angry at injustice and inequality – both perceived and real – too easily. I rage along with the headlines in *The Observer* on Sundays. I get hurt and I cry. But sentimental... not usually."

She smiled. Seemed lost in thought for a moment.

"I suppose you can't afford sentimentality in your line of work," she said. "We will spread the word. Do all we can. Give me your phone numbers and I'll call you. Whatever the outcome."

I walked back to the Healey, wondering if I really was on a mission.

* * *

Four days later, Rachel called me at home.

"No luck so far," she said. "No one we have talked with has any recollection of Lily. I am sorry, Jack. We will keep asking about her, however."

Short of ideas and getting nowhere, over the next twenty-four hours I ran out of purpose. There seemed no more I could achieve, and nothing I could fix.

So I spent the next two and a half weeks doing pretty much as I usually do when out of work. Gardening, which I'm not crazy about, but which I do because Emily liked the back garden looking the way she had planned and created it – I often feel she's at my shoulder, checking that I'm taking the proper horticultural care. I caught up with Chrissie and Adam, dog sat with Sam, spent time with Linda, watched films on TV, vowed to clear out the cupboard under the stairs but lost enthusiasm for the task the moment I began.

Then Rachel called again.

"We have found a lady who knew Lily. She won't talk to you, but she has given us some information. Lily's full name was Lillian Margaret Barrett. She has a married sister living in Sutton Berkeley."

"By that do you mean the Sutton Berkeley on the old A420?"

"That's our guess," Rachel said. "The sister's name is Marshall, or Maxwell. That's as close as we got. Apparently, Lily told all one night after they had begged enough money between them to buy a bottle of vodka. The street person we know said that Lily became falling down drunk and raged about her sister for a long time. Until they both fell asleep in a shop doorway. Does that help?"

"I hope so. Thank you, Rachel."

Sutton Berkeley. One of the richest little enclaves in northwest Wiltshire, just south of the M4. A village of probably less than a hundred and fifty souls. Maybe there was still time. Just maybe...

The Bristol Public Mortuary is southwest of the city, on the old road to Weston. Not a regular haunt for me these days, but I did visit on several occasions back in the day. I rang and got hold of a pathology technologist called Irving – his first name. He was polite and helpful. And as soon as he realised who I was talking about, deeply sorry.

"The lady was cremated yesterday," he said. "The police and the coroner had ruled that all efforts to find a next of kin had been exhausted."

"After three weeks?"

"I'm sorry, Mr Shepherd," he said. "I will inform the coroner's office of this new development. Perhaps you'll give me the information you have and—"

I disconnected the call, went out to the garage, and took the road atlas out of the Healey.

I was driving into Sutton Berkeley three quarters of an hour later. I called at the village shop, introduced myself to the lady behind the counter, and tried to be as user friendly as possible. She said there was no Mrs Marshall or Maxwell, but there was a Mrs Maxted. She gave me directions to a very imposing three storey house, set back from the road behind a regency red bricked wall. I tugged the bell pull. The bell jangled somewhere way inside the house.

After some time, the door was opened by a tall, attractive woman in her late 40s. She smiled at me. I asked her if she was Mrs Maxted. She confirmed that she was. I introduced myself.

"What can I do for you, Mr Shepherd?"

One of the worst jobs in the world becomes part of a policeman's skillset almost from the moment he joins the force. But no copper, however experienced, takes it in his stride. I can remember every second of the first time I rang a doorstep bell and asked if I could come into the house. And telling a nineteen year old girl and her sixteen year old sister that their mother had been bludgeoned to death by a crack addict, for the money in her purse.

I asked Mrs Maxted if she had a sister called Lily. She became agitated for a moment or two. Then she nodded without saying anything and beckoned me into the house. We sat down in the living room, or the drawing room, or whatever the fancy name was.

"I haven't seen my sister for twelve years, Mr Shepherd. I have no idea where she is."

"I'm sorry to tell you this, Mrs Maxted, but she died three weeks ago. She stepped into a lane in front of my car. I couldn't stop. I didn't see her in time."

"Where was this?"

"In Bristol."

Mrs Maxted stared at me for a long time, before she spoke again.

"So close," she said. "Oh God, so close." She sat up straight. "I searched for years. I've lost count of the missing persons officers I talked with; the agencies and detectives I employed. And... In the end she was living barely thirty miles away." She stood up. "Excuse me a minute, Mr Shepherd."

She left the room. I stayed in the armchair, not quite sure what I was supposed to do. I looked around the room. The fireplace was white veined marble, the porcelain was expensive and the grand piano was a Steinway.

Mrs Maxted came back with a photograph. She handed it to me.

"That was taken in Westonbirt Arboretum. The only picture of Lily and me together. Taken fourteen years ago. Before everything began to go wrong. I was thirty-two. She was thirty. And so, so beautiful. She was engaged to Raymond, loved him to distraction, but they had a huge row."

"Raymond?

"My husband."

"What did they row about?"

"To this day, I don't know. He never spoke about it. Neither did Lily. She just grew to hate me. It made things easier for her I guess. She disappeared the day before the wedding and I haven't seen her since. Raymond died last year, after nine months of heart trouble. He was on the list for a transplant, but he couldn't hold out long enough." She looked around the room. "You see how well I live? All the money in the world is not enough, if it can't get you what you need the most."

A little of it might have helped Lily, I thought.

Mrs Maxted apologised. "I'm sorry, Mr Shepherd. You don't want to listen to all this."

Listening was easier then talking.

"How was Lily?" she asked "Did she have friends? A family of her own?"

There were two choices by way of an answer. I opted for the truth.

"She was homeless," I said. "Living on the streets, sleeping in a Night Shelter."

"Oh Lily... Thirty miles away. So so close..." Mrs Maxted looked at me again. "Is it possible to see her? No, I suppose it's too late... Is it too late?"

"I'm afraid it is," I said. "She was cremated yesterday."

Mrs Maxted nodded. "I see."

"I had no idea who she was until, this morning. The Salvation Army located a friend of Lily's last night."

She said something, so quietly I barely heard the words. Then suddenly louder – "Oh I'm losing my manners. Would you like some tea?"

I said yes, for some reason. Politeness probably.

"My name is Elaine. I should have said before."

I drank my tea and left an uncomfortable ten minutes later, the last words Elaine said ringing in my ears.

"Thank you, Jack."

Chapter Two

*A*t exactly 5.30 on the morning of July 4*th*, *Three Fingers Banducci took a .38 slug in the back of his neck and a nose dive off Pier 13. The receding tide dragged him way out to sea. Four days later, what was left of him washed up on the beach in Summerville, fourteen miles to the south. The criminal career of Three Fingers Banducci was over. His funeral was a low key affair by gangster standards – two cars, half a dozen wreaths, the heads of the three families, and Rocco Gianelli, boss of the Stevedore and Longshore Men's Union, who had set up the hit. His relationship with Banducci was history.*

So was my interest in *The Family Affair*. Banducci should have smelled the set up from the other side of the bay. He was huge and slow witted, with an IQ that barely made double figures; but he'd been the Spitaleri family enforcer long enough to be able to put two and two together.

My own fault. I should have stayed with ITV's new 'cutting edge' drama about a murderer out on parole 17 years after chopping up his wife; and now a qualified solicitor, thanks to years studying in the prison library. I didn't mind the premise – as rehabilitation stories go it was promising – it was just that the actor's mannerisms irritated the hell out of me.

I dropped the book onto the sofa beside me, leaned back into the cushions and stared up at the ceiling. The phone rang out in the hall. I levered myself upright.

"Jack, it's May. I need your help."

I waited for her to say more, but there was a substantial pause.

"May...?"

"Something's happened to Bill," she said. "Can you come round?"

"Yes, of course."

"Thanks."

She rang off. I listened to the buzz on the line for a moment or two, then disconnected my end. I looked at my watch. 9.25.

I hadn't seen Bill Marsh for nine months or so. I liked him. He was sixty-six. A retired turf accountant. He had been in the betting business since the age of eight, long before the days of legal high street emporia. He worked as a bookie's runner for his Uncle Jimmy; who was run down by a Ford Consul in 1973, after consistently refusing to hand over protection money to a latter day re-creation of Pinkie Brown. The driver, in turn, suffered the same fate as Three Fingers Banducci. Bill always denied any association with the event. 'The man was foolish', was all that he said. At the age of twenty-five he took over Uncle Jimmy's business and prospered. I met him and May for the first time, during my days on the force; not long after I made Detective Sergeant. May, was getting nuisance phone calls, which gradually morphed into brutally menacing soliloquies. I sorted it out, and though we didn't meet often, the three of us became friends.

Bill and May lived in Syme Park on the edge of Clifton Down, home to big mansions and bank accounts. Bel Air in the Westcountry; the uber-expensive domain of the great and not so good. Situated above the Avon Gorge, close enough to the city for residents to eavesdrop on the world below, but far enough away for them not to have to care. It has great views, lots of money and its own private police force. I was offered a job, the day after I resigned from

Avon and Somerset Constabulary – as Liaison Commander, Street Section B – at twice the stipend I had just rejected. I thought about it. Emily didn't. She turned it down without a moment's hesitation. She didn't agree with my resignation either, but she accepted the why. I didn't join the police force to shoot anyone. Certainly not a seventeen year old out of his mind on angel dust. She said the resignation had substance; therefore what followed, must have so too. And there was none in spending my time protecting the insurance payments of those who never strove as much as one day for a just cause or the common weal. A private eye could choose – in most cases at least – which side he was on, and down which streets he should go.

There were no mean streets in Syme Park; at least in the physical sense. But mean, as in cold hearted and black spirited, they were a throwback to the oldest 'everyone else can go fuck themselves' attitude of all. They had laburnum hedges, gated security systems and manicured lawns. And Downs Avenue was truly exclusive. The longest and finest road of them all, which ran for a hundred and fifty yards to the cliffs overlooking the Avon Gorge.

A pair of stone lions flanked the gate to number 15. The house was set well back from the road and occupied more ground space than the average football pitch. Bill never ceased to enjoy the fact that a man resolutely old time working class, whose south Bristol accent was still as broad as the Avon Gorge, was living between a High Court Judge and some sort of money juggler, in a house bigger than both of theirs.

It was a starry, late April night. I rang the doorbell fifteen minutes after the phone call. There was no answer. I rang again. I heard footsteps inside the hall. May called out.

"Is that you, Jack?"

"Yes."

She opened the door as far as the chain would allow. Smiling in apology, but frightened nonetheless. She closed the door, unhooked the chain, opened the door again, and took a step backwards.

"Be careful."

I stepped into the hall. And almost into a pool of blood on the parquet floor. I stared down at it. Then up again at May. She breathed deeply, and blinked a number of times.

"Bill's not here," she said.

"Is he expected to be?"

May nodded. "Monday is his night in, my night out. I've been to a meeting in the Council Chamber."

"What time did you go out?"

"Just after 7 o'clock. I got back a few minutes before I called you."

I asked if I could look around. May nodded again. I checked all the bedrooms, dressing rooms and bathrooms. The living room, dining room, library, billiard room, and kitchen. A door in the utility room opened into the garage. The British racing green Jaguar XKR sat serene and quiet and locked. The bonnet was cold.

I found May in the kitchen, looking out of the window into the night. Three feet to her right the kettle was hissing and boiling. I moved to it and switched it off.

May turned to me. "Sorry, Jack. I was miles away."

"We should call the police," I said.

"Yes," she said, distracted and unfocused. "I'll make some tea."

Detective Sergeant George Hood was working late. A tough and quick witted DS on the Murder Investigations Team, run by an old friend of mine, Superintendent Harvey Butler.

"This might turn out to be way below the MIT remit," I said. "But there's a big pool of blood, and Bill Marsh isn't here."

"I'll come and take a look," Hood said. "It's a slow night. And this is something of a novelty – you calling in the police to investigate a crime."

He arrived, wearing a suit that clearly hadn't come from a High Street chain store, with a SOCO, a photographer and PC Eve Laker. She joined May. They drank tea and talked in the kitchen. The photographer and the SOCO went about their business. Hood and I sat, side by side, at the foot of the stairs.

"Have you looked around?" he asked.

"Yes."

"Touched anything?"

I stared at him. He apologised.

"Sorry..."

We both looked at the pool of blood once more, silent for a long time. Holding station like two of the three wise monkeys. Then Hood spoke again.

"I like Bill," he said. "He's got style. And his word means something. That's unique in these days of wannabes and second string crime lords. Pigmies by comparison with Bill, all of them."

That was some tribute coming from George Hood, the 'by the book' copper.

"However..." He turned and looked at me. "I hope you have no intention of getting involved in this."

"I don't know what 'this' is," I said. "No more than a missing persons case maybe. And finding people is what I do."

Although my recent track record was well below par. I hadn't unearthed the surfer daughter and the Salvation Army had found Lily.

Hood breathed in and out. He was about to lay down the law, when the SOCO called to him from the living room doorway.

"George, there's something in here you ought to see."

Hood stood up. Looked down at me. "Don't move. We have to discuss your concept of private sector involvement a bit more."

He walked across the hall. The photographer who had been crouched and staring at the blood through his macro lens, straightened up to his full height.

"All I can do, George."

Hood nodded his thanks and disappeared into the living room.

I got to my feet and walked into the kitchen. PC Laker stood up and moved into the hall. I sat down at the breakfast bar, opposite May. She was silent, a cup cradled in her hands. Two or three months younger than Bill, five feet four, with dark blue eyes, natural fly-away dark hair, and the sunniest disposition anyone was ever likely to encounter. Not so, at this moment, but she was holding on.

"That might not be Bill's blood in the hall," I said.

In all truth, not really much of a rationalisation, but it was at least a possibility.

"Okay, Jack," she said. "Then where the hell is he?"

Hood walked into the kitchen. May smiled a greeting and put the cup down in front of her.

"Will you come into the living room?" he asked. "There's something I'd like you to see."

May stood up, moved to the sink, turned on the hot tap, rinsed the cup and turned it upside down on the draining board. Hood waited patiently.

"I have to ask you not to touch anything," He said. "For the moment, we are treating this house as a crime scene."

May and I followed Hood out of the kitchen and across the hall, both of us unable to resist a glance down at the blood pool. May paused in the living room doorway. I stepped to her side. Hood moved to the SOCO who was standing by the fireplace. He looked down into the fire grate.

"Will we get anything out of those?"

The SOCO shook her head. "Unlikely."

"What?" May asked. "Those what?"

She moved to the fireplace. Hood gave me his best 'stay where you are' look. I stayed.

"Why did he light a fire?" May said softly.

"Hardly that," the SOCO said, like she was correcting an obvious mistake.

Hood stared at her. The SOCO looked suitably chastened. May didn't notice.

"We never have this fire on," she said. "Bill likes the temperature a couple of degrees lower than most people. So we set the thermostat over there and leave it." She looked into the grate again. "Bill never lights this fire…"

The SOCO spoke again; this time more user friendly.

"Somebody burned something tonight. Letters, notes, something like that." She pointed to the tiny flecks of blackened paper in the grate. "Not exactly a novel. But maybe twenty, twenty-five sheets, at a guess."

May shook her head – a gesture of disbelief. I asked if I could step into the room. Hood said that would be okay. I moved to May's side. She took my hand. Hood asked if there was anything out of place.

May shook her head again. Pointed to the sofa beside her.

"May I sit down?"

"Yes, of course," Hood said.

I sat next to her. Hood made himself comfortable in the matching armchair to the right of the fireplace. The SOCO picked up the conversation.

"Mrs Marsh… Can you tell me your husband's blood group?"

"AB Negative. It's rare."

Hood looked at the SOCO, who nodded in confirmation.

"So how soon can we get an analysis of the stuff in the hall?" Hood asked.

"Is this request urgent?"

"Yes it is."

May looked at Hood and mouthed 'thank you'. The SOCO got the message.

"If I take it into the lab myself, wake up some technician and stand over him while he analyses the stuff, I can let you know within an hour."

Hood nodded his thanks. "Call me on my mobile."

The SOCO and the photographer went into the hall and out of the front door. Hood turned his attention back to May.

"Is there somewhere else you can stay?"

"Why? Can't I stay here?"

Hood chose his next words carefully.

"We're in a bit of a quandary... If the blood in the hall isn't Bill's, it can be cleaned up and Missing Persons will take over the investigation. If it is his blood, then we have to consider more serious matters. And we'll have to do a full forensic sweep of the house before anything is touched. In either case, we'd rather you weren't here. At least until lunchtime tomorrow."

May listened to Hood without a trace of emotion in her face. When he had finished she didn't reply. So I suggested she stay with me.

"Yes," she said. "That will be fine. Thank you, Jack." She looked at Hood. "And thank you, Detective Sergeant, for your consideration."

"We'll do everything we can, May," he said.

May stood up. "I'll just get a few things."

"Okay. But PC Laker will have to go with you." He looked at her and raised his hands. "Sorry..."

She left the room, picking up PC Laker along the way. Leaving two detectives, public and private, staring at one another.

* * *

I live in an Edwardian semi in a quiet road in Redland. The first and only house I ever bought. I mean, we bought – Emily and me. May commented on this, as I ushered her into the hall.

"This is a comfortable house," she said. "Welcoming."

I hung her coat in the hall and took her suitcase upstairs to the guest bedroom. Downstairs again, I asked May if she wanted a drink. She said no and we sat down on the living room sofa. I put the phone handset on the coffee table in front of us.

"Our first house was half this size," May said.

The remembrance seemed to catch her by surprise. She scrolled back through the years. It took a while, so I waited.

"A two up two down, in Bedminster," she said. "We didn't have a bean. Bill had just started working for his Uncle Jimmy – officially that is. And he gave us the deposit."

She breathed in and out. Lost in days gone by and once upon a times. She shivered back into the present.

"God, that's a long time ago."

Willing the phone to ring, neither of us said anything for a while. Then May remembered Lily.

"I heard the Salvation Army found someone who knew her."

It was a useful change of subject for May, so I took up the cudgel. I asked her the question no one had been able to answer so far.

"Why would she be wandering around a well-heeled suburb like Redland?"

"She might have had nowhere to sleep. Or she might not sleep much. Many homeless people don't. They spend the night on the move. Some of them have the stamina to walk miles."

"She was a regular in a night shelter," I said. "But she hadn't been there for a while."

"Then something out of the ordinary must have happened in her life," May said. "Sometimes people disappear and we hear no more about them. That's not always bad news. So we hope for the best and try to believe they have had a change of fortune."

The handset rang on the coffee table. I picked it up.

"The blood is AB negative," Hood said.

"Hold on, George..."

I looked at May, anticipating the news, shaking her head.

"I'm sending a full team back to the house first thing," Hood said. "It'll take most of the morning to cover the rooms the SOCO thinks necessary. I'll have someone clean up the blood, then call you when May can go home. This looks like it might be an MIT matter. But I can't stop you working for your client. Just be careful that nothing you do ends up with both of us regretting it. In return, I'll keep you in the loop as much as I can."

"Thanks, George."

I ended the call. Looked at May.

Composed once again, she looked down at her hands, resting on her knees. We sat as though we had settled on this forever. Then May lifted her head.

"Will you try and find him, Jack?"

"Of course."

"Thank you."

I looked at the clock above the fireplace. 10.45.

"You should get some sleep," I suggested.

May got up out of the chair, moved to the living room door, then stopped and turned back to face me. It seemed she had something important to say but couldn't recall what it was. I tried to help out.

"May," I said. "At the moment, Bill is simply not at home. Hang on to that. Don't start imagining 'what ifs?' And remember, he's a tough old bugger. Not easily fooled and well capable of taking care of himself."

"All that sounds like you believe he'll walk in through the door at any moment," she said.

"Why not? He might do just that."

May stared at me. Like an illusionist's assistant who knows the trick is a stinker and the audience will see right through it.

"Goodnight, Jack," she said.

I watched her leave the room. Listened to her footsteps as she climbed the stairs. Waited for her to reach the guest bedroom.

And I pondered... Bill as I remembered him, was an uncomplicated, sensible man. Not one to disappear taking nothing with him and leaving behind his blood on the floor. So what sort of state was he in? He hadn't packed anything or taken his car. So he walked somewhere? No, he was driven somewhere. And then what?

I decided to go to bed too. Picked up the phone, intending to return it to the hall. As I left the living room, it began ringing in my hand. I pressed the call button and put the receiver to my ear. May appeared at the head of the stairs, still dressed.

Chrissie asked me how I was. I looked up at May and shook my head. She moved out of sight again. I talked to Chrissie.

"I'm er...doing something?" A faintly ridiculous thing to say.

"What?" Chrissie asked. "Something fun, something good?" Then a little alarmed, she asked. "Something dangerous?"

I was slow to respond.

"Dad?"

"No no no. May Marsh is here." I said. "It looks like Bill has disappeared."

"Looks like? Don't you know?"

I told her the story of the evening. She asked how May was.

"Showing immense control. But she's scared to death."

"Would you like me to come round?"

"No, don't do that. She's gone to bed. Best to leave her trying to sleep."

"Okay. Call me in the morning," she said. "Goodnight, Dad."

I switched the phone base to silent, took the receiver upstairs with me and put it on a bedside table. I took my shirt off and stepped towards the bathroom. The phone trembled and buzzed.

"I'm not calling too late am I?" Linda asked.

"No not at all," I said.

Linda is the sexiest accountant I have ever met. Five feet six, long brown hair, dark blue eyes and great legs. She has the office next to mine; on the third floor of a red brick converted tobacco warehouse by the river. It's as swanky as any red brick ex-warehouse can be, but by no means a show place. Linda's fellow accountants work in the city's business quarter in serviced executive suites, hold conferences in well upholstered meeting rooms, and have lunches in quayside bistros. Linda is smart and funny and constantly being head-hunted, but she is comfortable with her surroundings, has an appreciative client list, and no desire to labour among the denizens of tofu Bristol. She was, before Emily died, one of her closest friends. It took eighteen months for us to acknowledge the relationship that was growing between us. Currently, we were still exploring the possibilities.

I asked her if she was at home.

"No, I'm still in London. Meetings went on all day. I'm going to stay here tonight, with my brother. Just wanted to hear your voice before I go to bed."

"That's good to know."

"How was your day?"

"The day was alright. Boring actually. Paperwork. The evening's been something of a kicker."

"Why?"

I told Linda all I had told Chrissie.

"And you're going to help, of course," she said.

"Of course."

"Okay. But at least, contrive to stay in one piece until I get back."

"Will do."

"I love you," she said. "Goodnight."

I went to bed. Lay awake for an hour or so, listening to the sound of the house. On the other side of the wall, I heard May crying. Eventually I slept.

Chapter Three

I woke up at ten minutes to eight. Miserable and uneasy. I usually manage to park such first moments in the section of my brain which doesn't keep nagging at me. Not so this morning. And now I was wide awake, miserable and uneasy. I got out of bed, showered – which helped a bit, but not much – and met May in the kitchen at 8.30. She was boiling an egg.

"I hope that's okay," she said.

I laid another place on the kitchen table. She took a long look at me and asked if I was alright. I told her I was.

"Are you sure?"

I reflected that under the circumstances the counsellor in this situation ought to be me. I tried to brighten up.

"Yes," I said. "Coffee or tea?"

"Is the coffee real?"

"Absolutely."

The egg timer buzzed. May scooped the egg out of the pan and into an egg cup. Transferred the egg cup to the table.

"Where did you find that?"

"The egg? In the egg box on—"

"No. The egg cup. I never know where they are. Can't remember where they go, or where I've put them. Thinking about it though, I always had to ask Emily where they were."

I spooned an egg into the pan and switched the timer back to four minutes. May sat down at the table and watched. There was something she was working up to. I sat down opposite her.

"Go on," I said. "Say it. Whatever it is."

She picked up the tea spoon and tapped the top of her egg. Paused for a moment or two, then put the spoon down again.

"I er... was going to ask about Emily. Well actually, more than that."

"Go on..."

"How did you get through the weeks, months, after she died?"

I was about to say that she was jumping the gun, but for some reason I stuck with the script.

"With a great deal of help from my friends, Chrissie and Adam, Linda, Auntie Joyce and Uncle Sid..."

"Who are they?"

"My guardians. Well they were, way back then."

Back then... Hedley Park Infants School, in January 1974. My parents were driving over the Mendips in our new, second hand, two-tone blue, chrome trimmed, Ford Zodiac. It hit a patch of ice, spun off the road, slid through a gap in the fence, plunged into a brick quarry and exploded on impact with the quarry floor. After school, I walked the few hundred yards to Auntie Joyce's house for tea. She said Mum wouldn't be coming to pick me up.

Uncle Sid and Auntie Joyce, took me into their home and gave all the love it was possible to bestow on a sad, frightened little boy. Now retired, they live in Suffolk. Auntie Joyce sings in a choir in Southwold and runs the seriously off message local WI. Uncle Sid, an engineer by trade, recently took a course in welding at Lowestoft College and now creates huge metal works of art, in a shed which has massively reduced the size of the garden lawn.

"We phone or skype every weekend," I said. "No matter where we are."

"That's good..."

May levered the top off her egg and looked at the yolk inside the shell.

"It's a bit runny. I should have left it boiling a few seconds longer."

We finished breakfast. I went out and bought a newspaper. May found a copy of Kate Atkinson's *Case Histories*.

"Is this a good read?" she asked when I got back.

"Yes," I said. "It's about a private detective. I like to keep an eye on the competition."

May smiled. She sat on the sofa. I occupied an armchair. Began with the sports section of the *Guardian*, which seemed the lightest read to concentrate on. Not that either of us did. I read and re-read the headlines, but didn't get into the copy. On the sofa, May shuffled and changed position a number of times.

I thought about Mrs Maxted. I picked up the phone and dialled Irving. Apologised to him for rudely ending the conversation last time we talked. He said that was alright. He had discovered that Lily's ashes had been scattered in the Garden of Rest at South Bristol Crematorium.

I rang Mrs Maxted and gave her the information. She thanked me.

I went back to the *Guardian* but I couldn't focus. May and I continued to sigh and shuffle and fidget.

George Hood rang just after 11.30.

"The team is finished here," he said.

"Find anything?"

"Nothing out of the ordinary. A series of finger prints. Two sets all over the place, which must be from Bill and May. And odd ones, here and there, we might be able to make something of. Could pick up somebody known to us."

"What odds would Bill give you on that?"

"Let's hope we get to ask him," Hood said. "The bloodstain has been scrubbed out of the parquet. May can go home now. And tell her, we have a lot of people working on this."

* * *

My car is quartered in a garage at the bottom of the back garden, and opens onto the lane in which I had encountered Lily. The 1966, three litre Austin Healey convertible is my one indulgence. It's had several head gaskets, two gear boxes, replacement valves and countless hours in Mr Earl's Workshop in Southville. But when it's in tune, it rumbles softly in neutral and roars impressively at speed.

It sang its way across northwest Bristol, to Syme Park. I turned into Downs Avenue and coasted towards number 15.

We stepped, somewhat nervously, into May's house. Both of us looked at the place where we thought the bloodstain had been. A kind of memory reflex. There was nothing at all to see. George Hood's cleaner was someone to be recommended. There were no residual signs of a police investigation. The house was exactly as it should have been. Except that Bill wasn't there.

May took her suitcase upstairs. I took a look in Bill's office.

It was clearly signposted 'this is Bill's space'. As ordered, neat and tidy as his range of bespoke suits. With a huge modern lacquered desk, matching two-drawer filing cabinets each side of it, a big swivel chair behind it and three grand's worth of leather corner sofas with a lacquered low table inside the L. On his desk was a fabulous Victorian silver and glass standish and a Versace crystal Medusa paperweight. Christ knows what Bill had shelled out for those.

In my twenty-one years as a detective, public and private, I have encountered a plethora of premiership villains and hard cases; rich beyond the dreams of avarice, living in staggeringly expensive faux mansions with a conspicuous lack of style. But not Bill. He may have started his working life as a bookie's runner, but no one could deny he had class.

I spent five fruitless minutes exploring the desk drawers. They weren't locked, because there was nothing personal or secret in them.

The filing cabinets were unlocked too, and the reason why became clear. Names and addresses, letters and faxes and email print-outs, went back ten years in some cases – basically covering the decade since Bill sold his business. But there were no secrets, no diaries, no hidden agendas. Except for a note, paper-clipped into the Y folder behind half a dozen sheets of Y business. A list of nine or ten digit numbers and letters. Passwords probably.

There was no trace of a laptop or a mobile. With Bill somewhere, I presumed. Unless...

I walked back into the hall. Above me, May arrived on the landing, clothes changed and considerably refreshed. She moved on down the stairs, a new resolution in her body language. I asked if she had a spare key to the Jaguar. She collected it from a small wooden box, on the wall by the front door, next to the alarm.

I found Bill's mobile in the arm rest console between the front seats of the Jaguar, and his laptop under the passenger seat. I took both pieces of hardware into the office and returned to the kitchen. May was making a second round of breakfast coffee. She had also written me a cheque. She slid it along the work surface.

"I want to retain your services for a few days."

I picked up the cheque and looked at it. A thousand pounds.

"I'm not taking this."

"Yes you are," May insisted. "You charge 250 a day don't you?"

"Not to you," I said. "This is too much."

"Not for Bill," she said.

I slid the cheque back along the work surface. May shook her head fiercely.

"I want you to work on this, to the exclusion of all else. So take that cheque. Go on. Put it in your wallet." She looked straight into my eyes. Her voice dropped almost to a whisper. "Please, Jack..."

I reached out and gathered up the cheque again. I asked her if she knew the lock code for Bill's mobile.

"3344," she said.

We took our coffee into the office.

"When Bill retired, he vowed to leave all work behind," she said. "And it seemed to me he did."

"Who bought his business?"

"I don't know. He never told me, and so I didn't ask."

"Is that how it usually works?"

"Yes," May said. "He tells me things he knows I'll be interested in, but he never talks business in this house. I always stayed away from the betting shops. Not my thing at all." She looked round the study. "He spends a couple of hours a day, at most, in here. Reading stuff and making phone calls."

"Is he well? I mean in good health."

"Yes. A slight blood pressure problem, but that's all?"

"And he hasn't appeared worried or stressed recently?"

"No. I would have known if he was."

I unlocked the mobile. It offered two voice messages from Len somebody. *Call me, it's urgent*, he said. The first time at 4.20 yesterday afternoon, the second at 5.35. I asked May if she knew who Len was.

"No idea," she said. "Sorry."

I fiddled with the phone buttons and got into the contacts box. It was empty. There were no numbers on speed dial either. Something wrong there. Nobody with a mobile has an empty contacts box.

I found the outgoing calls log. One call only. Yesterday evening to a mobile; timed at 6.54. If there were others, they had been deleted.

May peered at the phone display. "So is that this Len bloke's number?"

"The timing's right," I said. "Could be that Bill called him back after the second message."

I pressed the recall button. The line was live, but Len didn't answer. I heard the first eight bars of *The Magnificent Seven* title theme, before his voice interrupted.

This is Len Coleman. Leave a message. Short and sweet.

There were five L Colemans in the phone book. The first was a lady called Lynette, the second a young sounding bloke called Lawrence. There were two voice messages from a Lucy and a Louise. And then a live response from an old man who took ages to get to the phone and sounded if he had emphysema. I apologised profusely.

"Now what?" May asked.

"I think you should leave this house for a few days."

May shook her head. "No. I won't move out."

She meant it. I looked at the determination in her eyes.

"Okay. Then will you invite someone to stay?"

She nodded this time. "My friend, Helen. She likes Bill and we get on well enough when we're together."

I had met Helen half a dozen times. She was five years younger than May. Widowed eighteen months earlier, having already won her own battle against breast cancer. Her terrific sense of humour had survived the surgery and the long nine months she spent nursing her husband. Like May, she had truckloads of passion and determination. She lived on her own in Bedminster; three streets away from the house she was born in.

"She copes with Syme Park, in small doses," May said. "I'll call her."

She looked at me, more like the May before all this began, her trademark resolution front and centre.

"I'll call you regularly," I said.

"Thank you, Jack."

Armed with Bill's mobile, laptop and list of passwords, I set off sleuthing. In the direction of Trinity Road Police Station and Detective Superintendent Harvey Butler.

* * *

I called from the Healey. Harvey was in his office. The uniformed PC at the car park barrier recognised me. He leaned close to the open window of the entry booth.

"Mr Shepherd. Good afternoon. A pleasure to see you."

A guileless young PC whose face looked familiar. I tried to match his politeness with a degree of my own.

"Thank you. Er... I do apologise. I can't recall your name."

"David De'Ath," he said.

How the hell could I forget that? I thanked him again and asked him to tell Superintendent Butler I was here.

"Yes indeed." He pressed a button to the left of the window. The barrier began to rise. "Please park in one of the visitor bays along the lane to the right."

I found a space, locked the car and walked back to the barrier.

"Detective Superintendent Butler will meet you in the lobby," PC De'Ath said.

Harvey was coming along the corridor to my left as I stepped into the building. The slow, rolling gait is deceptive. Although he carries a kilo or two more than he should, he's lighter on his feet than any man I know. Harvey is probably the best copper in town. Tough and clever and so straight it hurts. He was a dead ringer for head of the Murder Investigations Team when it was re-structured four years ago. He was able to hand pick his crew. The drawback was having to report, more often than he wished, to a group of uniformed officers with scrambled egg on their caps. He has to work in unimpeachable plain sight, although he's not above improvising if the occasion demands. As to private investigators... he regards them mostly as vigilantes, and at best, wayward knights errant. We have remained friends however down the years – since the shooting and my acknowledgement that I was never going to be a career copper.

We shook hands, but he was grumpy. I asked him what was wrong. He led me along the corridor.

"I am a man under siege, Jack. The new Assistant Chief Commissioner has an obsession with high profile policing. You've probably seen him on TV recently, speaking on behalf of the new order. Two days ago, he stole my top inspector to head up his new Task Force. He's squeezed the budgets of every department in the building to pay for these buggers. And for some reason, he keeps inviting me to attend meetings to discuss the 'challenges of a new age of policing' – whatever they fucking are."

We stopped walking. Harvey reached out and opened the door into the MIT squad room.

"Meanwhile the members of this elite bunch are charging around my manor like designer commandoes."

He led the way across the room to his office at the far end.

We sat on opposite sides of his desk, drinking coffee. Eventually, he leant back in his chair and asked me what I was after this time. I looked as hurt as I could. Harvey pointed at the carpet with his right hand and traced the distance between me and the door.

"A well-trodden path, Jack."

Which was true, all irony aside. I decided it would be best to get straight to the point.

"Len Coleman…"

"Never heard of him."

"He may be on your database nonetheless."

"What does he do?"

"I've no idea."

Harvey sat up in his chair and placed his elbows on the desk.

"Is that the sum of your rehearsed plea? Or do I get to know anything else?"

"He might have been the last person to speak to Bill Marsh last night."

"Ah. Once again, you want the public purse to pay for part of your current investigation."

This was another well-trodden path.

"Do we really have to go through all this dancing around again?"

"Not at all. You could desist from imploring us to help you do your work."

"I just need his address, Harvey."

He looked me straight in the eyes. Hood walked into the office, picked up the vibe, turned and walked out again. Harvey called him back.

"Len Coleman, George?"

Hood doubled the length of the pause, before he responded. "Never heard of him."

Harvey beamed at Hood, then at me. "There you have it. We know not the man."

I decided getting thrown out was better than getting nowhere.

"Come on, both of you. This tired routine is all bollocks." I pointed at the screen on Harvey's desk. "PC, keyboard, tap tap, database. The work of moments. I'm simply asking the guardians of law and order to help a council tax payer."

Harvey looked across the office to Hood. "Fun this, isn't it?"

"Unhelpful is what it is," I said.

Harvey grinned. "What the hell... Find out what you can, George."

Hood left the office. Harvey changed the subject.

"How's Chrissie? Did she decide to do her PGCE?"

"Yes, she did. Two thirds of the way through it now. Bloody hard work."

"She'll make it," Harvey said. "She's got the genes. Stubbornness, grit, persistence, bare-faced cheek... Want some more coffee?"

Five minutes later, Harvey, George Hood and I knew as much as the police computer. Len Coleman, aka Leslie Chisholm, aka Laurence Charlton, was a con artist with a Maths degree. Since achieving his majority, he had done three stretches at Her Majesty's pleasure, totalling five years. He was now in his 60s, and free and clear since 1998. He'd beaten the odds so far. The database said he was living in a garden flat in Bishopsworth.

Chapter Four

That was bigging it up somewhat. It was a two room basement with a bit of lawn out the back.

I rounded the corner of the house as a man a couple of inches taller than me, stepped out of the flat doorway. Long grey coat, fair hair, dark eyes, slim straight nose, and a semi-automatic which materialised in his fist. He took a couple of steps forwards and waggled the gun at the wall, advising me to get out of his way. I was about six feet from him, I dropped my head, lunged forward and met him hard at the base of his ribcage. The breath left him in a mighty rasping wheeze. Back-pedalling furiously, he came up against a big stone planter with some sort of mini tree in it. He fell backwards but managed to swing his body away from the planter. I landed on top of it, chest first. The tree collapsed, my ribs made contact with the rim of the planter and I slid head first into a big green plastic bin.

For a nano-second I felt okay. Then the pain arrived and washed all over me. My heart began thumping and breathing was agony. I rolled onto the lawn, taking a long time to focus. The man who had just introduced himself fared better than I did. By the time I got to my knees he was hovering over me. He brought the pistol down hard on the back of my neck, the pain switched to the base of my skull and I slumped face down into the grass.

The man slipped away.

I rolled onto my back, stared up at the sky and waited for my heart rate to slow down. My ears were ringing, and what vision I'd had a few seconds ago, was lost in a haze. My back, neck and shoulders hurt like nobody's business. There was a pain under my left eye. I probed gently at the spot. No injury, no torn skin, but I could feel a bruise already under way. I closed my eyes and lay still for a while. When I opened them again, the view out of my left eye was in cinemascope.

I turned my head and squinted towards the garden flat door. It was open and glass seemed to be missing from the top half of it. A few moments staring, gave rise to the conclusion that, as I was here, and not responsible for the breaking and entering, I might as well go into the place and explore.

Getting to my feet was painful. I swayed, regained my balance, and aimed myself in the direction of the door. My vision began to clear.

The top half of the door had been glazed. But at that moment most of the glass was lying in segments and shards on the hall carpet. From where I stood, it seemed that the far end of the hall opened into the living room. There was one door on the left hand side of the hall, the bedroom maybe, and two doors on the opposite wall – kitchen and bathroom, if I was right with the first assumption. I stepped into the hall, my shoes crunching the glass into smaller bits.

In the kitchen, I turned on the cold tap stuck my mouth under the spout and sucked in gulps of water. I straightened up, turned off the tap, breathed deeply, and looked around. The kitchen was small, but graced with furniture and appliances way above the price range of B&Q.

The bathroom was actually a mosaic tiled wet room, with an expensive German shower system. I ran some water into the wash basin and splashed my face.

The bedroom was a small slice of Arts and Crafts style. William Morris was undoubtedly the inspiration for the wallpaper and there was a print of one of Edward Burne-Jones'

Arthurian paintings on the wall to the right of the door. An iron framed bed with a gleaming brass headboard sat between two oak bedside tables with a leaf design carved across the faces of the two drawers. The same design was matched by the doors of the wardrobe standing against the wall opposite the foot of the bed – a graceful piece of Edwardian carpentry.

The living room was clean and tidy. Sanded and oak stained floorboards, and minimalist modern furniture ordered from one of the weekend colour supplements. Unlike the others, this room was totally without character. No personal stamp anywhere. I assumed that the man with the automatic had either come to the same conclusion, or had pocketed all the evidence available. No pc, no personal papers on the desk in the window alcove. Nothing declaring that the place was the home of Len Coleman.

Other than his body lying on the floor, in front of the fireplace.

The day surged into melodrama. I moved to the fireplace and looked down at Coleman, flat on his back on the hearth rug. His head lay on one side, a lumpy, bloody mess where his left ear should have been, holes gouged out of his cheek. In spite of the damage done to him, he was still recognisable from the picture on the police computer.

I groped for the mobile in my jacket pocket, found it, and called George Hood. He refrained from castigating me and said he was on his way.

My head was beginning to clear. So, Len Coleman...

Hardly a major villain, judging by his criminal history. Living low profile at an address which would attract no attention, although furnished with a serious amount of money. Clever. I sat down, as far as I could from the body, in an armchair by the window. It felt better staring at Len from a distance. Whatever he had been hit with wasn't lying around.

There was a single, heavy, brass candlestick about a foot high sitting on the left end of the mantelpiece. It probably had a companion piece stationed at the right hand end. If so, it was missing. Coleman's killer must have used it and taken it away with him. More sensible than washing it in the kitchen sink. I gave up thinking about it, leaned my head back and closed my eyes.

Hood, a female DC – younger and a little bit shorter – and two uniforms, arrived ten minutes later.

"This is more like it," Hood said. "Us finding you with a corpse at your feet. Did you do this?"

I stared at him. He grinned, and introduced the woman standing next to him.

"This is DC Holmes."

There was moment of silence. As if we were all on *Qi* and trying not to say the obvious. I thought what the hell...

"I suppose everybody calls you Sherlock," I said.

Holmes looked at me as if she had a headache.

"My friends do, Mr Shepherd."

Hood grinned again. He pointed at my face.

"You're getting a bruise there," he said.

He handed me over to DC Holmes and went for a prowl around the rest of the flat. Holmes looked straight into my eyes. Hers were green.

"Do you know Len Coleman?"

"Only as a corpse. We haven't actually met."

"But you had arranged a rendezvous?"

"No."

Holmes squinted at me. "I've been told about you, Mr Shepherd. A fully paid up member of the awkward squad."

I decided as she was on Harvey Butler's team, and therefore a smart copper, I'd help all I could. Which wasn't much, unhappily.

"All I know about Len Coleman is what the police database kicked out." I looked across the room. "I came here hoping to talk to him."

"About what?"

"A friend of mine." I gestured towards the hall. "Your boss will tell you about him."

My jacket pocket began ringing. I looked at Holmes. She nodded at me and turned back to Coleman. I thumbed the mobile receive button and raised the phone to my right ear.

"Have you had lunch?" Chrissie asked.

"Not yet."

I looked at my watch. Just after 1 o'clock. Chrissie issued an invitation.

"We're all here. Adam's working at home this afternoon."

Adam is a senior journalist on the *Bristol Evening Post*. He is twelve years older than Chrissie, who was nineteen at the time she informed Emily and me she was moving into Adam's house. I made my position clear. A rushed and ill-considered response, which sparked a series of family rows and ended up with Chrissie moving anyway. Throughout the nonsense, Adam sensibly stayed in the background and let us get on with it. Within days, Emily was diagnosed with cancer, whereupon all the wasted energy of the previous weeks paled into insignificance. It was clear Adam would run into an inferno for Chrissie if he had to. And he was at her side during the eight months it took Emily to die. There had been some talk recently of getting married as soon as Chrissie left university.

"I'm just finishing up here," I said. "I'll get to you as soon as I can."

I spent another fifteen minutes answering questions about the tall man and the automatic. Holmes looked aggrieved when Hood dismissed me.

"Mr Shepherd will make a statement at Trinity Road later," Hood said. Then looking at me, he stressed every syllable in his next sentence. "He can be trusted to do that."

* * *

I discovered more bits that were hurting as I eased myself into the Healey. Everything above my waist basically.

Twenty-five minutes later, I pulled up outside Adam and Chrissie's house – one of twenty in an impressive Victorian terrace on Dial Hill in Clevedon. I had stiffened up during the journey. Getting out of the car proved to be as painful as getting in. Upright I was okay. I walked slowly up the garden path.

The house greeter is hairy, a little over two feet high, with four legs, matchless enthusiasm and boundless energy. Sam the Bearded Collie is five years old and a stunner. He began barking when I rang the bell and didn't finish until we were lying on the carpet in the hall and I had him imprisoned in a head lock. I let him go. He reversed away from me and sat down, panting like an idling steam engine, delighted with the tussle we had just had.

Which was more than I could claim. Getting up from the floor was no easier than getting out of the Healey. Chrissie watched this manoeuvre, then studied the bruise developing nicely below my left eye.

"What have you been doing?"

I told her. About the tall man, but not about the corpse.

"Jesus Christ, Dad!"

She shook her head and retreated to the kitchen. Sam followed her.

Adam ushered me into the living room. He is always the perfect host; welcoming and disarmingly urbane – qualities I don't readily associate with journalists. The three of us concentrated on the meal. I had no clue as to the assault that was to follow. I was enjoying Adam's cognac when he volunteered to make the coffee and disappeared into the kitchen.

Chrissie was up to speed in seconds. "Are you ever going to learn?"

I stared at her. "The risotto was terrific," I said.

She grimaced, opened her mouth to go on. I beat her to it.

"May and Bill are old friends. Your friends, too. I have to find out where he is and if he is alive."

"Which entails, of course, fighting with gunmen on garden flat patios."

"Not necessarily..."

Her exasperation boiled over. "I mean, look at the state of you."

"Late 40s, straight backed, all my own teeth..."

"Shit, Dad. You look like you've just done two rounds with Joe Calzaghe."

No argument there, but logic has no emotion. And emotion was driving this discussion. Both sides of it. We were stamping on old ground, and dangerously close to the kind of face-off we thought was consigned to history.

"Finding people is what I do," I said. "And May and Bill are almost family."

"No. You and I and Adam and Sam are family."

She stared straight into my eyes. I couldn't argue. I chose to remain aloof. So Chrissie went back to the beginning.

"Please stop this," she said. "You are an investigator, not a brawler."

"Oh come on, Chrissie, it doesn't happen every day."

"No, but it happens. You take on too much, Dad. You shoulder other people's burdens and you give yourself away by the shovel full. Are your clients really so deserving?"

"If we waited until people were deserving, the world would go to hell."

Undeniably a truism, but nonetheless, a needlessly smart remark. And with reason, not well received. The cushion from the chair next to her frizbeed its way across the room. I caught it.

"Howzatt?" I appealed.

Chrissie yelled in frustration and began throwing at me everything she could reach. I raised my arms to my head. Three magazines and a hard-back from the coffee table bounced off my elbows. I was trying to make myself as small as possible in the chair, when she picked up the glass paperweight which had slid off the table and onto the carpet. I looked up at her.

"The proverbial blunt instrument."

Chrissie looked at the paperweight and then at me.

"One day," she muttered through clenched teeth. "One day..."

Sam was in the hall, peering round the living room door frame, staying well out of the way. Adam came into the room as if nothing was going on, put down a tray of cups, nodded cheerily at me, and reversed back into the hall. Chrissie retrieved the books and the magazines, re-arranged them on the table, picked up the cushions one by one, then sat down again and glared at me. I felt I ought to respond to all this, if only to keep my end up. Chrissie intercepted the move.

"Don't. Not a word. Clever or otherwise. Give May her money back and leave this to the police."

I shook my head. "I can't do that."

Adam arrived with the coffee. He sat down at the table and grinned at us.

"Help yourselves," he said.

Chrissie picked up the coffee pot. Put it down again and left the room.

"Do you take sugar?" Adam asked. "I never can remember."

* * *

Chrissie and Sam went out for a walk. I finished my coffee, thanked Adam for his hospitality and left too.

I drove up to the top of Bay Road and parked the Healey facing the sea. On cue, the sun came out and down below me the Bristol Channel morphed from uninviting dark brown into seaside steely blue. I got out of the car, walked east along Bay Road out to Layde Point and gave myself a talking to. The argument with Chrissie had been all too familiar. We should have moved on. I should have moved on. Emily had got us back together. She would have despaired had she witnessed that re-run after lunch. Must do better Shepherd...

Back at the Healey, I climbed in and drove to my office on automatic pilot.

Chapter Five

The one time tobacco warehouse has five floors. It sits on the north side of the Avon, facing the river and backing on to the Cumberland Basin. Inside, it's not as brutal as it appears from the outside. The bricks have been steam-cleaned. The reception space is friendly. There are four big sofas and two low tables sitting on the re-constituted flagstone floor. And the inevitable huge Yuccas to give the place a sense of 'green'.

Jason was on duty at the security desk. Recently a sports student at Bath University and a brilliant kayaker, he missed 2012 qualification by eight tenths of a second. He joined *Harbour Security* to help pay off his student loan, while he figured out what to do next. He set his sights on the 2013 World Championships in North Carolina. Found some local sponsorship – there was no money from UK Sport, as he wasn't considered an elite athlete, and thus, a medal prospect. So to teach the suits and time-servers a lesson, he smashed the world qualifying time. He started training four hours a day alongside his eight hour shift, in order to up his effort and his medal prospects. Then *Harbour Security* woke up to the possibilities. Took on board the promotional opportunities and bought Jason a Renault Espace with piles of interior space for his kit, and a roof rack big enough to carry two kayaks. He went to north Wales and trained eight hours a day. In North Carolina he aced the preliminary round, and grabbed silver in the final; just 1.257 seconds short of gold. The European Championships were fourteen months away, so Jason was currently in light training and back at reception. He was unfailingly polite, smart and funny. A real asset.

He gave me the morning's post. Three white envelopes with windows in them.

"Have a nice day, Mr Shepherd," he said.

I took the lift up to the third floor. The doors opened in front of me like a pair of curtains doing a reveal. My office was about 20 yards along the corridor straight ahead. And once again, I slid into discussion with myself about the sense in having some place to work I didn't really need. When Emily was alive and Chrissie was living at home, *Shepherd Investigations* was evicted from the spare bedroom. Linda announced that the office next door was empty, so I moved in – an arrangement no longer necessary, now that I had the house to myself. I unlocked the door. A good shift psychologically. The place looked, felt, and smelled like a workspace. Therefore, as I said to myself the last time we shared this dialogue, *Shepherd Investigations* operated better from here.

Which in turn led me back to the current commission. This case had all the ingredients for a grade A unhappy ending. Often, missing persons don't stay missing for long. They turn up again within days. Sometimes they just want to say "I'm fine I don't need you anymore." Or worse, "I've found someone else." Sometimes they turn up dead however, having left a pool of blood on the parquet floor.

I put Bill's laptop on my desk and switched it on. It fired up and demanded a password. Arguably as the first one needed each day, it would be top of the list on the Y file notes. The desktop opened. I clicked the internet icon and in seconds the laptop was mine to play with.

I spent an hour going through Bill's files.

They weren't helpful. There was no direct line to anything remotely nefarious. No names of hard line villains I had heard of, although there was a character or two I wouldn't spend time with by choice. I got the impression that a lot of stuff in these files had been deleted and the hard copy shredded. Or burnt maybe, in the living room fireplace.

I opened the envelopes in my post and threw the contents into the waste paper bin at the side of my desk. I checked my own laptop. Nine emails, none of them to do with work of any sort. I created a new file and labelled it Bill Marsh. I made some notes on the day so far, and saved them on a data stick.

* * *

I have a place to go when I can't make sense of anything.

Emily's memorial stone lies in a quiet corner of St Edward's churchyard, underneath a three hundred year old yew.

I coasted to a stop by the lych gate, at the end of a lane lined with beech trees. I climbed out of the Healey and looked around. In the stunning peace and quiet, it was hard to believe that the clamour of the north end of the city was only a few hundred yards away. I opened the lych gate. The daffodils were over and the tulips were clinging on to another day's welcome sunshine. There was the rich, sharp smell of new mown grass.

In memory of Emily 1969 to 2011.

I looked at the stone, fringed with grass cuttings. I knelt down and brushed them away. Emily was my life and my strength and my motivation for twenty three years. When the cancer took her, I was totally lost. I had no idea how to go on; moments when I didn't want to. What saved me was her voice. Telling me I had things ahead of me I had to do. She was the love of my life; still in my heart and head, chastising me every time I appeared ready to give up.

We talked for a while. Then I said goodbye.

I stepped through the lych gate again, and got into the Healey. I glanced in the rear view mirror. A sporty looking silver Audi nosed into the lane and glided up behind me.

I stayed in my seat and watched the driver climb out. He was big. Bigger than he had seemed in Len Coleman's garden. He moved alongside the Healey passenger door and in the process, blocked out the light. I waited to see what would happen next. He opened the door, bent down a couple of feet and looked into the car

"May I speak with you, Mr Shepherd?"

"About what?"

"Please get out of the car."

Behind me the Healey sagged on its springs as something weighty dumped itself onto the boot. My interlocutor spoke again.

"Pretty please..."

I opened the driver's door and slid out of the car. When I stood up, I was able to confirm the man was three or four inches taller than me; and considerably wider. I looked back to the rear of the car. His associate, who appeared to have no neck, grinned at me from a face which sat on his shoulders like a beach ball in a trough in the sea.

The man at the passenger door asked for my attention again.

"Mr Shepherd..."

I turned back to him. His neck was solid, like a racing driver's. But then, he looked strong all over. And his smile was a revelation. He beamed at me, by way of some truly expensive dental work.

In return, I tried to be gracious.

"We didn't have time for introductions last time we met," I said.

He smiled again. "My name is Smith."

I turned to the man sitting on the boot lid. "And you must be Mr Jones."

By the passenger door Smith said, "He's called Smith, too."

"Ah," I said. "The Smith brothers."

"You're obviously going to keep us in stitches," Smith Two said.

"I try to stay bright, in spite of the company," I said.

I turned to face Smith One. He reached inside his jacket. I froze. He produced a large white envelope and passed it across the roof of the car. He didn't have to stretch at all. It seemed he had long arms too.

"What's this?" I asked.

"Ten thousand pounds," he said.

I took some time over the next sentence.

"And what do I have to do for this ten thousand pounds?"

He smiled again. The sunlight flashed on his teeth.

"Nothing," he said. "My employer simply requests you do absolutely nothing."

"And who is he?"

Smith One gave a shrug of regret. I looked at the envelope in my hand. Time to be resolute.

"Well, 'nothing' is a problem," I said. "You have to be careful with 'nothing'. 'Nothing' can take you over. Then where are you?"

To my left, Smith Two sighed deeply.

I looked at him. "Difficult is it? This concept?"

He pulled a .45 automatic out from under his armpit. Obviously...

He stood up and the car rose on its rear springs. He stepped back, took his time, aimed the .45 at the rear window in the soft top and pulled the trigger. The roar was deafening, even in the open air. The bullet went into the car through the plastic rear window and out again through the windscreen; leaving a hole in the centre of it and the rest of the screen opaque, a web of jagged lines barely holding it together.

Smith One spoke. "My apologies..."

He took a couple of steps to his left, bent down and retrieved the spent cartridge case. Experienced and careful.

"Mine too," I said. Stretched over the top of the car and handed the envelope back to him. He shrugged once more and returned it to his pocket.

"The offer won't be made again," he said, emphasising every word, and slammed the Healey passenger door.

The damaged windscreen disintegrated, showering glass over the front seats.

The Smiths walked back to the Audi. The car reversed along the lane, swung to the left, disappeared for a moment or two, re-appeared, drove past the lane end and out of sight again. I cleared the driving seat of as much glass as I could, eased myself carefully into the Healey, turned on the ignition, and looked into the rear-view mirror. There was a neat, round hole in the rear window, about half an inch in diameter and right in my eye line.

I drove home with the wind stinging my face, crying like I was peeling onions. In the house, I called *Autoglass*, ran a bath and eased myself into it. The bruises from my first encounter with Smith One were now well established. But the twenty minute soak helped a bit. The man from *Autoglass* arrived half an hour later, apologised for being so tardy, and explained it had taken a while to find a match for a Healey windscreen. He nodded at my face and asked if I had walked into something. I thanked him for his concern, guided him through the house, out of the back door, and pointed him in the direction of the garage. Where he installed himself and set about his business.

At 4.45, I was sitting in my living room, on the way through a large whiskey and contemplating the latest turn of events.

What had I stirred up? Who was interested in me? Why was Len Coleman dead? And what the hell had Bill got himself into? This had to be about him. Two wide shouldered types

51

leaning on me and my car, drenched in menace, wasn't an everyday occurrence. There was a marker next to my name in somebody's ledger.

Not brimming over with ideas on how to improve the day, I decided I'd had enough of it.

I made some coffee and switched on the TV. It came into life tuned to Film 4. The afternoon western was into its fifth reel and too confusing for me to pick up. On BBC1, a middle aged couple from Rotherham, in search of a haven by the sea, were failing to get interested in an 80s built bungalow in south Devon. On BBC2, a man in the Methodist Hall in Ely, was offering the *Flog It* porcelain expert a hideous piece of Moorcroft for his assessment. I left them to it and looked elsewhere; and realised that people were dealing all over the medium. Antiques dealing, *Dickinson's Real Deal, Deal or No Deal...* I tried Five. Another film was on offer. A US made for TV movie, about a woman trying to drive her stepson insane – for some reason I failed to grasp – underscored scene by scene, by a relentless music track. In the meantime, ITV1 had changed programmes. But sticking firmly to the demographic, the channel was now re-running a fifteen year old episode of *Poirot*. I've never been a fan, so I went back to the western a second time. The hero was dying of his wounds on a dusty street, while the mayor was making the townsfolk ashamed of what they had let happen.

I was contemplating diving into the mire of cable offerings, when the man from *Autoglass* called to me from the kitchen. He said the screen was now fine, but there was nothing he could do about the rear window. He scrutinised my insurance certificate and agreed all was in order. I wrote him a cheque for £55 and he took his leave.

I called Mr Earl.

His grandfather had arrived in England on the *Empire Windrush* in 1948. So two generations later, Mr Earl is now twenty-five percent Jamaican and seventy-five percent south Bristol. Instinctively laid back and totally unfazed by the complexities of the world around him, he lives above his car workshop in a cul-de-sac in Southville, with his wife Alesha and his son Hamilton. The Earls are a singular example of how to get through life with the minimum of aggravation. Each time he presents me a bill, Mr Earl shakes his head sadly. But I've had the car fifteen years and long ago resolved not to give it up.

"Hi there Shepherd Bra," he said. "Healey broken down again?"

I described the hole in the soft top rear window and asked if he could repair it.

"It needs mending with a new one," he said gravely. Without a trace of indulgence.

"But in the meantime...?" I asked.

"Stick a piece of sellotape over the hole," he said, in all seriousness.

"Can't you accomplish something a little more robust than that?"

"Hang on," he said.

There was a clunk as he put the phone receiver down. Somebody was banging something in the background and I could hear Bob Marley singing *No Woman No Cry*.

Mr Earl came back on the line.

"I've got some toughened plastic here, and some heavy duty adhesive. Bring the Healey in first thing."

"Thank you," I said.

"You're welcome," he said and rang off.

I switched on the 6 o'clock news and found myself plugged into an ongoing litany of misery. The top story was hard to watch; another scenario from central Africa, which was unfixable because nobody but Bob Geldof and Richard Curtis and their friends cared enough to tackle the problem. An all too familiar sight of young children dying because adults put ambition, crossing the road to the other side, and 'why the hell do I have to care?' before simple compassion. By contrast, the second item bordered on farce; a cabal of UKIP leaders, broken down MEPs and a gathering of right wing Poles, with yet another reason why Europe wasn't working.

I sat through the rest of the news, and through *Points West*. I mistakenly caught the intro to *The One Show* – something about local council responsibility for rat infestations – and gave up on the evening. I went into the kitchen to find something to cook. I looked out across the garden into the gathering dusk. The clocks had embraced British Summer Time three weeks ago. It had been a bright, sunny afternoon and dusk was only now making an effort to close down the day. I trawled the fridge and the kitchen cupboards and decided on chilli.

My mobile rang. I found it in the inside pocket of my jacket, draped over the newel post at the foot of the stairs.

"Where are you?" Linda asked.

"Home."

"I've got one chore to do here in the office. I'll be with you in the next half hour."

The bath earlier, may have improved how I felt, but not the impression I was giving. I stared at my reflection in the hall mirror. The bruises on my face were livid enough to frighten a class of mixed infants. I put the thoughts of chilli to the back of my mind and made some more tea.

The front doorbell rang. Linda greeted me with a smile as I opened the door.

"I left my key at home, not used to the..." The smile morphed into a grimace. "My God! What have you been doing?"

I moved to one side. Linda stepped into the hall and I closed the front door. She pointed at the bruises.

"I've got them round my ribs too," I said. "Mr Smith did that. And his friend, also called Mr Smith, shot a hole in my car."

"He did what?"

"Well actually, he shot a hole in the back window, but the bullet went straight on and—"

Linda interrupted me. "Stop stop... Somebody shot at you?"

"Not me, the car. Smith Two did it, because I turned down an offer of ten thousand pounds from Smith One."

"I don't believe this."

"That's probably best."

"No, Jack. I mean that you—"

"Yes. I know what you mean. It was just a warning shot."

"Who from?"

I told her I had no idea, and regaled her with the events of the day. She stepped forward and wrapped her arms around me. I winced. She unwound herself and stepped back.

"I came here for a bout, no several bouts," she said, "of unbridled sex. And I find you in no fit state to join in."

"I'll be alright lying down," I suggested. "If you do all the work."

"How many times have the sisters heard that, I wonder?"

Chapter Six

I woke just before 8 o'clock with an eighteen carat headache. The bruises on my cheek and across the left side of my ribcage were now glowing yellow and purple. I found some codeine in the bathroom cabinet, took as big a dose as the bottle label would allow and stepped into the shower.

As I emerged from the steam, the sun came out. I gingerly towelled myself down in the warm light refracted through the bathroom window.

Linda was still asleep. I unhooked a pair of jeans and a shirt from their coat hangers in the wardrobe, picked up a pair of socks and my gardening trainers, and left the room, avoiding the creaky floorboard in the doorway. I dressed in the kitchen, opened the back door and walked into the sunshine. I sat down on the garden bench, raised my arms and looped them over the back rest, lifted my head into the sunshine and closed my eyes. The lead in the morning chorus was a blackbird, singing the sweetest heart stopping song.

Somewhere in the distance a phone rang.

I slipped into another 'how far have we got' moment and struggled a bit with it. There was no answer in the discovery department; although some ground had been covered in the menacing and beating up departments. While Len Coleman was dead, and no help at all.

Linda's voice rescued me. I looked back towards the house. She was standing in the kitchen doorway, dressed in light brown chinos and a cream shirt. She called to me.

"Adam rang a couple of minutes ago."

I got up off the bench and walked towards her. She looked terrific and I told her so. She said 'thank you'. I took the phone receiver out of its cradle on the kitchen wall and called Adam's mobile.

"I'm at the Post," he said. "Got your pc switched on?"

"No. Why?"

"Get to it. Google newspost dot local dot co dot uk slash Bristol. You're the headline this morning."

"What?"

"You, and Bill Marsh. Take a look. I'll stay on the line."

I went upstairs to the pc on a desk in the small bedroom. A minute later I was reading the post. *Prominent Syme Park Millionaire Disappears*, the headline yelled, *Private Eye Discovers Blood In Empty House*. And there were pictures. A recent one of Bill at a charity function and lower down the page, a grainy blow up of me, taken God knows where and when.

"Where the hell did they get all this from?"

"Don't know. No one here has a clue as to the source."

"Will newspost dot whatever know who is responsible?"

"Probably not."

"Will they care?"

"No. They cherry-pick from thousands of emails they collect, then upload them. No names no pack drill, no editorial, no taste, no concern for the truth, no censorship."

Adam paused. I was thinking. He continued.

"I expect the paps will get onto this soon. Stay at home until you work something out. Then call me. I'm not doing this story, but I'm about to be swamped by scribblers asking questions about you."

"Where's Chrissie?"

"She's in some school somewhere, on a teaching placement. I'm going home around 1 o'clock to spend the afternoon with Sam. Talk to you later."

The doorbell rang.

It was Angela, the post person. She took a step backwards as I opened the door. My bruises and I must have been lunging with intent. She was the only visitor I could see. I apologised for surprising her. She recovered, stretched out an arm and offered me a padded envelope.

"Too big to go through the letter box," she said.

I took it from her, backed into the hall and closed the door.

Linda asked if there was anything oaty or crunchy to eat. Not in this house. So we made toast and scrambled eggs. I opened the envelope as I sat down to eat. Dug out four catalogues, courtesy of a group of companies I had indicated an interest in receiving mail from, apparently.

"Did you?" Linda asked. "Indicate an interest."

"Not that I recall."

"That's the problem," she said. "You respond to some deal from somewhere, and then it begins. You surface on some supplier's database. Post code, phone number, mobile number, email address. And within days, the whole bloody retail world assails you with offers you can't refuse. And you can't stop the bastards. Because the manufacturers are based in Holland, the stuff is made in the Philippines, the telesales department is in Mumbai and the customer services department is in another fucking inaccessible place altogether."

She looked a bit flushed.

"I've never heard you rant first thing in the morning. Should I log this away and beware?"

"Oh yes..."

I examined the paperwork. There was a country clothes catalogue; full of hacking jackets and hunting and fishing garments with special pockets for gun cartridges and tins of bait. Introductory offers on garden rotavators, strimmers and chainsaws from *Great Country Gardens* – I wasn't sure whether 'great' referred to size or to quality. And two holiday brochures, with the strap line *Sensational Singles Holidays in Thailand and Malaysia*; offering cheap flights on airlines I'd never heard of. Basically for sex tourists. A cut price opportunity to exploit young women, young men, poverty and moral misery without any noticeable attack of conscience.

Linda asked me if I was going into the office.

"I'm going to see Mr Earl first," I said.

I escorted her to the front door. She leaned into me, let me take her weight and enjoy the smell of her.

"Later," she said.

I opened the door. She glided out of the house and swayed down the path to the front gate. Fabulous...

I watched until she got into her car.

I locked the front door, walked through the house and let myself out of the back. Got into the Healey and drove to Mr Earl's workshop.

"That's a bullet hole," he said.

I couldn't deny it. He shook his head sadly.

"Go and get some coffee. Come back in half an hour."

Alesha was behind the counter of the *Soul Food Café* across the road. Like Earl, born and brought up in south Bristol; mother to their son Hamilton and the beating heart of the family engine. She was known by everyone within a half mile radius, and no one spoke ill of her. Tall and slim and darker skinned than Mr Earl, everything she did seemed to have a purpose. And you couldn't see the joins. She went about her daily business seamlessly, through excitement and joys and crises. She handled those imposters all the same. And she brewed the best pot of coffee in the city.

Labi Siffre's *Something Inside So Strong* was playing on the café CD player.

Alesha smiled, stepped out from behind the counter, embraced me, and sat me down in the window facing the street. The man at the next table had tightly curled grey hair, wide shoulders and was probably in his 70s. He swivelled in his chair, shook hands with me and said 'hello'. I didn't know him at all, but I was a friend of Alesha and that was just fine by him. Labi Siffre segued into Jimmy Cliff and *You Can Get It If You Really Want*. I had a second cup of coffee. The man tapped the soles of a pair of battered Hush Puppies on the laminate floor, and then swayed in his chair along with *The Harder They Come*. I finished my coffee, gave the man my best wishes and went back to the workshop. Mr Earl told me the repair would last for a while, but I ought to consider saving up for a new hood. I dug my wallet out of my jacket. He waved it away.

"Not worth opening the till for," he said. "Next time will do."

There was a message on my mobile. May asking me to call her. I did that when I got to the office. She told me she had found Bill's wallet.

"In the pocket of an old blue fleece he wears every morning when he walks into Stoke Bishop for his newspaper. Sergeant Hood's team missed it."

I asked what was in it.

"Sixty pounds in notes," she said. "Co-op Bank debit and credit cards, his bus pass, his Senior Rail card, and his *Silver Star Casino* card. He's been a member for years. Some of his old mates are too. He's there twice, maybe three times a month. Could this help?"

"It could, yes. Are you okay?"

"Fine. Helen's here. She just supplied the journalists at the gate with tea."

She ended the call.

There was something about the *Silver Star* that rang a bell. I'd never been in the place, but now the name was there. Like an invitation to join *Linked In* from somebody you could just about remember, who had connections to another 300 hundred other people you didn't want to know.

I googled the casino. Moments later, the website sprang into life. And so did the hairs on the back of my neck. The owner operator of the establishment was Frederick Arthur Settle.

Not one of nature's noblemen, Freddie. A genuine south Bristol hard case. An expert in all aspects of law breaking, menace and violence. With a deft side-line in jury tampering. I arrested him once – in the days when I was a DS – for extortion and aggravated assault. The trial lasted three days. The jury was out for all of twenty-seven minutes. Settle walked and the CPS got a bollocking from the judge.

What the hell was Bill doing in such company? Hopefully just having a game of blackjack now and then. After all, he was once in the gambling business himself, and he could afford to lose a little here and there.

But I could feel a stirring of panic, mixed with a dose of anger; like a comic in front of a full house who knows there's a joke in what he's about to offer, but can't find the way to deliver the punch line. Not a 'matter of life and death' moment, but a shamefully inadequate one. Those moments happened, usually under stress. And Freddie Settle could manufacture other people's stress in his sleep.

Whatever... All conjecture was ludicrous. In order to discover how much Settle was involved in what I had got myself into, I would have to pay him a visit. Freddie Settle. Christ... Why would any person in his right mind, regardless of his profession, bravery or foolishness want to confront Freddie Settle? The outcome of any direct encounter was pre-ordained.

I'd always regarded myself as a decent detective and a useful bruiser. I owed May some effort. And maybe, for my own satisfaction – how the hell was I was convincing myself of this? – I needed to find out what Freddie was up to these days. Forewarned is forearmed, and other platitudes. Surely, as long as I was polite and didn't diss his soft furnishings...

For some reason, I showered, changed into lightweight trousers, put on a clean white shirt and a cream linen jacket. Maybe because I was calling on money. Maybe because I was a hell of a detective and cool as iced vermouth. Or maybe because, in lightweight clothing, I was less likely to sweat.

Chapter Seven

The Silver Star was located on Welsh Back. Converted from a row of two storey quayside workshops, the place looked very ordinary in the afternoon sunlight. A man in jeans was waving a wash leather at the street level windows. I asked him if the Boss was in. A pair of watery blue eyes looked at me from each side of a broken nose. He grunted and said he thought I might find her in the office.

Her...?

I was still distracted by this revelation when I bumped into an old acquaintance inside the foyer. Smith One. The bearer of ten thousand pounds, on behalf of – now no longer in dispute – Freddie Settle. My heart rate soared and I began to sweat.

"Mr Shepherd..." Smith One smiled graciously. "I'm sorry, but we are not open for business this early in the day."

"I appreciate that. But I would like to talk with the Boss if I may."

He considered the proposition. Decided it might be possible, and moved to a phone on the wall to the right of a pair of huge padded doors.

"This is Gareth," he said. "Shepherd is here."

I left him to his conversation and looked round as he talked. The foyer was a handsome art deco statement and designed with some imagination. The door to my left opened. A cleaner pushed a trolley full of brushes, cloths and cleaning materials over the threshold. She stopped, left the trolley to prop the door open and reached behind her. She picked up a vacuum cleaner hose and hauled it into the foyer. I had time to look into the room behind her – the bar, as sumptuously art deco as the foyer.

The cleaner pushed and dragged her tools across the floor. I moved ahead of her, opened the door left of the house phone, stepped into the gaming room and waited for her to pass by. She thanked me. I surveyed the room. More art deco.

I heard Gareth speak to me. "This way, Mr Shepherd..."

He beckoned me back into the foyer and pointed up the staircase. A polished wooden handrail swept round the white walled curve, supported all the way up, by a series of interlocking art deco motifs. The stairwell was lit by an oval skylight in the ceiling at the head of the stairs.

"Gareth what?" I asked.

"Thomas," he said.

"And your partner?"

"He really does have the same surname. We call him Dylan. He doesn't get the joke and we haven't explained."

He waved me on up the staircase.

Dylan appeared on the landing and waited as I climbed up to him.

"Good afternoon, Shepherd," he kind of grunted.

It was a few steps to a walnut, zigzag patterned door, with the name 'Settle' on it. Dylan knocked on the door, opened it and ushered me into a large sitting room. A redhead, wearing a dark blue silk shirt and designer jeans flowed towards me. She held out her right hand.

"Frederica Settle," she said. "You can call me Freddie." She shot a look over my shoulder. "Thank you, Dylan."

I heard the door close behind me. I couldn't take my eyes off the hostess. The coolest of cool elegance. Mid 30s, five feet nine, slim build, long legs and sensational dark eyes. She turned her attention to me.

"I know. Dylan doesn't ring out 'enforcer' does it? But he likes it. So we all refrain from taking the piss."

She smiled. I smiled back.

"It's a pleasure to meet you, Mr Shepherd."

"You can call me Jack," I said. It seemed best to enjoy the informality while I was still in a position to do so.

There were two sofas in the centre of the room, with a low satinwood table between them. She waved me to one of them. I sat down, lower than I had anticipated, and was embraced by the soft cushions. Getting up out of the sofa again swiftly, should the need arise, would be difficult.

"Can I get you a drink?" Freddie asked.

"No thank you."

She moved to the other side of the table, dropped into the sofa, relaxed, raised her right arm and rested it on the top of the cushion behind her. Crossed her left leg over her right and waited while I looked around me. This room was the best of the recce so far. I'd always believed that Freddie Settle wouldn't recognise taste if it wrote him a cheque for a million pounds. It looked however, like he'd spent close to that in here.

"It's not exactly my style," Freddie said. "I prefer lean looks and clean lines. But Dad likes it."

"Where is he?"

"He's retired. I'm the Boss now. You're surprised of course."

I had to admit I was. But I pulled myself together sufficiently to qualify the consideration.

"Not that you're in the job, specifically. Rather, that Freddie has managed to produce such style and refinement. I include you in that assessment of course."

"Benenden and the LSE," she said. "I was born into this business and groomed to run it. It's not about threats, broken kneecaps and protection any more, Jack. Those days are consigned to retro TV. This is a creative, post twenty-twelve, high investment company. Dad's money wasn't wasted. This is where we both want me to be."

I couldn't think of anything to say. So Freddie moved things along.

"Now what can I do for you? I was given to understand that you and my associates failed to get on."

"A question of ethics, Freddie."

"Yes that's how I heard it. Still you're here now. So...?"

"Why did you offer me ten thousand pounds?"

Freddie pasted the smile back on her face and crossed her right leg over her left. "Do you really expect me to answer that?"

"I guess not. But I am a detective and I'd fall short of my job description if I didn't ask the question."

"And you'll also understand why I don't feel disposed to explain. Suffice to say, I'd hoped you'd look upon it as a windfall and accept."

'Less is more', is an often tested concept. This lady was the best at it I'd ever come across. So, clinging on, I changed the subject.

"How are you on other information?" I asked.

"Okay, probably."

I tried the intro I had rehearsed.

"Len Coleman," I said.

"Who?"

"Len Coleman," I repeated. "He was a member here."

"Was he?"

Freddie stared at me. I managed not to blink.

"Okay," she said. "Let's see..."

She reached for the phone on the desk. Pressed the speaker button on the base. Then a couple of numbers. Somewhere in the building, a man called Cyril answered the call.

"Yes, Ms Settle..."

"Cyril, do we have a member called Len Coleman?"

"Give me a moment."

"Of course."

A moment later, Cyril came back with the answer.

"We did. He's no longer with us."

That was open to many an interpretation. Freddie also in the moment, grinned at me.

"Since when, Cyril?"

There was a beat. Which turned into several bars rest. Freddie and I waited. Cyril came back to us.

"He was invited to renew his membership ten days ago. As yet, he hasn't done so."

Freddie looked up at me. "Do you want to ask him anything else?"

I talked to the speaker. "No. Thank you, Cyril."

"Is that all, Ms Settle?"

"Yes, Cyril. Apologies for disturbing you."

"That's alright," Cyril said.

Freddie switched off the speaker, leaned back against the sofa cushions once more and shrugged.

"So there you have it."

I moved to get to my feet. Squeezing out of the cushion's embrace was as tricky as I had expected. Freddie had all the time in the world to stretch a restraining arm across the table. I was left leaning forwards.

"Is that all?" she asked. "Surely not. There must be something else we can help you with."

She said that with consummate seriousness. I couldn't help but stare. Then she smiled again. She was really good at this stuff. I allowed myself to assume she was unlikely to summon Gareth and Dylan to rough me up in her office, and pressed on.

"Why was Gareth at Len Coleman's house?" I asked

"Was he?"

For a moment, it looked like she was about to do another phone check. But no. If ever there was a dead horse getting a good kicking, this was it. In slow motion, I got to my feet. Freddie watched me, waited until I was up straight, then matched the manoeuvre herself. The interview was officially over. She pressed a button on a wall beside a chunky sideboard with overlaid swirls on the doors.

"Any time you want to risk a few notes come back and see us. Free membership for you of course."

"Thank you. But I can't afford the losses."

"The downside of the detecting business," she said. "Prospects few and far between."

The Settle firm knew all about prospects. There were people propping up motorway intersections who did too.

The door opened and Dylan came back in.

"Please see that Mr Shepherd is escorted off the premises."

Dylan nodded, stepped to one side and motioned me to the door. Freddie, now once again uber-gracious, bade me farewell.

"I'll give your regards to my father," she said. "I'm sure he will be interested in how you are. Take care now."

An image of her father grinning at me from the dock in Bristol Crown Court, was seared onto my retina.

"I'll do my best, Freddie," I said.

Dylan escorted me back to the head of the stairs – he was clearly the first storey man – where he pointed to Gareth waiting for me at the bottom.

I stepped out into the sunlit street, shaking from head to toe. I walked to the Healey, fished the keys out of my pocket and dropped them on the pavement. I picked them up again. Fumbled them into the door lock, got the door open, climbed in and sat behind the steering wheel, my heart thumping.

Chapter Eight

I drove to the office, picking up a sandwich and a salad on the way. In the lobby, Jason handed me an envelope with a note in it.

"Ms Barnes said you were not answering your mobile," he offered, by way of explanation.

I read the note. Linda was off to Plymouth, not likely to be back until late. She suggested I meet her later, at home in Portishead. For which, I now had a door key, and about which, I wondered from time to time.

I was married to Emily for twenty-two years. The relationship was exclusive from the day we met. She was unfailing in her understanding, total in her concern for us both and tireless in her efforts to make sure we worked. She was the love of my life. Emily was... Emily. Unique. Linda was altogether different. She was taking time and care to build the relationship we were currently embarking on. But I was still dithering.

I took the stairs up to my office. I made some coffee in the kitchen along the landing, ate the food and fell to talking the situation over with myself.

Bill had disappeared without his car and his wallet. The plan Bill and Len had worked out, had gone to rat shit in the face of intervention by a person or persons unknown. The musing was interrupted when the phone on my desk rang.

"What do you know about Walter Cobb?" Adam asked.

Walter Cobb... Entrepreneur, impresario, football club director, and scrap metal merchant. Alleged to owe money all over the county in guise number one, implicated in a series of concert ticket scams in the second, derided in equal measure as idiot and buffoon in the third, and richer than Bernie Ecclestone courtesy of the fourth. Bristol's original kipper-tied wide-boy. More old-fashioned chancer than serious villain. Something of a poker player however. Legend has it he won the scrap business in a game of five card draw, one night in a motel out on the A38. There is a stonking caricature of him, complete with medallion and chest wig, adorning one side of the only gentlemen's public convenience still functioning in Southville. His sworn enemy on the city council fought for years to prevent the cleansing department clearing it up. Now the work of art is something of a landmark. *"How do I get to Ashton Gate?" "Second left and straight on past Walter Cobb."*

"I know as much about the man as anyone else," I said.

"Can you meet me?"

"Haven't you got to get home?"

"No. Chrissie and Sam are doing their weekly hospital visit. This evening, it's the Oncology department at the BRI. Sam's a star. Shows off like the clappers and the patients and staff love him to bits. I'll meet you at the *Nova Scotia* in fifteen minutes."

The pub is a short walk from my office. It sits on the Cumberland Basin dockside at the western end of the floating harbour. It's a place to drink and eat, a rendezvous, and a harbour ferry stop. Old and comfortable inside, with tables and seating on the dockside for summer days and lazy afternoons. The late afternoon sun was warm enough to sit outside. Adam bought the tea and we sat down. I thanked him and opened the conversation.

"So... The local hero we were talking of earlier."

"Indeed," Adam said. He raised his cup, took his first sip of tea and went on. "Walter Cobb is about to go broke. Spectacularly.

No business, no dosh, and soon, in all probability, no roof over his head."

"Refreshing to know, but er..."

"What does it have to do with you?"

"In essence."

"Indulge me for a minute. Tomorrow morning, everything he owns is being taken away from him. The Bailiffs will be in by noon."

"How do you know all this?"

"I've seen the paperwork. Courtesy of his PA. A lady called Bridget Dean, who by all accounts has kept Cobb's business afloat almost singlehanded in recent years. He owes her four months' wages. Which in itself is not the problem – Cobb has been short of readies before – but this time, he's been paying his personal bills, with money Bridget put into the company. So, understandably, she's mad at him."

"Okay..."

"Yes, sorry. I'll get to it. A swift eye cast across the paperwork reveals the list of major creditors. Among them, Bill Marsh."

"How much is he owed?"

"A little short of fifty-two thousand."

"Christ..."

"And meanwhile, according to Bridget, Walter was in hock for a time to the *Silver Star Casino*. The owner-operator of which, is the one and only Freddie Settle."

He waited for me to respond to the last sentence. Expecting me to turn a whiter shade of pale and shift in my seat. But I had already done that bit.

"No it's not," I said. "The place is now in the hands of his daughter, Frederica." Adam stared at me. "She says I can call her Freddie."

Adam struggled to find something to say. I moved the conversation along.

"Bill is a *Silver Star* member," I said. "I went there earlier today."

Adam, amazed at the idiocy of such a move, managed one word. "Why?" Then added another three. "For God's sake why?"

"I wanted to get a feel of the place," I said.

"Feel of the..."

He lapsed back into speechless. Took in air and blew out his cheeks.

"I know it was a little ill-advised," I said.

"Actually not to be advised at all," he said.

We both took time to contemplate that. Adam spoke again.

"So come on. Explain."

I gave him chapter and verse. He listened without interrupting. At the end of the story he went back to the subplot.

"Well, Walter ought to be a breeze after Freddie," he suggested. "There should be no threats, real or implied, from a man who glories to such an extent in the image he pedals, that he's happy to allow himself to decorate a bog wall."

"How bright is he?" I asked. "Really."

"Bright enough at poker. Bright enough to get by, until now. What I mean is, he's not a total buffoon."

I must have looked at Adam in disbelief, because he elaborated.

"Just don't think he's a pushover. His hyper-opinionated, on the edge of foolishness schtick, hides a devious mind. A bit like Boris Johnson."

* * *

The headquarters of Cobb Business Ltd was situated in Whiteladies Court, a four storey building of serviced offices across the road from the BBC. Inside the entrance hall, a man behind a marble desk pointed me at the doors of an exclusive lift. Inside it there was one button only. Top Floor.

I stepped out of the lift directly into the top floor lobby. A blonde with blue eyes and a brunette with hazel eyes were stationed behind a huge walnut desk. Hazel Eyes was wearing a telephone head set and attempting to pour oil on troubled waters.

"I'm sorry, Mr Satchell. Would you like to speak to Bridget?"

Blue Eyes smiled at me. "Can I help you, Sir?"

"I want to see Mr Cobb," I said.

"I'm afraid he's just gone out," she said.

"How long will he be?" I asked.

The smile faded. She looked to her left for assistance. Hazel Eyes wound up her conversation.

"No... I'm very sorry... Please do. Goodbye, Mr Satchell."

She pulled off the head set. "Dear God!" Then she registered my presence and apologised. "I beg your pardon."

I told her not to worry. Blue Eyes helped out.

"This gentleman wants to know when Mr Cobb will be back."

The brunette sighed. "I'm sorry, Sir. I'm afraid I have no idea."

"Then I'll pop in and see Bridget," I said.

Hazel Eyes pointed across the lobby. "First left along that corridor, Sir."

A brass plate on a walnut door said *Bridget Dean*. I knocked on the door. There was no response from the other side. I opened the door and stepped into an office about fifteen feet square, with a suspended ceiling, hidden lighting and more walnut furniture. There was no sign of Bridget. The door which I assumed to be her access to Cobb was closed. I walked across some extremely expensive carpet and opened the door. Something weighty zoomed past my head and on into

Bridget's office. A second later it hit something which crashed to the floor.

"Oh God I'm sorry," Bridget said. "I could have killed you."

Five feet two or three, with cropped auburn hair, she was wearing a white tee shirt, blue jeans and trainers. She was breathing heavily and she looked fierce in spite of the apology. She was standing behind Cobb's desk; a monster piece of walnut like the desk in reception, in front of a huge window with a view across Whiteladies Road. Bridget seemed to be ransacking the place.

"Forgive me. I thought he was back."

"You should have taken a moment to check," I suggested.

"Yes, I'm really sorry."

"Where is he?"

"He's gone out, the fucking shit."

That assessment chimed with all that was known about him. And Bridget was on a roll.

"He just sacked me, do you know that? Fucking bastard!"

It seemed discourteous not to ask why. So I did. Bridget shook her head ferociously then stepped back and slumped down into the chair behind the desk.

"None of your business," she said.

I took time to look round the office. It was a bit of a mess. The drawers of two walnut filing cabinets were pulled out. The doors of a quartet of custom built walnut cupboards were open, contents strewn around the place.

I asked Bridget if this was her work. She confessed it was. I asked her what she was looking for.

"Something expensive. He owes me something expensive?"

"Did you find anything?"

"I think the bronze I threw at you was it. Do you fancy a drink?"

"What has he got?"

"No not here," Bridget said. "I wouldn't drink his whisky if I was dying of thirst. Over the road."

She led the way out of Cobb's office.

The franchisees of the eateries, bistros and bars on Whiteladies Road change often these days. We sat facing each other across a table in a window booth in *Brunel's Bar* – all velour covered foam and laminated surfaces. No walnut anywhere. A couple of months ago, the place was an overpriced restaurant called *Filippo's*. When I used to spend money here, three or four years ago, it was a pub called *The Engineer*.

Bridget had downed her first house cocktail in one, now she sipped at her second. I was drinking a glass of beer and taking a long look at her. She knew I was doing so but she was clearly confident enough to let that sort of thing happen. I guessed she was around the same age as me. Her hair colour came out of a bottle but the rest of her looked absolutely genuine.

"Is there a Mr Dean?" I asked.

"No," she said.

"Was there ever?"

"When I was twenty-one. It lasted a couple of years. Then he joined the army and went to Iraq the first time around."

"Oh I'm sorry."

She grinned at me. "No no... He didn't get himself killed, although that would have been the decent thing to do. He came back, told me he was suffering from post-traumatic stress and went off to find himself."

"Where is he now?"

"God knows..."

She sipped at her cocktail again. I sipped my beer.

"Okay," she said. "Who are you?"

"Jack Shepherd," I said. "I come to you via Adam Leslie. He's my daughter's partner. I'm a private detective, looking for a friend."

"A friend. That probably counts as important."

"Thank you. Unfortunately, he may have got involved in some deal with Walter."

"That's not good. Presumably Walter owes him money."

"Yes."

"And his name? A straight swop. In complete confidence," she said.

"Bill Marsh."

Bridget sighed and sat back in her chair. "I remember. Fifty something thousand pounds."

"Yes. That's what Adam said."

"I like Bill," she said. "I've known him since he took over his Uncle Jimmy's business. He gave me a job when I desperately needed one. A bit of a wide boy, not entirely straight, but proper south Bristol."

"So how long have you worked for Walter Cobb?"

"Almost ten years."

"That's long enough to get close."

Now she shot an angry look at me.

"Close...?" She looked as if I'd just asked her to eat something foul. "If by that you mean close enough to second guess his every move, to tidy up the wreckage he leaves behind him, to smile at the people he needs to impress, to side track the people he needs to dodge. I know the business version of him inside out. But close? Nobody gets close to a man like Walter Cobb. His daughters knew that better than anyone."

"Where are they?"

"Lauri is dead. The other two are in New Zealand. That's the farthest away you can get, before you start coming back."

"So what's going on over the road?" I asked.

"Nobody was paid last month," Bridget said. "Walter's broke."

"That's just relative," I said. "There's a difference between broke and over-extended. People like him are always short of cash."

"No, really. He's flat broke. Bust. Down and out. He owes money all over the city and beyond."

"How much money?"

"A few hundred thousand."

"Is he going to survive?"

She snorted. "*Cobb Business Ltd* isn't. But you're right, there's no doubt Walter will get by. There'll be something stashed away somewhere."

I asked Bridget where Walter lived.

"Moorend," she said. "The other side of the M4. At the bottom of a lane appropriately named Fortune Avenue."

I asked for his telephone number. She recited it to me. I logged it.

"Aren't you going to write it down?" Bridget asked.

"I don't need to. I remember numbers."

"Just in case however..."

She called a waiter over, borrowed his pen, asked for a page from his order pad and wrote on it. She passed it to me.

"Mine. And my mobile," she said, looking me straight in the eyes.

"Thank you," I said.

There was a pause. Then Bridget wound things up.

"Just remember this. Walter fucking Cobb is as cold as the Russian Steppes in February and slippery as a boatload of eels. Be careful."

She downed the rest of her drink and stood up to leave. I let her go and watched through the window as she crossed Whiteladies Road.

Chapter Nine

Late afternoon now. Whiteladies Road was gridlocked. And there was only one way to go; onwards and up to the Downs. It was twenty minutes before I cleared the traffic, and 6.30 by the time I turned the Healey into Fortune Avenue. The lane was two hundred yards long or thereabouts and led straight onto Cobb's front drive. The black and gold painted cast iron gates were open. I considered this an invitation to proceed, so drove on through and parked the Healey behind the black Bentley in front of Cobb's garage doors. The house was a mock Tudor affair; half-timbered and hideous.

Cobb had seen me arrive. He opened the front door before I reached it. He was shorter than me, but heavier. Mid 60s maybe, greying hair, dark eyes under heavy brows and a moustache which would have looked better on just about anybody else. He wore his blue denim shirt outside his jeans to hide the extra couple of inches round his waist. The thick-soled, soft leather loafers on his feet were expensive. He wasn't in a good mood.

"Who the hell are you?" he asked.

I told him.

"A journalist?"

"No."

"I mean, look," he said. "The fucking excitement's over. I'm going broke and that's it. End of."

"Maybe not," I suggested.

He ignored that and asked what I was doing on his doorstep.

I told him I wanted to talk with him. He asked me about what. A friend of mine, I said.

"Who?"

"May I come in?"

He must have decided he wasn't over-burdened with things to do. He stepped back and waved me into the hall. Floor to ceiling dark oak panelling with two rooms off to the right. And a misguided attempt at a country house staircase, which began on the left and wrapped itself around the hall as it rose upwards. Somebody had made a list of period features required and installed them in all the wrong places. Cobb ushered me into what he must have considered the drawing room. Although the dimensions were different, it looked just like the hall, the mock Tudor motif continuing to run riot. The fireplace took up most of one wall.

"So... The money's all gone," he said.

"Do you care?"

He glared at me. "What the hell is that supposed to mean?"

"Simple question," I said. "Are you upset?"

"Of course I'm fucking upset."

"I ask that, because you may also be taking the friend I mentioned with you."

"Yeah? Who?"

"Bill Marsh."

Cobb grinned at me. "Dear oh fucking dear... Hardly. Bill Marsh could buy my debts three or four times over."

He threw that line away like a professional. In fact he was delivering a performance of some quality. He continued.

"Look. I'm devastated by it all."

"Which explains," I said, "why you're doing a passable imitation of a man who doesn't give a toss."

He looked for a moment, like he was weighing up the pros and cons of throwing me out. Instead, he decided to be hospitable. Asked me if I wanted a drink. I told him 'no thank you'.

There were two padded armchairs facing each other in front of the stone fireplace. He moved around the table, sat down in one and pointed me to the chair facing him. I chose to stay on my feet. He looked offended for a moment, then settled back in the chair cushions and stared up at me. I stared back. There was a long pause. He gave up first.

"So... How is Bill?"

"I'm not sure," I said. "He's disappeared."

He looked blank. Scrunched up his face, like a child making a big show of thinking. I asked him where he was on the previous Monday night.

He smoothed his face out. "Can't remember."

"Try."

He sniffed. "Alright, I was here."

"Were you alone?"

"Unfortunately."

"All night?"

"Yes. Counting the last of my money."

Probably in plastic bags under the bed. He waited for me to go on. Looked confused when I didn't. I stared into his eyes. And the phoney politeness suddenly evaporated. Cobb stood up and pointed at the living room door.

"Right that's it. I've had enough. Get out of my fucking house."

So I did. As I walked to the Healey, Cobb yelled at me from the doorway.

"And fucking stay away!"

I got into the car; not sure if I had improved the shining hour at all. I reversed out of Cobb's gateway, u-turned, coasted a few yards along Fortune Avenue and stopped. I took my mobile out of the glove box, called Adam and relayed the conversation to him.

"I don't know what the score is. Cobb didn't act like the man with brains you suggested he was."

"I told you, that's his schtick. You're supposed to fall for it."

On the road back into the city, I switched on the radio and found *5 Live*. The 7 o'clock news bulletin top story was about a crash on the northbound carriageway of the M5, north of Taunton. A Ford Escort burst a rear tyre, while travelling way over the speed limit. The car slid into the central reservation barrier and bounced back into the traffic. Cars and vans following, plunged into the chaos.

I wondered if Linda had begun her journey back from Plymouth. Probably not yet. In which case, she would have to drive much of the way up the A38.

A long evening alone with the TV, looked odds on. Or I could spend the time making some notes on what this case had yielded so far. And even if I ended up with more suppositions and questions than currently in the log, something might surface.

Or I could worry about my relationship with Freddie. I'd get shorter odds on surviving it than an apprentice wire walker's first attempt to cross the Avon Gorge. We both knew exactly what the rest of the world did about Bill and Len Coleman, thanks to newspost dot whatever. Freddie could monitor my progress, pop up every now and again to enquire about my health, confident that the time would arrive when frustration would drive me to tell her what she wanted to know – whatever that was – or do something foolish.

Walking from the garage across the back lawn, I had a minor brainwave. I poured a generous double malt, sat down in the living room and phoned Adam.

"Accepting that Bill Marsh is at the top of Freddie Settle's 'Things to Do' list," I said. "Do you think we could use the newspost blog to confuse things?"

"Blogs are always good for that."

"Can we set up an email address untraceable back to us?"

"There's no such thing as a completely safe email address. But we can do enough to give us a little time to play, before we're rumbled."

"Could we concoct some story, outrageous enough to appear to be true?"

"Such as...?"

"Something that implicates me in Bill's disappearance."

"Why? Bloody hell, Jack..."

"See if we can drag something wicked out of the woodwork."

Adam was quiet for a few seconds. I listened to the buzz on the line.

"We'll need a laptop," he said. "Can't use yours or mine."

"Is that a problem?"

"Shouldn't be. There's a shop in Bedminster which sells re-conditioned pcs. Chris Gould, the bloke who runs it, has a workshop at the back. We don't need anything fancy. In fact the older the software the better. I'll call him and get back to you."

I sat for a couple of minutes wondering how this mad scheme might pay out. I decided it was foolish to raise that question now. So I fell to considering how long it was likely to be before Linda got far enough up the A38 to by-pass the mess on the M5. I called her mobile. She didn't answer. I left a message, decided to stay on the sofa awhile, turned on the TV and discovered a re-run of Dennis Potter's *The Singing Detective* on BBC4.

Linda called at 9.20.

"I thought we were going to meet here," she said. "Are we not spending the night together?"

"I called earlier," was all I could think of saying. "Your mobile. I left a message."

"Ah right..."

"Twice," I said, as if that made the shaky ground more stable.

"But you're still not here."

That was clearly the case.

"Shit, Jack... I was stationary on the M5 for the best part of an hour. Then on the A38, dribbling along for another hour and a half. Looking forward to being greeted by you, holding out a glass of chilled something or other."

"I didn't think it was..."

I stopped. Whatever I was about to offer, was going to be a mistake. I was indisputably at home on my own sofa. The fact I had been side-tracked by the genius of Dennis Potter, and assumed that Linda would call me from somewhere along the way, was probably no basis for negotiation.

"Didn't think it was what?" she demanded. "Worth coming over?"

"I'll come now," I said.

"Don't bother," Linda said.

"I did ring..."

Her voice went up a couple of notes, which is what happens when she is being severe. Only she was about to be more than that.

"The battery was dead actually. Because I had left it in my briefcase, switched on, all day." She took all the full stops out of the next sentences. "I appreciate how stupid that was I know it's not your fault but I'm stressed and hot and tired and all the way up the fucking A38 I was ticking off the miles thinking about later expecting you to be here and you weren't and that pissed me off."

She stopped and gave out a weary sigh. It was followed by a lengthy silence.

"I'll come over now," I repeated. But the night was lost to us.

"Best not," Linda said. "I'll have a bath and a drink and find a movie to watch in bed. I'll see you tomorrow. Goodnight."

"Goodnight."

Linda ended the call. I was left listening to the dial tone. Another rousing hit Shepherd...

Chapter Ten

Adam rang at quarter past eight the following morning. I rolled over in bed and reached for the phone.

"We're up and running," he said.

I was still not fully awake. "With what?"

"Chris Gould has an old laptop, with the absolute minimum of software; no games no apps, no shit like that. Run by Windows 98, amazingly. We're going to use a no-reply address. He suggests we work from his place."

"Which is where?"

"The old trading estate off Bedminster Parade. I'll email you the address and Chris's phone number. Meanwhile, we need to think about the tone of this diatribe."

"Where are you?"

"At home. Chrissie and Sam have gone out for a walk. I was going to go into the office."

"Come round for breakfast," I suggested. "We can talk across the coffee and doughnuts."

"Doughnuts?"

"Fresh from the bakers on the corner."

* * *

We were eating the custard filled doughnuts thirty-five minutes later.

"Did you see Linda last night?" Adam asked.

"It's considered not done to speak with your mouth full," I said.

"That's obviously a 'no.'"

I glared at him. He swallowed and put down the doughnut he was working on.

"I've been thinking of something along the lines of... *Bristol PI, Jack Shepherd, appears to have solved the mystery of disappeared bookie, Bill Marsh. His investigations led him to a one hundred percent reliable source of information. And Shepherd is now in the process of liaising between this source and police officers involved in the case...* What do you think?"

"I think we'll get arrested for attempting to pervert the course of justice."

"What justice? No copper is actually hot on the case. You won't get anything approaching justice at the hands of Freddie Settle. And the conspiracy, if there is such in this case, begins with Bill Marsh and his mate Len Coleman. We, or rather you, are simply after the truth. And along the way, unfortunately, a serious bollocking from the women in your life."

I offered him a look I hoped defined the stress I was feeling.

"Okay, let's really examine this," Adam said. "What, do you think, is the accepted credibility rating of the newspost site?"

"I guess a bit less than the late unlamented *News of the World*."

"Exactly. And as such, it will be devoured by all the people who actually want the story to be true. Around here, that could amount to tens of thousands. You will be hot news for days, if we can keep it up."

"Or on the run, like Bill," I suggested.

"Yes, well, let's not dwell on that at this stage," Adam said. "We have three sets of people whose interest we need to retain. Bill, Freddie Settle, and the Murder Investigations Team."

"Actually four," I said. "Walter Cobb is in play."

"Four then," Adam said. "Bottom line is, we don't care whether any of these people believe us, so long as the post creates an itch irritating enough for them to scratch. Freddie is in no position to discount this material. As far as she is concerned, this scurrilous shit might just be true. In which case, she will upgrade her interest in your welfare."

"Something to cherish."

"And I guess that Harvey Butler might ring up and ask a question or two. You will of course berate him for taking notice of such imaginative rambling, and tell him, in no uncertain terms, that none of it is true. The ideal phone call will come from Bill, concerned that increased public interest in whatever he's doing, will be no help to... well whatever he is doing."

None of the possible reactions to this nonsense was comforting. But in the absence of leads, theories, or hunches, desperate though this endeavour was, it was plan A.

Adam looked at his watch. "I've got to go." He stood up. "Thanks for breakfast. I'll call you as soon as Chris calls me."

I was left alone to consider the day's schedule. Going into the office might give rise to the opportunity to apologise to Linda. The phone rang again, as I stepped out of the back door. I turned back into the kitchen, took the receiver off the wall phone.

"Jack, it's May. We have a bit of trouble here."

She was agitated and not altogether in control of her breathing.

"Trouble where?"

"The Drop In Centre. We seem to have had a break in."

"Are you alright?"

"Yes, I wasn't here. No one was. It happened sometime overnight."

"Have you called the police?"

She said she didn't wish to do that.

"If you come down here I'll explain. Behind the building, there's a loading yard we share with the bakery. Park there and use the back door."

The Drop In Centre used to be a branch of Stead and Simpson. A three storey, terrace building in Bedminster, between an electrical chain store and a local bakery. I drove into the loading yard, parked the Healey and found the door to the tiny back yard behind the Centre. There was a tiled brick outhouse to my left, obviously once the outside loo. To the right of the rear door was a window with very little of the bobbled opaque glass left in the frame. May was on the other side of it, sweeping the floor. She looked up, disappeared, and the door opened a few seconds later. She stood back and motioned me inside. We were standing in a narrow corridor which opened up and led into the old shop space. I looked into the room May had been sweeping. There was glass all over the floor.

"Just a store room," she said.

"Anything missing?" I asked.

May shook her head. "Not from in here."

"And this door to the left?"

"It's a shower room and a toilet."

I looked in the direction of the shop space. "And in there?"

"Come and see," she said.

It was the first time I'd been in the place. The old shop floor was fifteen feet wide, and maybe twenty-five feet deep. It was mainly a seating area, with four old, re-conditioned sofas, a dozen armchairs and some low tables. There was what passed for a reception space to the left of the front door. An old civil service desk with pedestals and a plastic inlaid top, had chairs both sides. A door at the rear of the room led to the stairs.

I turned back to May, the unspoken question hovering between us. I answered it. Told her I'd made no progress with the search for Bill. She said she'd seen the piece about Len Coleman on *Points West* the previous evening. It had shocked her a bit. I asked her how she was getting on. She said she was keeping busy and that helped. This morning's discovery however...

She gave me a tour. The first floor had a dining area the same size as the main room downstairs, and a kitchen behind it, taking up the same space as the ground floor storeroom.

"There's not much room to swing the centre's cat," May said. "But running at full steam, we can cook lunch and an evening meal for sixty-five. Sometimes we have more guests than that. We don't turn anyone away, but the hospitality suffers a little. We're open from 11 o'clock in the morning until nine at night."

There was another bathroom directly above the one downstairs, and at the back, a small office. The door was open. The architrave around the lock catch was splintered.

"Did you come up here earlier?"

"Yes, but I didn't go into the office. I called you downstairs from my mobile."

There were four rooms on the top floor. The smallest housed two desks and two chairs; the room next to it, a couple of football tables; the other two, some floor cushions and shelves with small collections of books. I asked May why she hadn't called the police.

"That's the last option, Jack. We have a lease from the city council, who took over this shop when the business closed. It's renewed every year. There is a lot of opposition to our tenancy. Some people would be delighted to see the back of us."

"And it's time to talk about the lease?"

"Yes. Another six weeks until we sign again. We have always kept a low profile, Jack. A Drop In Centre in this street is a problem for some of the rate payers and their customers. Although, surprisingly, our adjoining neighbours don't seem to mind. Others however, live uneasily with the idea that this place is undesirable at best. A break in would give them a chance to take the moral high ground. And a police investigation would trigger that."

Outside the office again, I pushed the door open with my elbow.

"Have a look," I said to May. "But don't touch anything."

May stepped into the office, stood in the centre of the room, looked around 360 degrees, then backed out into the corridor.

"So what do you want me to do?" I asked.

"I don't know really," she confessed.

Downstairs again, I looked at the alarm sensor above the front door and along the corridor to the one above the back door.

"These are triggered if the doors are forced?"

"Yes. One of the bakery employees lives in the flat above the shop. He used to be a visitor here, when he was on methadone. He went through the misery with a crushing amount of hard work. And he made it. Got his job, and volunteered as unofficial caretaker here. He has a key and the alarm code."

"So what happened last night? Did the alarm go off?"

"Yes. But there is no sensor above the store room window. A major error, as I now appreciate. We have money to extend the alarm system, but the work isn't being done until next month. When the baker got down here, the back door was open and... whoever... had gone."

I walked to the back door. May followed. We stepped into the yard. I looked towards the old privy.

"Do you keep anything in there?"

"Stuff to be re-cycled, that's all. Take a look."

I opened the outhouse door.

There was a man – 40 something maybe, but he might have been younger – wearing an old brown woollen coat, lying on a pile of flattened boxes. The coat seemed too big for him, the cloth cap on his head, too small. He might have been taller once, but I guessed if we pulled him upright, he would fold like an old concertina. I got closer. He smelled of booze and damp and loneliness.

"May..."

She stepped to my side. Looked into the shed. "Oh God..."

"Do you know him?"

She took a while to reply. "Martin. He visits often. Sleeps a couple of streets away."

"Not last night." I spoke to him. "Martin..." Then a little louder. "Martin..."

His head was tilted towards his right shoulder. I felt for the carotid artery on the left hand side of his neck. No pulse. I checked for a second time. Nothing. Behind me, May let out a long quiet sigh.

"He's dead isn't he?"

"I'm afraid so." I stood up. "You can't keep this from the police."

* * *

"Was Martin a regular visitor?" George Hood asked May. "How well did you know him?"

We were sitting in the main room. The venetian blinds over the windows were closed. The blind on the door, was pulled down. The SOCO and his associates were out in the yard. A Forensics Officer came down the stairs.

"I've finished in the office," he said, and held up a plastic evidence bag with the pc mouse in it. "Can I take this with me?"

Hood and I looked at May.

"Yes, yes of course. We have others somewhere."

The FO left in the direction of the storeroom. May answered the first part of Hood's question.

"Martin was a regular, yes."

"Do you know much about him?"

"Not much, no."

"His second name?"

"No. That's the case with a most of our visitors. And we don't insist they tell us."

In spite of being detectives and, by definition, people alleged to have a grasp on the world most ordinary mortals don't, Hood and I were listening to stuff new to us.

"Practically all of the people who walk, and sometimes stagger, through these doors have no recorded history," May went on. "Some of them can't tell us who they are, however much we frame questions we hope they'll understand. Whatever name they offer us, we accept. Unreservedly. This place is just a step away from the end of their world. We try to make it as welcoming as possible. For drinkers, drug addicts, street people, the shoeless, the unknown, the beaten, the lost..." She stopped talking. "Sorry I'm on my soap box." She went on. "Like Martin, many of them drop in regularly. But we rarely learn anything more about them, regardless of the number of times they visit."

"Has Martin ever spent a night in the shed out there?" Hood asked.

"Not that I know of."

"Would you? Know I mean."

May nodded. "I think I would, yes." She blinked furiously as tears built up in her eyes. "What is going on here gentlemen?"

"The break in might be the only issue to address," Hood offered. "We won't know anything about the death of Martin until the post mortem is done. There is no obvious link between the two situations."

May looked at Hood again. "But there might be, you mean?"

"I mean, there's no obvious link. But it's something we might have to take a view on later."

I changed the subject. "Can we look in the office now?"

May led the way upstairs. The room housed a desk with a keyboard and a screen and a telephone. A three drawer metal filing cabinet stood in a corner, by the window which overlooked the courtyard. The FO had outlined the space where the mouse had been with white, plastic tape.

"And are you sure you were the last person in here yesterday?" Hood asked.

"Yes, I locked up. And I still have the key."

"Are there any copies?"

"The volunteers have one each."

Hood asked May to find a spare mouse. She fished one out of the bottom drawer of the filing cabinet. He told her to place it where the other mouse had been and plug it into the keyboard.

"So is that how you left the desk last night?"

"What do you mean?"

"The papers, the pencil pot, the phone, the mouse... Is anything in the wrong place?"

Hood asked her to sit in her chair. She did. And the inspection directly from her point of view worked.

"The mouse pad," she said. "And the mouse. They are not the way I left them. When I finish with the pc, I push the pad away to the right. And I always leave the mouse on top of it. The pad and the mouse have been moved."

"Someone used the pc after you closed up and left." Hood said.

"But that person would have to know the password," May said.

"Where do you keep the piece of paper you wrote it on?" She looked at him sheepishly. "Everybody does the same thing," he said.

May bent down, opened the bottom drawer in the desk pedestal and dug a small piece of paper out from under all the other papers. Then looked down at the pc.

"There are no real secrets in here. Just stuff on how the Centre works. Records of donations and finances, lists of people who support us... well some of them. And of course the meagre knowledge we have managed to assemble on our visitors.

She was close to tears again.

Hood ordered us out of the way while he looked around. I made coffee in the kitchen below. May sat at one of the dining tables, staring out of the window, occasionally shifting in her chair.

Fifteen minutes later Hood walked into the room. He said 'no thanks' to coffee, and the three of us moved to the ground floor. We met the FO, who delivered his verdict on the storeroom.

"The place is covered in prints," he said. "And some glove smudges. Left by the thieves, I guess. If you're serious, we ought to print everyone who has a connection with this place."

"No no," May said. "I want us all to pretend that nothing has happened in here. I appreciate that you must discover the cause of Martin's death and investigate whatever turns up. But please, please, make as little fuss as possible."

The FO looked hurt.

"Write your report and give it to me," Hood said to him. "No one else."

The FO shrugged. "You're the boss."

He turned and walked towards the back door. Hood said 'goodbye' to us and followed him. May waited for the back door to close, then waved me to one of the sofas.

"Is our relationship confidential?" she asked. "I mean between client and investigator?"

"Absolutely. Except perhaps under torture."

She smiled and sat down next to me.

"Since the Lily business, I've been doing some thinking and checking. Looking at faces, counting heads. Visitor numbers have dropped, in ones and twos, during the last nine months or so. I'm going to go through this with Harry when he's in here tomorrow."

"And what's the problem with that?"

"No problem at all, if the missing people have moved on to other places, and, hopefully, better things. Doesn't make any difference to us in organisation terms. Actually it helps to make the money go further."

"Will your donors approve of that?"

"Of course. They give us what they do without conditions. We have some still with us after almost twenty years. One of whom, has a considerable personal fortune. Most of them remain anonymous. And in the end, unfortunately, those who stop coming here, will be replaced by others. The current estimate is there may be three hundred people living rough in Bristol."

The locking gizmo outside the front door buzzed; then beeped as a series of buttons was pressed. The door opened and a lady, in her 50s, with shoulder length silver hair, stepped over the threshold. Monica, one of the volunteers. May introduced us, before regaling her with the events of the day so far.

I spent the next half hour at the Centre, as the volunteers arrived and prepared to open for business. May and I talked in one of the top floor rooms for a while, sitting on the floor cushions.

"Why do you do what you do?" May asked

"It's my day job," I said. "If I don't do it, I don't eat."

"There are other endeavours which could probably deal with that."

"I don't know how to do anything else."

"Oh come on, Jack, that's too flip, even for you. You do what you do because you believe in it."

"Not to the superhuman extent that you do," I said. "You fight the good fight on a daily basis, it seems to me."

"Okay. Why did you spend all those days on Lily's behalf? And don't offer me any guff about knocking her down."

I thought about it for a while. May waited.

"Some while ago, I saw a film called *Life And Nothing But*. The story of a French officer in the aftermath of the Great War, charged with establishing the names and histories of thousands of dead soldiers. His job as he saw it, was not to find the Unknown Soldier, but to make sure he didn't." May was looking straight into my eyes. "It made an extraordinary impression on me. Hell, I can't claim to have done anything close to one percent as important. But even in the small things, somebody has to care."

"Ask me why I do what I do," May said."

"Okay. Why?"

"Because somebody has to care."

I grinned at her. She shuffled into another position on the bean bag.

"You agreed to try and find Bill because I asked you to. You didn't believe you could do that. You don't believe it now."

"Actually, I don't believe it's a lost cause at all. Yes, Bill has disappeared. I've no idea where he has gone, or why. But others are looking for him too. People who wouldn't be doing that if they thought he was dead."

May opened her mouth to say something. I beat her to it.

"Dangerous though these people might be, they are no more clued up than I am. I just have to stay one step ahead and find Bill before they do."

There seemed sense in that. May nodded her head

"And his mobile," I said. "There are no numbers in his contacts box. No one in crisis, spends time deleting phone numbers, unless he's working to some agenda."

May processed all that. I wound up.

"The odds are long I know. To be honest, I think Bill might give us two hundred to one. However, Adam and I have a plan for changing the odds. Not tried and tested I have to admit, but it might just work."

There was a call from below. The chef had arrived to begin preparing lunch. May led the way downstairs.

My mobile rang as I crossed the courtyard. Adam said that Chris Gould wanted us to meet him at 2.30.

Chapter Eleven

The room behind Chris Gould's shop was little more than twelve feet square but packed with used hardware. There was a work bench against one wall and racks along all four, built with dexion and shelved with plywood. A wooden table with an old laptop on it, sat in the middle of the floor with bentwood chairs on opposite sides.

Chris was probably around the same age as Adam. Five eight or nine, thin as a barber's pole, with sparse, light curly hair. He shook my hand and explained that most of the hardware was in the process of being renovated, before being shipped to schools in Malawi.

He pointed at the laptop. "Windows 98," he said. "A no-reply email address. Nothing else. No files no folders and no frills. Difficult to trace."

He left the room and went into the shop. Adam sat down in front of the laptop and began to type.

The story of the Bristol PI and the blood-stained parquet floor grows curiouser and curiouser. The man he is seeking, is now hiding from him, the police, and a city crime boss. It's only a matter of time, surely, before the investigator's client is caught by one team or another. The blood on the floor was just the prelude to something more bloody and brutal. Fascinating though it is to speculate on which way this will go, my money is on the crime boss.

Adam typed the newspost email address into the box and pressed send.

"Bingo," he said and swung round in his chair.

"Do you really think that Bill or Freddie will read that?" I asked.

"Can't fail to, if they're keeping an eye on the local news."

We thanked Chris. Adam went back to the *Post*. I went to my office.

Linda was in her office too. I stood outside the door rehearsing what I hoped would be an acceptable apology. It just sounded puny. I knocked on the door. I heard her say 'Come in.'

She looked up at me from behind her pc screen. "Hi..."

"I'm sorry," I said. Seemed simpler than beating round the bush.

She nodded. "Okay..."

I sat in the chair in front of her desk. She waited for me to go on.

"Yesterday was a bit confusing," I said, lamely.

"I spent seven hours of yesterday in my car," Linda said. "Most of them not moving."

"I got involved in stuff."

"Really? What sort of stuff? And how would you rate the involvement level? It's clearly pretty low in our thing. Or rather, in your section of it."

"I have your front door key."

That provoked the response it deserved.

"So why didn't you fucking use it last night? Christ, Jack. All you had to do was take a twenty minute drive, make yourself at home and pour me a drink when I arrived. Which I did, knackered, pissed off and hungry, only to find the significant other in my life conspicuous by his absence."

"I er..."

"Don't bother, Jack. I don't want to hear the explanation. I lost several hours of working time yesterday, which I'm now trying to catch up on." She nodded in the direction of the door. "So if you don't mind..."

As I opened the door she said, "And you might like to think about returning the front door key."

I went back to my office. I remembered Chrissie once telling me how useless I was at this stuff. "You mean well, Dad," she said. "But you've got a pretty small skills base to work from." This from a fifteen year old. I thought it way off the mark at the time. I talked to Emily who was a little more gentle with me, but clearly at one with our daughter. At which point, I began to appreciate that Emily was the driver of the family engine and I was just the fireman. And not truly successful at that. I mastered the major task but failed to keep up with the small things. I realised how important they were when Chrissie and I started to fight. By the time she moved out of the house I was up to speed, but of course it was too late. We had lost years of precious time.

And now Linda was suffering from my lack of resolve.

I had nothing else to do but wait out the day. I caught up with emails. Run of the mill stuff, none of them exciting. I made some coffee, drank it, typed and sent three emails in return. Then I waited for something to happen, like the refugees in *Casablanca*.

At 5 o'clock I rang Adam.

"Nil desperandum, old man," he said. "We've held on to the idea that Bill is not dead, but making a serious attempt to convince the rest of us he is. So let's be patient now. I'm going home. I'll call you tomorrow."

"Yes, thanks. Give Chrissie my love."

"Sleep well, Jack."

"And you."

I pressed the red button and put the phone receiver back in its base. I decided to get my notes up to date. An hour later, the last four days were chronicled on six sheets of notepaper. Including one whole sheet of questions. About the blood on the parquet, the papers in the fire grate, Bill and Len, Walter Cobb and Freddie Settle, and was this all some bloody conspiracy?

It was at this point, that I came up with a scheme to move things along. I called Harvey Butler with a proposition.

"You want me to do what?" he asked, incredulity hurtling down the phone line.

"Bug my phones," I repeated. "All three of them. Home, office and mobile."

"Why?"

"Well..." I began.

Harvey interrupted. "I know. You want me to agree to this exploitation of the public purse, without asking too many questions and not getting involved in whatever it is you're doing."

"Yes. But it's likely to work for both of us," I insisted.

"Okay, one question only, Jack," he said. "What has provoked this request? No flannel or bullshit. Just a direct answer."

"I'm hoping Bill Marsh will call me during the next twenty-four hours. And whatever I can prise out of him, might lead to some real evidence gathering. I know this is not a Murder Team case. Not yet. But it might turn out that way."

Harvey was silent again. I pressed him.

"I'm not suggesting anything unofficial or off the books here. Just what you do all the time. These are my phones we're talking about and I agree to it. I'll sign whatever piece of paper I have to."

Harvey responded. "Okay. Come round here now, and we'll set it up."

I left my office. Linda's office door was locked. In the car park, there was a stream of water running from the Healey to the boundary fence. I unscrewed the radiator cap and peered inside.

Dry as a bone. There was no point refilling it, only to have it boil over again on the way to Trinity Road. I called Mr Earl.

"How many times is this, Shepherd Bra?" he asked

I didn't know whether he meant the number of phone calls lately, or the number of times the Healey had broken down. One and the same really. He dismissed the suggestion I ring the AA and have the car towed to his garage. Insisted he'd pick up the car himself. He arrived in less than ten minutes. Towing a dark green Landrover Defender on an A bar. It looked familiar.

"Bought this from young Jason Bra. When the security firm gave him the Espace," he explained. "New gearbox and new diff. It purrs man, it purrs."

He hooked up the Healey and drove out of the car park. And he was right. The Defender did indeed purr. I was in Harvey's office at 6.30.

"What's the matter with your face?" he asked.

"I tripped on the hall stairs and made contact with the top step."

Harvey shrugged and didn't pursue the matter. He offered me some forms to sign. He counter-signed them, and I was out of his office five minutes later. Home at 7 o'clock.

Waiting again. Just like earlier.

My mobile rang. It was Bob Carlton, a whiz-kid from surveillance. He was a kid too, comparatively speaking. A year younger than Chrissie. But something of a genius with pixels and digits.

"Just called to test that everything is working at both ends, Mr Shepherd," he said. "I guess you know the drill. Keep him on the line, don't make him nervous, and we'll pinpoint where he is. Hang on."

The background office volume rose as he took the receiver away from his face. He shared a sentence or two with somebody else, then talked to me again.

"It works; we are in business," he said. "Good luck."

How many clichés can you muster to reference how time passes? Stuff about waiting for trains, watched kettles, paint drying, grass growing, and of course waiting for some bugger to call. To avoid interruptions, I switched the landline into answer mode; ready to pounce and go live if it did so. Chrissie rang a few minutes after nine, leaving a message. Linda called just before ten, sounding stressed and wanting to talk. Which was my fervent wish too. I listened to her, weirdly at odds with myself and counting the seconds, until she stopped abruptly and said, "Hell I'm just rambling, talk tomorrow." and rang off.

Carlton and I spoke again at 10 o'clock, before he went off duty. He was surprisingly upbeat about the whole business.

"Your man will call the moment you stop looking at your watch and pacing up and down. I suggest you go to bed, Mr Shepherd."

That seemed like sensible advice, so I did. And instead of sitting on the sofa wide awake, I lay in bed wide awake. The last time I looked at the bedside clock, it said 2.56.

Chapter Twelve

The front doorbell woke me up. Or rather, the persistent knocking which followed. The clock on the bedside table said 7.15. Dressing gown wrapped around me, I yelled to whoever was out there that I was on my way.

The milkman was standing on the doorstep. He handed me a pint of milk and a bill for £65.42p.

"Four months," he said, with some menace.

I promised to give him a cheque the following day. He said that wasn't the way it worked if I remembered. The billing was all done on line. Before I could ask him why he was, therefore, standing on my doorstep with hard copy, he said that in extreme cases, it fell to him to act personally to collect money owing. An enforcer driving an electric milk float. No getting away from that combo. He ordered me to log in and pay *Milk Direct* before noon.

I made some coffee. Poured milk into the mug from my brand new pint. Drank the coffee, went back upstairs, and took a shower. Minutes later, soaking wet and reaching for the towel rack, I heard the phone ringing in the bedroom. I grabbed the towel and dripped swiftly from shower to bedside, to answer the call.

George Hood asked me what I was doing. It told him I was soaking the bedroom carpet. He said that was the mistake he had made. Using *DriFoam* was the best way to clean a carpet. No water and no shrinkage. I didn't bother to correct him, laid the towel on the duvet and sat down on it. And immediately began to feel cold. Mercifully Hood moved on quickly.

"Do you know the burger van parked on Durdham Down?"

"Yes."

"How long will it take you to get here?"

"Once I'm dressed, ten minutes."

"I'll buy you breakfast."

* * *

The sun was up and awake. Hood was sitting at a plastic garden table, eating a bacon sandwich.

"What can I get you?" he asked.

"Just coffee thanks."

I sat down while he organised that. He put the mug in front of me and returned to his sandwich. He finished eating. I waited. He wiped his lips with a paper serviette.

"The mouse we took from the Drop In Centre didn't give us anything," he said. "But I have some news about the man in the outhouse. The pathologist reckons he died around twelve hours before you found him."

"Died of what?"

"Heart attack. At least, his heart stopped." Hood sat up straight in his chair. "But here's the thing. Martin whoever he is, is missing a lung."

He paused long enough to let that sink in. In return, I stared at him. Then found a question to ask.

"Can you live with only one lung?"

"Apparently. As long as everything else works and you look after yourself. Take it easy, walk don't run. Sport is out of the question, naturally. In fact anything which makes you breathe heavily. Although Martin was never going to make it in any case. The remaining lung was in very good health, according to the pathologist. But the same can't be said for his liver, his kidneys and his lower bowel. Somebody relieved him of one of the few major organs in good nick."

"Somebody qualified to do it presumably."

"The pathologist said it was a truly professional job."

"So what did Martin do?" I asked. "Did he sell it?"

Hood shrugged. "I've been pondering on that."

"What's the going rate for a healthy lung?" I asked.

"Anything up to fifteen thousand pounds, to buyers in wealthy circles. Maybe Martin was paid a few hundred. Not much, but a lot to someone with no money and no roof over his head."

Hood swallowed a mouthful of coffee.

"So someone picked him off the street," I said. "Examined him, found out what was working and relieved him of it?"

Hood put his mug down. "Improbable though it may seem..."

"In which case, that person has an operating theatre at his disposal."

"And facilities to keep the lung alive between harvesting and transplanting," Hood said."

"And how wide is that window? A few hours?"

"Sometimes longer than that. Nonetheless, it means the harvesting was done to order and they lucked out with Martin. They were looking for a lung in working order. And he had two of them."

I took a drink of coffee. Hood went on to explain all he had discovered about body part surgery.

"If you carry donor notification, at your demise, any hospital can harvest all organs that are useful. At any time in your life, you can donate a kidney or bone marrow to a relative or friend, providing you are a match. You can also donate your blood, your skin, or your hair. Actually the law allows you to sell those bits if you can. But nothing else."

"And there's a black market for the stuff you're not allowed to sell or buy."

"People like Martin could be prime targets for those engaged in the trade," Hood said. "No addresses, therefore no records. Few people who know who they are. And those who do, with rare exceptions like May and her friends at the Drop In Centre, don't give a toss. The Martins of this world are multiple losers. Not that he was a drain on the public purse. He died of natural causes."

"In a manner of speaking," I said. "So what do you do now?"

"Nothing," Hood said. "Not in the Murder Team's purview, street people. Unless they die unlawfully. More your line of work, I'd say."

He looked at me steadfastly.

"Should I take that look to be one of some significance?" I asked.

Hood changed the subject. "Len Coleman, however, he's definitely my pay grade." His eyes remained glued to mine. "So what is it you know about him that I don't?"

That was easy to answer. With the whole unvarnished truth.

"Absolutely nothing," I said.

Hood grinned in disbelief.

"Slit my throat and hope to die, George. Someone else was looking for Coleman and got to him before I did, obviously. Why are you asking this now?"

"Because the question begging for an answer is, 'who is this someone?' And was he, or she, spurred into action by your enquiries?"

I didn't say anything.

Hood sat back in the chair. "Someone else is in the loop, Jack. Who is it?" He beamed at me across the table. "There's a gang of people working on this now. I can sit here all day. Actually I wouldn't mind another mug of coffee. Your shout."

In this mode, George Hood is like Banquo's ghost. He won't go away.

I ordered two more mugs and took them back to the table. We took sips. Hood said it was good. He looked around Durdham Down. At the joggers, the women with kids in pushchairs, the dog walkers. The sun was now beginning to warm the day. We sipped coffee again. Hood looked at his watch. He said the morning was flying by. Clearly he was able to cultivate an immensely high boredom threshold when required. Not one of my accomplishments however. My resistance was disintegrating like a beach sandcastle overrun by the incoming tide. Hood decided we had fannied around long enough.

"Jack. Who did you go and see concerning the whereabouts of Len Coleman? Give. Or I'll take you to Trinity Road and get the Boss to work you over."

I looked at him. He sat forward in the chair and began to count on the fingers of his right hand.

"Obstructing the police, interfering in the course of an investigation, conspiring to pervert the—"

"Ah come on, George..."

He looked at me dead centre. Unblinking.

"Who is it, Jack? Who did you talk to?"

I took a couple of beats. Then I told him. He stared at me, gobsmacked.

"Not the Freddie Settle we have grown to despise," I added. "Apparently he's retired. Daughter Freddie has taken over the family business."

Hood breathed in and out. "Right..." He looked at me again and waited for the whole explanation.

"Bill is a member of the *Silver Star Casino*. Len Coleman used to be, until a fortnight ago. Freddie told me she had no idea as to his whereabouts."

We sat in silence for some time, each of us considering the problem from opposite ends. Clearly we were both attached to the proposition that Freddie Settle was orchestrating this business. But confronting her would yield absolutely nothing. Visited by the police or the private eye, the outcome was likely to be the same. A display of cool but outraged innocence, and all the time she needed to check that everything was locked down tight.

Hood spoke as though he had been reading my mind.

"Okay," he said. "Assuming Freddie ordered the Coleman killing, she might have over-cooked this a bit. Coleman dead is a statement of intent. Crystal clear. He's out of the way and you're in the clarts. But now the rest of us public servants are in this too. She must know that. And it may be the one thing that keeps you out of her clutches."

That was kind of comforting.

"But it might be best to stop the bollocks you're pedalling on the net. That will swiftly irritate your allies as well as your targets."

"I don't know what you're talking about George."

"DC Holmes reads everything. And she's known for her imaginative leaps."

He drained his mug and got up out of his chair.

"As to Ms Settle," he said. "No point poking a hornet's nest with a stick, unless you have everything ready to control the outcome. But should we unearth something solid, it will give me the greatest pleasure to steam in and put the cuffs on her. In the meantime, Jack, stay out of trouble."

He turned and walked to his car. I watched him get in and drive away.

The trail to Bill was getting colder with every ongoing event. Following it was leading me nowhere. And Martin was just another lost soul. No family, no friends, no life. He was what he was.

I am. Yet what I am, none cares or knows
My friends forsake me like a memory lost.
I am the self-consumer of my woes...

109

I first read that poem by John Clare when I was a young copper, during an investigation into a teacher's suicide. I was searching his bedroom, and there was a copy of Clare's collected works on the bedside table. I'd never heard of him, but I opened the book and was drawn into his personal darkness. His poetry is heart breaking stuff. And it echoes down the years to me, still. John Clare knew more about loneliness, loss and despair than most. Like Martin, and, somehow, my teacher suicide case, he lived among the forsaken.

I drained the coffee mug, stood up, waved my thanks to the burger van proprietor and walked to the Healey.

Chapter Thirteen

Detective. The job description couldn't be clearer. The work is all in the name. But with it, comes a host of unpredictable elements. So when the going gets tough, do something easy...

Back home, I sat down in front of the pc, googled *Milk Direct* and paid my bill. I could look the milkman in the eyes next time we met.

I drove to the office, thinking about Freddie. I had said no to the largesse she had offered. So she had simply reversed her strategy. Instead of receiving money for doing nothing, I was now going to get nothing for doing all the work. The odds on a successful outcome were risible. Every sensible bone in my body said, 'Go on holiday and send Freddie Settle a postcard to show how far away you are.' It was just plain daft to upset her.

By comparison, Walter Cobb seemed no more than a minor sub plot. He was under siege from bailiffs, the Inland Revenue and the VAT Man. He was broke and desperate, but he had no reason I could see for being involved with Bill's disappearance. Fifty-two thousand pounds was a lot of money, but not enough, surely, to risk the consequences of doing away with his major creditor.

I parked the Defender behind the office building, walked along the riverbank, around the corner and into the lobby. Jason was at lunch. His oppo, Eric, was an efficient though charmless character. He liked the uniform he wore, and on quiet afternoons, was given to walking the floors like Mr Mackay in *Porridge* – slow and straight backed, checking that the cleaners' work was up to par.

Right now though, he was dealing with an unwanted visitor.

It was difficult to guess how old the man was. Somewhere between thirty and forty maybe. Tallish. Long hair and a moustache which made him look like Frank Zappa. Wearing a blue anorak over a woolly shirt, battered corduroy trousers, and on his feet, brown shoes with thick soles. He was begging for money. Eric was trying to escort him outside. Neither was giving ground, but Eric was the stronger of the two. He dragged the man past me and shoved him out of the door. I watched the man swing round, trip, stagger a few yards, then regain his balance and move slowly across the turning circle in front of the building. Beyond that, he disappeared into the gloom and the maze of concrete pillars supporting the road which funnelled traffic onto the bridge over the Cumberland Basin.

"Filthy, useless git," Eric muttered. "There's a bunch of them living over there."

He moved back to the reception desk, brushing imagined dirt and disease off his uniform jacket. The encounter gave me an idea. From my office, I phoned George Hood.

"Can I have a copy of the photograph your man took of Martin?"

"Er... Why?"

"No concern of the Murder Team you said."

"Until you stumble over another body."

"But in the meantime... Come on George, speed is of the essence."

"I'll email it to you," he said.

I was printing out copies when Linda knocked on the office door and stepped over the threshold.

"Have you time to talk?"

I should have said, 'of course, sit down', and made her welcome. I should have said I was truly glad to see her. I should have poured oil on trouble waters. I should have said anything but the sentence I did say.

"Not right now. Sorry. There's something I have to do. We can talk as soon as I get back. Yes?"

"And when will that be?"

"I don't know. Depends on what I find. Sorry..." I gathered up the copies of the picture. "I have to chase up someone. It might be important."

"Of course," she said, without a trace of emotion in her voice.

She stepped into the corridor. I apologised again, closed the office door and set off towards the lift. I pressed the call button and looked behind me.

Linda had gone into her office.

I followed the steps of the man Eric had thrown out. Across the turning circle, over a wide pavement backed by a low concrete wall, and into the cavern under the flyover. A huge space, supporting four road lanes into and out of the city over the Cumberland Basin Swing Bridge; with lines of concrete pillars growing from short props to twenty feet columns as the road rose up to bridge level. Way beyond, the river flowed westwards under Brunel's suspension bridge. I walked towards the view. In front of me the space opened out. I was now directly underneath the traffic, the noise magnified by the concrete echo chamber around me.

There was a grubby makeshift village built under the flyover. Put together from wood, cardboard boxes, chicken wire, blankets and old tarpaulins. The remains of a fire smoking on a metal grill, rested on a circle of bricks. Two broken armchairs – one on three feet so it leant over at an angle, the other on no feet at all – a couple of empty fruit boxes and a wooden stool, sat on the concrete surrounding the fire. It was a dismal and desperate place. The kind of alfresco shithole that most of us don't want to think about.

I counted seven people. Three men and two women – including Eric's evictee – who looked like they might be inhabitants of this place; and two men who were clearly visitors, standing at the rear of a Transit van which had backed into the space from the access road.

There was a discussion going on – mostly drowned out by the noise of the traffic from where I was standing – accompanied by lots of arm waving. They were all too busy to notice me. One of the visitors opened the Transit rear doors. Visitor Two, reached out to the tallest man in the group and gripped his arm. The man tried to shake him off. He was swung round through ninety degrees and pushed towards the Transit. At which point, one of the women detached herself from the rest of the group, picked up a length of timber and launched herself at Visitor Two. He turned back to face the group and failed to dodge the piece of 2 by 2 as it swung towards him. It thumped into his shoulder. The tall man shook himself free from Visitor One, who grabbed him again, pointed him at the nearby concrete pillar and shoved him at it head first. The man crunched into the pillar, staggered back a step or two and sank to his knees. Visitor Two, meanwhile had wrenched the piece of 2 by 2 from the woman. He pushed her away from him. She staggered, over balanced and fell back onto the concrete.

I fished the mobile out of my jacket and thumbed the office reception number; raised the phone to my ear and got Jason, back from his lunch. Visitor One saw me as I dropped the mobile back into my pocket. He called out to his associate, who swung to face me, still holding the chunk of wood. He shifted the timber from his left hand to his right and re-arranged his grip on it.

I stepped forwards slowly, counting the time I figured Jason would take to materialise behind us. Six seconds to cross the lobby and get out of the door, five seconds to cross the turning circle, another five to cross the low wall, another six or seven to arrive on the scene...

Visitor Two nodded at his partner. Twenty yards behind us, Jason hove into view. It was now two against two. And the visitors had to decide how important their mission was. They decided to tough it out. It was a mistake.

Jason was at my side moments later. Standing straight and tall, he was an imposing presence. He crabbed to his left, taking with him the attention of a suddenly much less confident Visitor Two. I crabbed the other way and inched towards Visitor One. No weapon appeared from anywhere; obviously no hardware was required for a trip to a group of down and outs under a flyover. Taking comfortable strides, I closed the space between myself and Visitor One. He wasn't sure what to do. He swayed from left to right and bounced a couple of times, like a goalkeeper preparing to face a penalty. He allowed me to walk straight at him, concentrating on my face. He raised his arms and took up the stance of a nervous southpaw. I swung my right leg and kicked him in the crotch. He yelled in pain and sank to his knees.

There was a roar of agony to my left. The piece of timber was on the ground. Jason had Visitor Two in a half nelson, his right arm under the man's chin. He heaved his arm upwards, pushing the man's face up and back. The man started to choke. Jason released his grip. Visitor Two staggered forwards grabbing at his throat. Jason picked up the length of 2 by 2, raised it and thumped it down on the back of the man's head. The man yelled, raised his arms to the source of the pain, and keeled over.

There was a ragged cheer from the village inhabitants. Eric's evictee moved towards the injured man. Another man found some rope. We sat the visitors down, tied them together back to back, and with the amount of rope left, tethered them to the Transit trailer hitch. I asked the villagers if they objected to me phoning the police. This was greeted, not un-naturally, with some suspicion. They had all been demoted to an un-fixable underclass and none of them expected to receive anything but trouble from those who didn't give a toss about them. The woman who had brandished the 2 by 2 was nominated spokesperson. As she moved towards me, I had time to notice how she looked. Short brown hair, closely cropped; dark eyes, cheeks more hollow than they should have been. She was wearing a dark blue boiler suit and a scruffy denim cap. She looked every inch like a Brecht heroine.

"We would rather not have anything to do with the police," she said; no accent in her voice, her words carefully chosen.

"Okay."

I looked at the Transit and the trussed up visitors. I asked Jason to go back to the office, get into the Defender and drive it round to the front of the building. I gave him the keys.

"Leave them in the ignition," I said. "And wait for me to arrive."

He didn't object or ask any questions; simply nodded yes. He said a genuinely felt 'goodbye' to the villagers and moved away. I watched him until he was out of sight, then gathered the villagers around me. The injured man had stopped bleeding from his forehead and insisted he was okay.

I showed them the police photograph. The lady with the piece of 2 by 2 shivered.

"That's Martin," she said.

"What do you know about him?" I asked.

There was some discussion; followed by some whispered moments I couldn't hear under the traffic noise. The 2 by 2 lady spoke to me again.

"Martin didn't live here. Do you know the old engineering factory off Parson's Road in Bedminster? That's where he was sleeping. Under some boxes at the back of the car park. The other people there might help you."

She gave the photograph back to me. I talked to the group again.

"One more thing," I said and pointed at the Transit. "Help me to untie those two and we'll let them leave."

Happy to be left to themselves once again, they set about the business. The 2 by 2 lady produced another blunt instrument – a length of metal gas piping – and offered it to me. We stood shoulder to shoulder, acting as menacingly as we could, while two of the men released the visitors. Number one was tallish, brown haired and wearing a cheap, black suit. His associate was shorter, shaven headed, clad in jeans and a blouson jacket, trainers on his feet. A of pair of cut price heavies. They did as instructed. I committed the registration number to memory. Gave the iron bar back to my new friend and wished her luck.

"My name's Molly," she said,

The Transit doors slammed and I set off like Dwain Chambers. Across the open space, over the low wall, and out into the daylight. The Defender was parked in front of the office building, engine idling, driver's door open. About fifty yards to my left, the Transit drove out into the sunshine. I reached the Defender, yelled my thanks to Jason, slid into the vehicle, found first gear and pulled away.

Ahead of me, the Transit was turning on to the road which fed traffic up and round and onto the swing bridge. The van turned into the stream, when the driver of a mini slowed and flashed his lights. I slid into the traffic three cars later. The roof of the Transit was clearly visible and easy to follow. We drove over the bridge, kept to the left and slipped down the ramp onto the Portway – the route to the M5 and Wales and all points west.

The thickening traffic was never going to allow the Transit to reach enough miles per hour to break the speed limit. We trundled underneath the suspension bridge and cruised along the Avon Gorge. Five minutes later we reached the sprawling M5 motorway junction in Shirehampton. The Transit drove straight on and into Avonmouth.

No place to visit for an afternoon out.

Fuel depots, a massive container terminal and cold storage warehouses line the dockside. Inland of the dock complex, the industrial estate creeps northeast from the mouth of the Avon for a mile and a half and spreads eastwards back to the M5. The northwest corner is appropriately named Smoke Lane Industrial Estate. There's a huge chemical plant in the middle of the acreage, which does its best to help boost the smoky skyline, and alongside that a sewage treatment works. Around these places, occupying a series of industrial zones, is the mandatory gathering of DIY centres, furniture outlets, electrical stores, car parts distributors and storage facilities.

We turned north into the massive trading estate which runs parallel to the dockside. I dropped back and let the Transit open up space between us. It turned left into a cul de sac of small warehouses, swung into the car park in front of one with number 9 above the roll up door and stopped. Alongside a familiar black Bentley – Walter Cobb's motor car.

I pulled up at the road entrance and switched off the ignition. The two men climbed out of the Transit and went into the warehouse. I sat in the Defender, listening to the ticking of the engine block and settled back in my seat to wait.

I was bored within minutes and invented something to do. I got out of the Defender and walked back to the map of the estate standing on the corner. The tenant of number 9 First Avenue, was an outfit called *Futures Ltd*. The name didn't give any clue as to what the company did or sold, which was probably the intention. I walked back to the Defender and decided to try using whatever credit I still had with George Hood.

Hood wasn't at his desk and the call was diverted to Harvey Butler's office.

"Jack," he cried, joviality zooming down the line. "Nice to hear from you. I imagine there is something we can do for you."

I decided not to rise to the bait. "I need you to track a registration number for me," I said.

"Okay," Harvey said. No argument, no attempt at irony. "What is it?"

I recited the details I had read on the back of the Transit. He repeated them back to me and told me to hang on. The line clicked, then clicked again. I waited. There was one more click and Harvey came back to me.

"The Transit belongs to a roofer we know as second storey man Reginald Pearce. Are you by any chance near this Transit as we speak?"

"I'm looking at it," I said.

"In which case, Mr Pearce isn't in it," he said.

"That's right. He and his mate are in a warehouse in Avonmouth."

"No, Jack, I mean Mr Pearce is not there. He's in court today. Right about now, I'm told, pleading guilty to seven counts of earning money under false pretences, and two counts of illegally taking lead from a church roof in Brislington. He will be in Horfield prison by the close of play, beginning an eighteen month stretch at least."

I absorbed the information.

Harvey broke the silence. "Does that help at all?"

"No."

"Can I help you in any other way?"

"No."

"Then have a nice day."

He was about to end the call.

"No wait a minute," I said. "Why are you in such a jovial mood?"

"We've had a re-shuffle," he said. "And a new DC added to the squad. George is currently on the top floor, having a conversation about a promotion."

"That's progress," I said.

Harvey asked how May was. I told him she seemed okay the last time we spoke, and asked him about progress on the Len Coleman murder. Which changed his mood slightly.

"There is none," he said. "How are you progressing with finding Bill?"

"I'm not," I said.

I heard another phone begin to ring.

"Sorry, Jack," Harvey said. "I want to take this. Go gently."

And that was that. Another dead end. Well not entirely, but I couldn't see where two men in a borrowed Transit was going to lead. So I tried road testing an assumption... Men in the employ of Walter Cobb, visit the miserable domain of a group of people with no assets, no self-esteem and nowhere to go. They attempt to persuade one of the group to leave with them. Failing to do so, as the result of the unpleasantness that follows, they drive to their boss, to fess up.

Well that worked as a scenario, but I had no idea why. And that was the issue. The people who could tell me, were sitting round a table across the road and would certainly not rise to shake my hand if I were to interrupt.

Assuming that Walter Cobb had no plans to flee the country, I could catch up with him if I needed to. And the time and effort involved in following his employees around until they did something unpleasant once again, didn't bear consideration.

I fired up the Defender, u-turned in the road, and drove back into the city.

Chapter Fourteen

Molly was alone, sitting in the three legged armchair when I ventured under the flyover again. She stood up as I walked towards her. She was wearing a bulky cardigan over the boiler suit.

"Are you going to do this regularly?" she asked. "Visit us I mean."

I told her not too often and asked if she would answer some questions. She responded by saying she would, providing I didn't pry too much.

"Is asking for names prying too much?"

"Not necessarily. I gave you mine."

"Yes you did."

"But I didn't get yours."

"Jack Shepherd. I'm a private investigator. Trying to locate a friend."

Molly considered that information. She stared across the concrete and beyond to the gorge and the river.

"His name is Bill Marsh," I went on. "You may know his wife, May. She runs the Drop In Centre in Bedminster."

Molly turned back to me, nodded, but said nothing. I went on.

"I think a group of people are trying to get the centre closed," I said.

"People are doing that constantly," Molly said.

"Alright... But I'm finding things which appear to be a lot more sinister. Which might be connected to the men who visited earlier. I know now who they work for. Their boss sent them here to find somebody, and they chose your friend. Can you tell me his name?"

"Why?"

"Because I need to join some dots. If I do, it may help lead me to Bill, and in the process, get to the source of what's happening at the Centre."

Molly knew there was more by way of explanation and waited.

"All of you here have visited the Centre, right?"

"Yes. Some of us still do so."

"Including the man the Transit drivers wanted to take away?"

"Yes."

"Will you give me his name?"

"Donald. Don, he likes to be called."

"His full name," I said.

Molly shook her head.

"I would ask him myself, but he's not here," I said. "I promise you this isn't about him. It's about the visitors you had. I'm trying to find out why Don should be a target."

Molly looked steadfastly into my eyes

"Alright," I said. "So that we don't single out Don, give me everybody's name."

A voice called from our left. "Weaver."

Molly and I turned and looked at the man we were talking about. He walked across the concrete towards us.

"Donald Malcolm Weaver," he said.

We stood stock still, three corners of a triangle. Above us, the sound of traffic rumbled on. Weaver stood straight and tall. His thick soled black shoes were scruffy, his grey trousers were dirty at the knees, but the heavy tweed jacket looked clean by comparison. He wore it well. Like a man who, at some time, had been able to afford a bespoke suit or two. Somewhere, he had washed his face and cleaned the wound on his forehead, but the skin was torn and needed stitches. He anticipated what I was about to say.

"I'm not going to a doctor." Like Molly, he spoke with no recognisable accent.

I looked at her. She shrugged. So I faced Weaver again and asked a routine question.

"Do you think the men in the Transit came looking for you, personally? Or were they on a fishing expedition?"

Weaver thought about this for a second or two. The wail of an ambulance siren faded up onto the soundtrack above us, passed over our heads, then diminished as it raced on.

"I don't know," he said.

"Does it help to explain things, if they did know who they were looking for?" Molly asked.

"Maybe."

"All of us here, are as anonymous as it's possible to get," Weaver said. He surveyed the cavernous concrete space that passed for home. "At least Martin's okay now. Way beyond all this."

Suddenly his eyes filled with tears. He sniffed and pressed the fingers of his hands into his eye sockets. Then he dropped his arms and apologised. Molly moved to his side.

"It's alright. You're allowed to cry for Martin. That's the one thing you can do for him now."

He talked to me. "Where will Martin be?"

"I don't know," I said. "He may still be in the morgue."

"Is there a chance that he's already...?"

Don wasn't able to finish the sentence. Molly gathered him into her arms. I tried to help.

"His body will still be in cold storage," I said, attempting to be upbeat, recalling my recent brush with the regulations.

"No vagrant is buried or cremated, until the local authority is satisfied that all attempts to trace a relative or the next of kin, have been unsuccessful. I'll find out what I can on your behalf." I paused. Thought about how to how to phrase the next bit. "In Martin's case, there is another consideration. He has only one lung. He probably sold the other."

Molly and Don stared at me; neither of them, it seemed, able to speak. I looked at Don. Asked him how old he was.

"Thirty six," he said.

"And in spite of living like this, are you well?"

"I think so."

"What do you do if you become ill?"

"We don't," he said. "Become ill I mean. Colds, flu, sprains, aches, pains... We try to ignore them."

"Seriously ill then. Where do you go?"

"To the NHS Walk In Centre, in Broadmead."

Molly intervened. "Why are you asking all this, Jack?"

"I'll tell you in a minute." I turned back to Don. "Is that where your medical records are kept?"

"I guess so. I've never thought about it."

"Okay. And the only other place which has information on you, is the Drop In Centre in Bedminster?"

"Yes."

"And is this the same with you, Molly?"

"Yes. Now will you tell us what this—"

I held up my right hand. "Just one more thing. And it's very important. Have there been other disappearances or deaths among the homeless groups that you know? Recently, I mean. Say during the last nine to twelve months."

Molly and Don looked at each other. I waited. Don spoke first.

"A man called Ted Morris used to live here with us. He disappeared during the summer last year. Late August." He checked with Molly. "Will that be right?"

Molly thought about it, then nodded. "I'd say so, yes."

"How old was Ted?" I asked.

"Late 20s," Molly said. "He had been living on the streets for seven years he told me. Just a day or two before he disappeared."

"How? How did he disappear?"

"He left here mid-morning, to see if he could find something to eat. And he didn't come back."

"And no one has seen him since?"

"No one."

"Could he be living with another group? Or on his own?"

Don answered this question. "That could be so," he said. "But he isn't. We don't have much of a network, but if Ted was around somewhere we would know. The Drop In Centre would know."

Molly was impatient now. "Jack, please, tell us what this is all about."

I looked at them both. Then told them about following the Transit.

"I think those men were supposed to collect you. Like they did Martin and Ted."

"Why?" Molly asked.

"This isn't much beyond an educated guess," I said. "But it could be that their boss has copies of your personal records, such as they are."

Molly opened her mouth to speak. I held up my hand again and talked to Don.

"You have no kin at all, right?"

Don shook his head. "No."

"No one to lay claim to your estate?"

He looked around the concrete shelter. "What estate?"

"How many people know who, and where, you are?"

"I don't know," he said. "A couple of dozen maybe."

Molly interrupted. "Come on, Jack. Explain."

"I believe you are on the list of those two latter day resurrection men. A list of people whose loss to the world will not cause the slightest ripple. Who are being offered money for body parts."

I waited while Molly and Don absorbed that rationalisation. Then I asked him if he would consider selling a kidney for five hundred pounds.

He looked at me, dead centre. "I might," he said.

I turned to my left.

"Molly?"

She responded with another question. "Are you sure about all this?"

"No," I said. "And I don't want to believe any of it."

"Because you're telling us," she said, "that someone, somewhere, is running his own private enterprise, from his own operating theatre. In secret."

"Yes."

"How the hell is that possible?" Don asked.

"I don't know," I said.

"And where would the money come from to set all that up?"

"I don't know that either."

"So..." Molly said. "Where does that leave us?"

"Did you have lunch?" I asked.

"No," Molly said.

"Let's go do that then," I said.

Sid Swift's Meals on Wheels van was a few hundred yards away, along the riverbank, parked at the entrance to a garden centre with no café. Sid conducted his business on the understanding that the garden centre staff could eat and drink at mates' rates, and a small percentage of his earnings went into a charity box.

I have known Sid for years. He's 50 something. A stocky character, broad shouldered, bearded and a devoted City fan. He cooks seven days a week, dawn 'til dusk, save for the Saturday afternoons City play at home, half a mile away. On those occasions, for a few hours, his sister takes over. She is the same height as Sid and the same width. With a beard she would look just like him. No side to either of them, no prejudice shown, no judgements ever made. When they had money, Molly and Don were regular customers.

He nodded a greeting at them and turned to me.

"Jack Shepherd, as I live and breathe."

From inside the van, a foot or so above me, he reached across the counter and extended his right arm. I shook his hand.

"How are you, Sid?"

"Never better, Jack."

Burger and chips all round was accompanied by large mugs of steaming thick brown tea. Molly and Don ate without speaking, as if any lack of attention would see the food whisked away. After we had finished eating and Sid had presented us with a second mug of tea, Molly and Don told me their stories.

Molly was forty-two years old; a nurse with two marriages behind her. Her first husband died at the age of 28; trying to save himself and the family dog, one bank holiday when they were trapped by the tide and the mud at Burnham on Sea. She had become addicted to anti-depressants as a result, then prone to serious mood swings. She was prescribed more pills to keep her stable, but had difficulty getting up in the morning and getting on with the day. She began to steal from hospital medication cupboards. She was fired. And lost in a regime of uppers and downers, attempted suicide. In the end she beat the drugs; but not her second husband, who at the slightest upset, beat the shit out of her. She left him. He refused to buy her out of the house, simply banned her from entering it again. Molly rented a flat and took the best job she could find, with an office cleaning company. She lost that job when the company downsized; ran out of money trying to keep body and soul together and was thrown out of her flat when she fell three months behind with the rent. She had been on the streets three years.

Don was a long distance lorry driver. He loved the job. Did it for fifteen years, until he ran down a seven year old child on a zebra crossing. It loaded him with guilt, destroyed the joy and the freedom the job gave him, and broke his spirit.

"It still comes back to haunt me," he said. "Through cold, wide awake nights, and long empty days."

"What about your family? I mean, way back."

Don unveiled a potted history, without any sentimentality.

"No parents anymore. My sister died when she was six. My mother died, weeks later, of a broken heart. My father jumped off the roof of the office building he was working in. I spent years in and out of foster homes. I left school as soon as I could, got an apprenticeship in a garage and trained as a mechanic. Then got an HGV licence. I've never really had a long standing relationship of any sort."

On the surface, there was nothing about Molly and Don which said 'victim'. Nothing about them, apart from the threadbare clothes, which said 'homeless'. Nothing about their conversation which said 'ignorant'. Nothing about them which said 'loser'. Ignored until forgotten maybe, but somehow, managing to stay alive under seriously brutal circumstances.

I asked if either of them knew a lady called Lily. "She had that name on a chain around her neck," I said.

Molly picked up the past tense. "Has she disappeared too?"

"Not disappeared no," I said. "She was run down by a car."

"Three weeks ago," Don said. "I heard about it. I knew her."

"From where? Can you tell me anything about her?"

"Not much. We shared a squat for a while. She told me she came from somewhere in the home counties. I lost touch with her after we were evicted."

"She became a regular at the Night Shelter in St Werburgh's," I said. "Until a month before she died."

Molly had her hands wrapped around the mug of tea. "Why are you concerned about her?"

"That's a good question," I said. "I guess because nobody should die unknown and un-mourned. And she was missing a kidney."

Molly sipped her tea. Don stared into the distance.

Thanks for your help earlier," Molly said.

"Is there anything else I can do for you?"

"You bought us lunch," Don said.

"I'll try and find out what's happening with Martin's body," I said.

I got up from the table, waved goodbye to Sid, and walked back to the office.

Chapter Fifteen

I drove to the Drop In Centre. There were twenty odd visitors in rooms around the place. Two volunteers were clearing the dining room. The chef was cleaning his kitchen. I sat in the office with May and Harry.

Over tea and biscuits I told them the story of the day. May agreed I could look at Molly and Don's records. She took a key out of a drawer in the desk and unlocked the filing cabinet. I read the meagre notes. Molly and Don had told me more over burger and fries. I asked how many people were on file.

"Seventy-six," Harry said. "No seventy-five now, without Martin."

"And all the hard copy was originated on this pc?"

"Yes."

"Information which was stolen during the break in," May said.

She looked at Harry. He nodded at me.

"I believe that, yes," I said.

And it focused our attention. The speculation that the Transit men were picking up to order, now had substance. I asked May and Harry the question about regular visitors disappearing from their radar.

Harry blew out his cheeks. "People do stop coming, of course. Sometimes, thankfully, it's because their situation has improved."

"And you get to hear about those cases?"

"Usually, yes."

"And the others?"

"Sometimes we hear of them living in other communities."

"And the rest?"

Harry shook his head and opened his arms.

"I understand," I said. "There are people who need to be here. Some who turn up every day. So who has gone missing recently?"

"Three I can think of," Harry said.

I waited. He looked at May, checking for his assessment.

"We last saw Alice Davis three or four months ago," May said.

Harry nodded. "January," he said. "Mid-January. I remember that because she told me it was her birthday in a couple of days. I told her we'd have tea and cakes. She smiled. It was a great smile when it arrived. Ear to ear. She left still smiling. But she didn't come back."

He looked at May, who said softly, "Yes I remember."

"Was Alice fit and well?" I asked.

"Yes, she was," May said. She searched the files in her head. "Somewhere in her 40s. She seemed to thrive on misfortune. No matter what she had to face. I don't remember anything getting her down."

"And the other two?"

Harry contributed again. "Ted Harris," he said.

"Yes," I said. "Molly and Don told me about him."

"Did they tell you about Brian Watson?"

"No."

"Brian was a gentle man," May said. "Self-contained. Listening to music the rest of us couldn't hear. The kind of person you have to look out for. He never told us where he lived. We tried to find out, of course, but that's a delicate exercise at best. The risk is the person you're trying to help will discover what you're doing, and then move on."

"Is that what happened with Brian?"

"No," Harry said. "We had given up digging into stuff about Brian. Just welcomed him without questions."

"And when did he disappear?" I asked.

"Between Christmas and New Year. We had a bit of a do here on New Year's Eve. Brian didn't show. And hasn't done so since. Does that help?"

"Yes, unfortunately."

* * *

In the office building lobby, Jason waved me to the reception desk.

"The old Defender sounds like she's running well," he said.

"New gear box and new diff," I said.

He handed me an envelope. "A note from Ms Barnes."

I opened the envelope while I was waiting for the lift to arrive. *This is so foolish Jack. I'm back late afternoon. Can we sit down and talk?*

I opened the office door with a lighter heart. Made some coffee, filled a mug, sat in my chair, leaned back and put my feet on the desk. The inside pocket of my jacket began ringing. I found the mobile and answered the call.

Bill Marsh asked, "Where are you, Jack?"

I swung my feet off the desk and sat upright in my chair.

"No no, Bill. The question is, where are you?"

"We'll get to that," Bill said. "You first."

"I'm in my office."

"We need to meet," Bill said.

"Fine. Name a place and I'll be there with bells on."

"It's just after four, yes?"

I looked at the clock on the wall. "Three minutes past."

"I'll meet you at 5.30."

"Where?"

"I'll figure that out and call you back."

"Why? What's to figure out?"

"Just go with this, Jack. Please."

"Do you know that Len Coleman's dead?"

There was a long pause. Difficult to tell whether Bill was absorbing the news, or trying to work out a reply.

In the end he said, "No more questions, Jack."

He ended the call. I switched my mobile off, placed it on the desk and stared at it. Thirty seconds later, it rang again.

"Bill called from an address on Rycroft Road," Harvey Butler said. "George is on the way. Holmes and a couple of uniforms with him."

"Have I your permission to join the posse?"

"Best I think. You'd probably go anyway."

"Is it a home or a business address?"

"We're checking that."

I called May. She wasn't at the Centre. I called home. Got the answering machine and left a message – "It's Jack. I've just had a call from Bill. He's alive and well. More later." I rang May's mobile. Same result. I left the same message. Harvey called again, as I crossed the car park and reached the Defender.

"We think Bill was calling from *Faversham Funeral Services*," he said. "Has he gone into the undertaking business?"

"Not that I know."

"Well if you get there swiftly enough, you might get to ask him."

I headed northeast, towards Filton. It took me nineteen minutes to get to Rycroft Road. A patrol car and George Hood's Vauxhall were sitting in the car park to the left of the funeral parlour. PC De'Ath was stationed at the door. He bade me a good afternoon and waved me inside. He was obviously not confined to Trinity Road gate duty. Although come to think of it, he was currently doing the same job outside an undertaker's.

Funeral parlours are odd places; the atmosphere part church, part morgue and part library. I haven't spent too much time in them, but they are always as I expect them to be – a breathless hush underscored by organ music. Like a reverent department store lift. The lighting in the lobby was low wattage, provided by small, soft glow bulbs. A dado rail stained in dark oak, ran all the way round the lobby at waist height. Below it some sort of textured lining paper was painted a silver grey. Above the rail and across the entire ceiling, the colour was a soft off white.

PC Laker was standing in the hall. She nodded at me.

"Nice to see you again, Mr Shepherd."

I returned the compliment, both of us speaking in hushed tones. PC Laker pointed along the hall.

"The Funeral Director's office is to the right."

It was a big room, with a big window clothed by a long vertical strip blind, and otherwise furnished in the accepted mortician's vernacular – polished light oak panels around all four walls, with discrete dado lights shining from a suspended ceiling. A dark brown upholstered chesterfield and two matching chairs made up the guest accommodation. The carpet was a lighter brown. The place was uber tidy. Sitting behind a big light oak desk and staring at Hood and DC Holmes, a tall man with a long face and an expensive haircut, was in vehement denial. All three looked at me as I slipped in through the doorway. Holmes nodded a greeting. Hood made the introduction.

"This is Mr Berling, Jack. The Senior Undertaker here. He says he hasn't seen his boss, Mr Faversham, since this time last week."

"Has he any idea where Mr Faversham might be?" I asked.

"He says not."

"Does he know if, or when, Mr Faversham is coming back?"

"He can't commit himself."

"So ask him if—"

Berling interrupted, irritated by the third person conversation. "I am in the room," he said.

Hood turned to him. "So make a contribution to the debate."

"Mr Faversham is the Funeral Director," Berling said. "This is his company. He is the man in charge."

Hood gestured to me. "This is Jack, a friend of the man who was here half an hour ago." Berling shifted in his seat. "So... Are you sticking to this story?"

"It's not a story," Berling said, smarting at the perceived insult. "Like you, the man asked if Mr Faversham was here." Berling looked at me. "And I told him the same thing. No."

"And you have never seen this man before?" I asked.

"No." Berling looked back at Hood. "How many more times...?"

"Okay," Hood said. "As we're here, do you mind if we look around?"

"Have you got a warrant?" Berling asked.

Hood stared at him, then transferred his attention to Holmes and me. We both looked suitably disappointed. Hood turned back to Berling.

"We usually find that those who have nothing to hide, agree readily to such a proposition."

"Ah yes... er Detective Sergeant. But this is something of a special place. You do understand? We have clients, lying at rest here. I simply cannot allow you to disturb the peace and tranquillity of any room in this establishment."

"We will do our utmost to respect that," Hood said.

We all watched Berling and waited for him to respond. He swallowed and breathed in and exhaled and swallowed again. Hood helped him out.

"I can send PC De'Ath to find a magistrate and get a warrant issued. And in the meantime we'll just sit here and wait for him to return."

Berling bowed to the inevitable and got to his feet.

"I must register a serious protest at all this."

"Noted," Hood said.

Berling moved around the desk, ushered us out of the room, and we embarked on a guided tour of the place. Beginning with two more offices. Followed by the embalmer's work place, and the 'Design Room', where the range of coffins and accoutrements were on display. We were then allowed to inspect the 'Dressing Room', the place in which the client was prepared for his last resting place. Berling allowed Hood to take only one step into 'Rest Room One' and 'Rest Room Two', both of which contained occupied coffins. Holmes and I stood well back in the corridor. Finally, we all got to see the store room; about fifteen feet square, stacked with a range of wood panels, drapes, gold plated coffin handles, corner plates, screw toggles, shelves of paraphernalia and tools of the trade.

"We design and build everything to order," Berling said, pride in his work getting the better of him. "In our workshop in Horfield. But we assemble the final bespoke product in this space. We have a first class carpenter and a fabric designer on contract. Now if you don't mind..."

He ushered us into the lobby and locked the storeroom door again.

"Well?" he said. A little belligerently for an undertaker.

Hood thanked Berling for his co-operation and allowed him to escort us into the street. Where Hood asked PCs Laker and De'Ath to recce the building's exterior. The exercise didn't reveal much. The curtains were drawn across the windows facing the street. Behind the building there was some architectural confusion. The funeral parlour had once been two semi-detached homes, re-modelled when the use was changed to business. The space which had once been the garden, now housed – as far as I could tell – the rooms we had just visited.

Hood, Holmes and I had a conference by the Vauxhall.

"Okay," he said. "Bill was here, looking for Faversham who wasn't. And that provoked the phone call to you. Which isn't much of a result, given that we are three clever detectives."

No result at all, in essence. We still had no idea where Bill was. And now, Arnold Faversham had joined the platoon of persons missing.

Hood spoke to Holmes. "Another house to house for you to organise, Sherlock. All doors within a fifty yard radius. Armed with a description of Bill and a picture."

Holmes collected Laker and De'Ath and gave them some instructions. Laker got on to her phone and called for reinforcements. I moved to the Defender, Hood alongside me.

"What the hell is Bill doing?" he asked. "I mean, look who we've dredged up so far. Freddie Settle, whose organisation is known for dealing in dead people, Len Coleman who is dead, and the disappeared Arnold Faversham, who has two dead people in his parlour."

"Presumably for reasons other than criminal," I said.

"Hard to assess, when he's not here to ask. Do you think Berling's in the loop?"

"Probably not," I said. "Seeing that he's still at work, and not in hiding somewhere."

I unlocked the Defender. Hood stared at it. I explained.

"It's a loaner."

* * *

I was back in my office by half past five, with nothing to do but sit and wait for Bill to call. He didn't. At half past six Adam did, offering to buy me a drink. I told him I didn't want to leave the office. That I was expecting a call, and if lucky, a visit from Linda.

"I'll come to you,"

I sat in the office and did some more waiting. Bill still didn't ring, and Linda didn't appear. Adam was the first to show.

"I've been digging around for the last couple of days," Adam said. "Downloaded everything the *Post* has on the Settles and called an Inspector I know in Serious Crimes." He waved a data stick at me and pointed at the laptop on my desk. "May I?"

He sat down in one of my client chairs, shuffled up to the desk, swung the laptop around and fired it up. Inserted the data stick, tapped a key or two and swung the screen back to me.

"The highlights," he said. "Take a look."

There were a dozen *Post* pieces on the stick. Stories about the Settle empire which cut close to the bone – though not close enough to make Freddie call his expensive lawyers – and a selection of photographs.

One featured a group of people at a charity fund raiser. Daughter Freddie on her father's arm, beaming into the camera lens. Another starred Bill and May, in company with Walter Cobb, the Regional Director of a major children's charity and Freddie Senior. A third displayed the two Freddies in the foyer of the Hippodrome, at a reception for the English National Opera, on tour with *Don Giovanni*. Freddie Senior was smiling that smile he had bequeathed to his daughter. There was a photo taken at a garden party to launch a new environment initiative, with Cobb, the Lord Mayor, the city council Finance Director and Freddie Senior side by side. And the most bizarre picture – celebrating the opening of a new hospital wing – was a line-up of two surgeons in dark blue suits, a nurse, and the Westcountry Hospital Trust Administrator standing in front of an ambulance. All of them smiling at the camera, with the nurse shaking Freddie Senior's hand.

Adam moved around the desk and looked over my right shoulder.

"Freddie paid for that," he said. "The hospital wing. Got his name on a plaque inside the entrance. Inspired isn't it? Money laundered courtesy of the NHS."

I looked at the next photograph, taken on Bill Marsh's front lawn. His sixty-fifth birthday bash a year ago. Two lines of local worthies. Bill and May front and centre, next to the two Freddies. The rest of the cast, a collection of dubious extras, alongside and around them.

"Look at them all," Adam said. "Is that really the sort of company we would expect Bill and May to keep?"

"Maybe," I said. "Maybe not."

The last photograph was the most interesting. Taken with a long lens across the floating harbour, it showed Freddie Senior sitting at a window table in a waterside bistro, facing a man I didn't recognise. Adam straightened up and moved back to his chair.

"That is James Warburton," he said.

I shook my head. "Doesn't mean a thing."

"He owns eighteen hundred acres on top of the Mendips. *The High Combe Estate.*"

"So Freddie Settle is having lunch with a well-heeled landowner," I said. "What can you make out of that?"

"Not much, if you have a cheerfully unsuspicious mind. However, if you know Freddie and are inclined to believe the worst of him, then all sorts of possibilities occur."

"Is this a *Post* picture?"

"Taken by a stringer."

"But you didn't use it?"

"No. We sent a reporter out to the estate to talk with James Warburton. On the pretence of doing a series on managing the countryside."

"And?"

"Warburton wasn't interested in talking to us. One of the subs put a researcher on the story. She discovered that a couple of the quangos helping to fund the estate had been dissolved; and the remit of two government agencies, also involved, had been reviewed. She believed that Warburton was about to run out of money."

"So, being the suspicious souls we are, we presume that Freddie was prepared to fill the financial holes."

"First response, yes."

"And...?"

"The trail went dead. The researcher couldn't find anything else. No plans or schemes to discover. Not so much as a single ripple on the Warburton ornamental pond."

I looked at the photograph again. Adam waited for my response.

"Alright," I said. "What would Freddie Settle want with eighteen hundred acres of woodland?"

"Perhaps he's gone into the conservation business."

"A complete reverse of policy thus far," I said.

"Something to think about," Adam said. He moved to the door. "I'll leave the data stick with you. Love to Linda."

He walked out of the office. I stared at the open doorway.

The phone rang. I grabbed the receiver. Jason asked me if I had any letters to post. I told him 'thank you but no'. He said he hoped I would have a good evening and rang off.

The time slid painfully on towards 8 o'clock. Evening was signalled by the sky darkening outside.

Bill still didn't call.

At 8.30, Linda appeared and tapped on the open door. Framed by the architrave she looked terrific. Blue silk blouse, and blue denim skirt down to an inch or so above her sensational knees.

"Hi," she said.

I swallowed.

"You are allowed to tell me how fantastic I look."

"You look fantastic."

I stood up and walked round the desk. Linda stepped into the office, closed the door, locked it, and leaned back against it. I moved into her arms. We kissed; hard and hungry. Linda arched her back, lifted her hips and pressed close. I started to shake. She felt it. Swung us both round and reversed our positions. The door took my weight. She leaned the whole length of her body against me and began, very slowly, to rotate her hips. I groaned. For a split second I thought "Christ, Bill, don't ring now." Linda pulled me away from the door, reversing slowly towards the desk, then eased out of the embrace. She dropped to her knees on the carpet. I did the same. She leaned into me again. I rocked back, slid my heels out from under me and lay down. Linda slid into position beside me.

"Now you," she said.

We rolled through one hundred and eighty degrees. I looked down at her. The silk blouse was tight across her breasts.

I have a history of buggering up great moments like this. 'Take it easy, Shepherd,' I said to myself. 'Just make it work.'

"Don't think about this, Jack, for fuck's sake," Linda breathed. "Just do it."

Chapter Sixteen

"Are either of us contemplating work today?" Linda asked. Saturday morning, five minutes past nine. We were lying with our heads propped up on pillows, looking out of the huge bedroom window at a vast expanse of the Bristol Channel.

Linda had moved into the best preserved bit of old Portishead, a year and a half ago. Woodlands Road runs west to east behind an avenue of houses built perilously close to the Severn Estuary cliff tops. Linda's home is midway along the road; a two storey art deco house, which feels as if it's hanging over the cliff edge. The windows in the ground floor living room and the bedroom above, are big and wide; like the view across the water to Wales. The spring equinox is always a bit of an adventure on this exposed bit of coastline. When the prevailing wind is blowing and the rain is streaming sideways, it hits the windows with some force, beating a tattoo on the double glazing. This morning, the wind was blowing with determination, but the sky was clear.

"I have tickets to a shindig at the Royal West Academy. Champagne and canapés at noon."

"In aid of what?" I asked.

She looked at me oddly, as if I was a child who had spoken out of turn. "Art," she said. "What do you think it is? It's the launch of a new gallery space and a celebration of an endowment from somebody. Take your wallet. We may be asked to contribute."

"No such thing then, as free champagne and canapés."

A mobile rang from somewhere. I looked at Linda.

"It's not mine," she said.

I sat up. My phone was ringing on the chest of drawers facing the bed. I got up to answer it.

Bridget Dean had news.

"I've found my late, greedy bastard employer's old iPad," she said.

"An old one. How many has he got?"

"Only one. Well two actually. But he thinks he has one only. In all the office upheaval, I found the one he thought he'd lost. I think we should talk."

"Okay," I said. "Now?"

"I think sooner is better than later," she said. "Have you had breakfast?"

"No."

"Come and have it with me."

She gave me her address. I looked at the bedside clock again, told Bridget I'd be with her before ten, and rang off. I turned back to face Linda.

"Where will you be before ten? And with whom?"

"Walter Cobb's secretary and long established right hand person," I said.

"That's a pity," Linda said, looking directly at my crotch.

Suddenly I felt vulnerable. No man can make rational explanations trouser-less. Linda eased out from under the duvet and crawled along the bed towards me. She extended her right arm, took hold of my penis and pulled gently. I could move nowhere but forwards. By the time I reached the bottom of the bed, all sorts of possibilities were available.

"You not going to breakfast with another woman without something to remember," Linda said.

I managed to extricate myself from the bed twenty minutes later, struggled into jeans and a shirt, and said I'd be back in an hour or so. The Saturday morning traffic was light and another twenty minutes later, I was across the Cumberland Basin and into Hotwells. Whereupon my mobile rang. I pulled over.

Helen was on the other end of the line, disturbed and frightened.

"May has disappeared," she said.

"You mean she's not at home," I said.

"I mean she hasn't been home since breakfast yesterday."

I sat in the Defender, staring through the windscreen. Helen took this hiatus at my end of the line, as less than encouraging. She broke the silence.

"What do I do, Jack?"

"Nothing until I get to you. Within the hour, I promise."

"Okay, thanks," Helen said and ended the call.

I decided I didn't have time to contemplate another disappearance right then. I swung the Defender out into a gap in the traffic.

Bridget's house sat on one of the narrow hillside terraces which run down from lower Clifton to Hotwells. She ushered me into the living room. A kind of mini *grande salle*, knocked through into the kitchen, and occupying the whole of the ground floor of the tiny house. It was simply and minimally furnished – it had to be – but the cushions were big, the fabrics and curtains brightly coloured, which made the room feel more substantial than it was.

"It's a pleasure to see you again, Jack," Bridget said.

I returned the compliment. She pointed at the sofa.

"Please sit down."

She was wearing a pale blue tee shirt and dark blue jeans. She went into the kitchen area and called back to me. "Cereal, eggs, toast...?"

"No breakfast," I said. "Just coffee please."

She took a mug from a mug tree to the right of the sink and poured coffee into it from a coffee maker. I asked her if she knew who was looking into Cobb's financial extemporising.

"The Receivers are on the way," she said. "They'll be in on Monday. And as I'm the only one who knows how the business works, they've kept me on the payroll temporarily."

"Is there anything you can tell them?"

"I've no idea, Jack. I don't know what he's actually doing, or how he's managing to do it."

She stepped back to me.

"It's only been made a few minutes," she said. Handed me the mug and sat down at the other end of the sofa, leaving two feet of space between us. "I appreciate this is Saturday morning..."

"Not a problem," I said, "if it's going to help find Bill."

And May, it occurred to me.

She reached behind her and picked up the iPad sitting on the side table alongside the sofa arm.

"A real house of secrets this."

She placed the iPad on the sofa, in the space between us.

"How did you get into it?"

She grinned at me. "I know all his passwords."

"Does he know you know?"

"Yes. A breach of security perhaps, but neither of us imagined he'd be in the shit and we'd be in this situation." She paused for effect, then went on. "And I've learned a lot over the past twenty-four hours." Another moment's pause. "I think Walter has been doing business in the Channel Islands."

"Since when?"

"Don't know. Not long I imagine. There is folder in there, created during the summer of 2013. Labelled *Cobb CI*."

"What's in it?"

Bridget shook her head. "Well here's the thing. Stuff to do with a place called *Channel Skies*."

"Is that all?"

"All I could find."

"No contact addresses or phone numbers?

She shook her head. We both pondered for a second or two.

"What the hell could *Cobb CI* be up to?" Bridget asked. Then answered her own question. "If *CI* means Channel Islands, that could be where Walter's stashed money he doesn't want any of us to know about."

"Can the Receivers get at it?" I asked.

"I doubt it," she I said. "That'll be why it's there."

I sipped at my coffee mug. Bridget put her hands between her knees and began rubbing the palms together. I sipped my coffee again.

"And..." she said. "There's another file, labelled *BM*. Not hard to figure out who that is. I found a series of emails between Walter and Bill Marsh." She reached behind her and picked a data stick off a side table. And some sheets of A4.

"I've printed them out. I didn't get round to other stuff. I thought I could leave that to the super sleuth."

The emails covered a period of five months over the late summer and autumn of 2012. They were about money – basically Cobb spending huge sums of it and asking Bill for more.

"For what, do you think?" Bridget asked.

I levered myself upright on the sofa. I read all the emails again. So did Bridget. Then I looked at her and she looked at me, both of us hoping the other might have a moment of revelation.

"What was going on between Walter and Bill?" Bridget asked.

"Whatever it was," I said, "it was secret. Which, given Walter's track record, probably means it was illegal. Can I take the iPad as well as the stick and the notes?"

"Do you need to? The receivers might want to see it."

"I'm sure they will. Let me have it over the weekend. I'll get it back to you before Monday. Scout's honour."

"Well, who could doubt that?"

We sat on the sofa in silence, for some time, shrouded in wondering. I drained the coffee mug. Then I told Bridget that May had disappeared too. She groaned. Leaned back into the sofa cushions and stared up at the ceiling.

"Christ..."

She stood up, moved across the room to her desk, found a pencil and a piece of paper. Wrote down the iPad and email passwords. I stood up too.

"Can you sort all this out?" she asked.

"I don't know," I said. "I'll try."

Bridget ushered me to the front door. I stepped outside and walked to the Defender. When I turned to look back, Bridget waved, reversed into the house and closed the door.

I drove to Syme Park going through the expanding list of missing persons. First Bill, still alive – at the time of yesterday afternoon's phone call at least. Len Coleman, dead on his living room floor. Arnold Faversham hiding. Walter Cobb, somewhere, counting his money. And now May, just somewhere.

I pulled up in Downs Avenue at 10.45. The press corps had melted into thin air. I told Helen Bill had called me, but it didn't diminish the stress levels much. I asked her if anyone had phoned to speak to May.

"No... Do you think she might have found where Bill is, and gone to see him?"

"Not without telling us, I would have thought. Unless that's another secret being kept."

Helen looked distressed again. I suggested she should go home.

"There's no point sitting here alone."

Helen nodded. "Yes that's probably best. Yes I'll do that."

"Do you want me to give you a lift?"

"No no. That's fine."

"You know where I am," I said.

I used the phone in Bill's office to call Chris Gould.

"How are you at getting into hidden files on an iPad?"

"Fairly useful," he said.

"I have the thing with me," I said."

"Bring it round and I'll take a look."

I drove into Bedminster and handed over the iPad.

"Are you looking for anything in particular?" Chris asked.

"Stuff on the Channel Islands. And anything you can dig out with the names of Bill Marsh, Walter Cobb and Len Coleman attached."

He wrote the names down. I told him about the police phone tap. He took an old 3G mobile from a drawer and handed it to me.

"Keep this for a few days. The number's on the piece of masking tape on the back. I'll call you on that phone until you tell me otherwise."

I left the iPad with him and got back to Portishead ten minutes before noon.

Linda was dressed and ready for the champagne gig. Smart casual was never so sensational. We drove in the Defender to my house. I changed into the closest I ever get to smart casual. We left at 12.30, for the heart of the city's gallery land.

* * *

The Royal West Academy is one half of a small outbreak of Victoriana at the end of Queens Road, in Clifton. The other half is represented by the Victoria Rooms, situated forty yards from the academy on the other side of a roundabout. The former is an understated, classically restrained, example of the oeuvre; the latter, all swirls and ridiculous detail, is an over-the-top gothic revival meets retro-Corinthian statement, fronted by lions and nymphs, a fountain and a statue on a sculpted plinth. Miraculously, we found a parking space behind the RWA.

Walking to the gallery, Linda fished the invitation cards from her hand bag. She stopped walking and froze on the pavement.

"Bloody Hell..."

I turned to face her. She held one of the cards under my nose.

"Look who the heroine of this little gathering is."

I read the card. Writ large was the name of Freddie Settle, philanthropist and art lover. Linda synchronised her deep breathing with mine.

"Does this revelation change our minds?" Linda asked. "Are we the sort of people to be intimidated by this?"

"Probably not. For we are strong and our cause is just."

Linda smiled at me. "Hell yes."

We walked into the front door of the Academy, past a life size photograph of Freddie dressed to the nines. By the time we reached the first floor gallery, she was drawing to the end of her welcome meet and greet. She was standing on a rostrum under a massive splurge of red and brown by an artist I didn't know. Relaxed and confident in front of her audience, flanked by her accountant Cyril and the Gallery Director. Gareth Thomas, wearing a light grey suit and a charming smile, was standing on the floor in front of the rostrum.

"That's a twelve hundred quid outfit she's wearing," Linda whispered.

"Bringing exhibitions of this quality to the Westcountry takes time and money," Freddie was saying. "And while I can't claim to have done any of the hard work, I'm only too pleased to take all the credit for paying the bills."

There was ripple of polite laughter from the assembled art supporters. Freddie acknowledged this and scanned the room.

"Unfortunately I have a busy afternoon ahead. So I can't stay long."

She saw us loitering at the rear of the gallery, stopped working the room, and aimed the smile in our direction.

"Please enjoy the reception and these glorious works of art. Thank you all for coming."

The art supporters applauded. Freddie shook hands with the Gallery Director and stepped off the rostrum. Cyril joined Thomas.

A raven-haired teenager with a smile to rival Freddie's thrust a plate of vol au vents at me.

"Can I tempt you, Sir?"

"No thank you," I said. "Perhaps later."

Linda stepped to my shoulder. "So what do we do now?"

"Do you want to be introduced?"

"I should say so. A once in a lifetime opportunity to meet the crime boss."

"Let's hope it is only once."

A colleague of the raven-haired teenager swung into position in front of us with a tray of champagne glasses. Linda took one and nodded her thanks. I was still looking at Freddie – glowing with delight and grace at the people around her. Linda picked up a second champagne glass and nudged my elbow.

"Jack..."

I took the glass. Freddie was flowing across the gallery floor. Managing to acknowledge everyone she passed, but clearly heading for us. Thomas and Cyril followed discreetly, two strides behind her.

"Jack," she cooed, and directed the nuclear powered smile straight into my eyes. Before turning to Linda. "Hello, Ms Barnes."

Linda blinked a couple of times, surprised that Freddie knew who she was. Freddie probably had biographies of half the people in the city. Linda took a deep breath and swallowed.

"Ms Settle," she said.

"Call me Freddie. So pleased to meet you. Unfortunately, I must fly."

"I had no idea you were a patron of the arts, Freddie," I said.

"Something my father did. So we carry on the tradition. Places like this would be forced to close without the support of local businesses."

It was hard to disagree with that. Nonetheless, Freddie's expansion, and the malignant growth of Settle influence over long revered city institutions, was no cause for cheer.

A mobile rang. Thomas took a phone from his inside jacket pocket and clamped it to his ear.

"Thank you," he said. He returned the phone to his pocket. "The car is downstairs, Ms Settle."

She looked at us and shrugged politely.

"Sorry. Come and have a drink with me, Jack. Soon. We have lots to talk about."

Had we? That was the most loaded invitation I'd been offered in a long while. Linda looked alarmed. Freddie flowed past us and out onto the landing. Thomas nodded at me as he followed.

"Mr Shepherd..."

Cyril offered no acknowledgement at all. Simply slid by. Linda grabbed my hand and leaned close.

"Some woman," she said. "She's good, really good. And she frightens the shit out of me."

"You're not alone in that. However..."

Linda thought that I was about to resolve something. She let go of my hand. When I didn't say anything more she changed tack.

"You've got that determined look in your eye," she said.

I stared at her. "What look?"

"The one you get when you're determined."

"It's only there to fool the public."

"Is there any chance that Freddie wants to discuss something constructive?"

"She actually said, 'we have lots to talk about'. It loses something in the translation. What she meant was, 'I'm still on your case."

Linda took that on board, then resolutely moved things along.

"Okay," she said. "In the meantime, let's have some more champagne and give this art the once over."

Chapter Seventeen

The art was exciting. Brand new. From painters and sculptors throughout Britain and Europe. The vol au vents were rather good, once we got around to them. I missed *Football Focus*, but maybe, now and again, you have to get a dose of what is good for you.

We had a late lunch at *Browns* on the southern corner of The Triangle. I drove us home mid-afternoon.

I turned the Defender into the lane behind my house and drove towards the silver Audi, parked outside my garage.

"Is that erm...?" Linda asked.

"Gareth and Dylan, yes."

Back to lean on my car and wave guns at me. No doubt a more substantial dose of menace guaranteed this time, with Linda included. I reacted with the first idea that entered my head. Slowed the Defender to walking pace, switched to four wheel drive, locked the diff and floored the accelerator pedal. Gareth and Dylan must have been too startled to act quickly. We were only a few yards short of the Audi when it began to hurtle backwards along the lane, weaving from side to side, as whichever Thomas was driving tried to match speed and direction. The Audi was barely a couple of car lengths away as it scorched out of the lane and vanished to our right, accompanied by an angry roar from the protesting engine. I stamped on the brake pedal and the Defender slid to a halt.

From out on the road we heard a loud tearing noise and the sound of buckling metal.

I unlocked the diff and looked at Linda.

"Can you drive this?"

"Of course."

"Then back it up to the garage, and leave it there."

I got out of the Defender and left Linda sliding across the front seats. Behind me I heard the engine revs rise, as I looked down at the skid marks sculpted into the tarmac by the Healey tyres three weeks earlier. Unhappily, only the first traffic involvement of the month. I thought of Lily whose life I had ended. And now, out in the road...

The Audi was crushed to about two thirds of its length and appeared to be jammed into the front of a number 85 bus. Or rather, the car looked like some huge concertinaed object which the bus had gorged out. Amazingly, the engine was still running. The left front wing of the bus had caved in and the front door was jammed shut. Passengers were exiting from the back of the bus. The driver managed to get out of the cab by squeezing through the space to his right where there had been a window. He fell, head first, onto the road. Rolled over and sat up, dazed and disorientated. A lady passenger collared him, helped him towards the pavement and made him drink from a bottle of water she took out of her shoulder bag.

The bus stop was a hundred yards from the lane end. The bus wouldn't have been up to cruising speed when the Audi slammed into it. But the revs would have been high and the bus using a lot of bottom end torque. It was a hell of a smash.

Inside the Audi, all four airbags had exploded into action. The boot had been pushed forward and was now sharing space with the rear seats. Everything inside had been shunted forwards too. The interior was a mess of bent plastic, broken glass, torn leather, tangled upholstery and twisted metal. The two front deflated airbags were streaked with blood. Both Thomases were unconscious. Gareth behind the driving wheel, his head way over to the right of his neck, glass and blood in his hair. Dylan, head down on his chest with an ugly wound in the side of his neck, which was bleeding steadily. One of the passengers, moved to my side clutching his mobile.

"I've just called an ambulance. The fire brigade is on the way too, with cutting gear."

Between us we tried to open the Audi doors. At least the front ones, the rear doors weren't recognisable as such any more. We couldn't do it. The bus driver joined us. Stared at the men in the front seats.

"Jesus Christ..." He looked at the two of us. "I'd only just... pulled away from the bus stop. The car came at me so fast..."

He turned away, lurched across the pavement and threw up in a garden hedge.

Linda walked out of the lane. I moved towards her.

"Go to the house. You don't have anything to do with this," I said.

"Neither have you," she said.

"That's something to be discussed."

"No no," she said. "The Audi driver reversed out of the lane and into the bus." She waved about her. "All these people saw it. And they are not injured."

"The Thomas brothers are."

"You were the last person on the scene. You didn't see any of it happen."

She was right of course. I didn't. And I could do without DC Reynolds back on my case – pleasant though he had been – as well as the MIT and Freddie.

Linda read what I was thinking.

"You didn't cause this," she said. "If anyone did, it was those two in the car. Freddie even. If she hadn't sent—"

"This is always a phoney argument," I said. "You can keep going back through any train of events, each one motivated by the one it follows. World War One didn't start with an assassination in the Balkans, it started with a hundred years of upsets and revolutions in Europe after Napoleon was beaten. And he did what he did because—"

Linda held up her arms and patted the air.

"Alright I get the point. However, the reality is here. And there is no need for you to be part of it."

"I'm going to wait for the ambulance. Find out how badly hurt Freddie's employees are. I'm not going to get implicated in anything. Everybody here knows when I arrived on the scene. Sitting in my living room and waiting for Freddie to ring and ask me what I did to her Audi and her two enforcers, isn't an option. She will lay all this at my door whatever. Please, go back to the house."

She stared at me for what seemed ages.

"Okay. I'll sit in your living room and drink your brandy. So don't be long."

She kissed me, turned and walked back into the lane. From somewhere in the distance the sound of an ambulance siren grew in volume.

* * *

The paramedics couldn't get at the two men in the Audi. While they were waiting, they checked all the bus passengers and treated the driver for shock. They wrapped him in a blanket and made him sit in the ambulance. It took another ten minutes for the fire fighters to cut away enough of the tangled remains of the Audi, to allow the medics to get inside. They managed to stop the blood flowing out of Dylan's neck. He regained consciousness, at least for a moment, then floated in and out. Gareth was still unconscious when the medics loaded him into the ambulance. A couple of police patrol cars arrived. Uniformed PCs talked to all of us about we had seen. I walked home a little later.

Linda moved into the kitchen as I opened the back door.

She leaned into me, wrapped her arms around me and held on tight. Then we moved into the living room. I poured a large brandy and sat down in the nearest armchair. I swallowed some of the brandy. Felt it go all the way down. I looked at Linda, sitting on the sofa like a maiden aunt waiting for the little boy who has spent the day getting into trouble, to fess up.

Chris Gould's mobile began to ring. I swallowed the rest of the brandy, found my jacket and retrieved it.

"*Cobb CI* is in Jersey," Chris said. "I'll email the folders and files to you. Not much I'm afraid. There is no communication with Len Coleman, and no more about Bill Marsh than you know already. But there are one or two emails between Cobb and somebody called Arnold Faversham."

I thanked him, and said I'd pick up the iPad first thing the following morning. Chris said anytime during the day would be fine. He ended the call.

"That's a new, very old phone," Linda said. "What is it, a spare?"

I changed the subject.

"How much do you know about banking in Jersey?" I asked Linda.

"A bit. Why?"

"It's where Walter Cobb keeps his money."

"You mean the money he's not telling the receivers about," Linda said.

There was a pause. I waited for her to assemble information.

"We tend to think of offshore, in terms of exotic sounding places like the Cayman Islands, Barbados, the Seychelles, Belize," she said. "But there's a long list of prospects closer to home – Andorra, Luxembourg, The Isle of Man, Jersey..."

"And all these places offer the same kinds of service?"

"Yes."

"And they are?"

"Basically, tax avoidance and serious opportunities for money laundering. Up until the mid-90s, in some places it was even possible to set up your own personal bank. A US mobster called Meyer Lansky did just that, to launder the money coming into his casinos from the rackets."

Linda paused for me to take that in. Then she continued.

"Jersey is an odd place. It obviously doesn't have the glamour you assume the exotic places flaunt. It's ruled rather like a medieval bailiwick, according to laws written in *Jerriais* – a kind of ancient sounding muddle of French and English. The islanders are British but not European citizens as Jersey isn't in the EU."

"Effectively, a foreign country then."

"And the island's business is no longer just about cows and tomatoes. These days, agriculture makes bugger all contribution to the island's economy. The finance business makes up close to forty-five percent. Ninety-something thousand people live on the island, or to be correct, in it. Two thousand of them are accountants."

She paused, to give that statistic weight.

"Compare that to Bristol," she went on. "A population of four hundred and thirty eight thousand. With maybe five hundred people working as accountants. And if you remember from *Bergerac*, Jersey is famous as the sunny well-to-do haven of retired old money, unscrupulous new money, chancers and law-benders and rich yacht owning non-doms."

"And you're saying that's not a far-fetched picture of the place?" I asked.

"It's close enough. Income tax is low, VAT practically non-existent. So if you can slide all you earn through your Jersey bank account, you're quids in."

"And setting up a bank account is no problem?"

"As long as you can prove you have the wherewithal to open one. All the UK High Street Banks are there. As well as a glut of private banks. Which provide anonymous bank accounts, low interest rate loans, and investment opportunities you won't find anywhere else."

"So, if you like sun," I said, "quaint place names, a touch of French life without having to learn a foreign language, a place you can circumnavigate in a morning, and all sorts of opportunities for tax avoidance, then Jersey is the place for you."

"In a nutshell," Linda said.

"So how do we find Walter Cobb's company?" I asked.

"You've got a name. Fly out there and mooch around. Shouldn't take you long to find. Even if you have to explore the whole forty-seven square miles."

I found my laptop and read Chris Gould's email. He said the retrieval was patchy. He had attached all he could get out of the deleted folders and there wasn't much. As to the main business of *Cobb CI...* "Care Homes," Linda said. "I don't believe it."

It did take a substantial leap to lock into the idea of Walter Cobb the carer.

"There's not much in the folder at all," I said. "The emails passing between Cobb and Arnold Faversham are interesting though. Lots of talk about plans kept close to the chest. Budgets full of massive costs for the tools of the undertaker's trade."

Linda looked at the pages. "They're euphemisms," she said. "Code words. Meant only for those in the loop. The budget cost for 'flowers' is £15,000. For 'disbursements', £38,000. For 'cleaning and maintenance' £17,000. 'Deliveries' £26,000. For 'materials A' £123,000, for 'materials B' £95,000."

"Arnold must be running a multinational undertaking organisation," I said.

"Whatever," Linda said. "If the ratio of profits to costs is 3 to 1 – the least you'd expect from a successful business – then he and Walter must be rolling in it."

I looked at her. "Do you fancy a weekend in Jersey?"

"At those prices, absolutely."

* * *

The flight from Bristol to Jersey takes forty odd minutes with the wind in the right direction, and costs twice as much as it does from London City Airport and Gatwick. And a clutch of other airports too.

I gave myself up to the vagaries of domestic flight tickets and shelled out £278 for two returns.

Chapter Eighteen

"Have you been up all night?" Auntie Joyce asked. "Why?"

"You look terrible."

"Nobody looks their best on Skype," I said. "How are you and Uncle Sid?"

"We're well," she said. "He's got grand designs for his new piece. He's thumping something right now. The noise is torture. I'm surprised you can't hear it."

"What about the neighbours?"

"They're away for the weekend, so he's getting some extra thumping in this evening."

This was our weekend hook up. It's a regular thing but never a chore. Uncle Sid is a mild mannered retired engineer, Auntie Joyce is a miracle, and they still love each other to bits. We always find plenty to talk about. I told her about the imminent Jersey trip.

"You could probably do with a break," she said. Then had second thoughts. "It's not a trip is it, it's part of some investigation."

"Linda is going with me," I said.

A bit lame that. Auntie Joyce thought so too. She took a deep breath and kept her own counsel.

"Ah the noise has stopped," she said. "I'll go and fetch Sid."

She moved out of shot and I was left with a view of the bookshelf in the study. Uncle Sid arrived thirty seconds later.

"You look a bit knackered," he said.

I told him we had done that bit and asked him about his new creation. He told me it was an abstract and would be a work in progress until he realised he had finished it. He feared however, that it might prove too big.

"All of them are," I said.

"Yes," he said. "But I fear this one may be a creation too far."

We talked for ten minutes or so. Then Auntie Joyce came back and we resumed our conversation. She asked about Chrissie and Adam and Sam.

"In genuine rude health. And Sam is... well he's just Sam," I said.

Then Auntie Joyce grimaced. "He's started thumping again. Take care in Jersey."

I told her it was no more than a fact finding mission. She said that was the sort of thing UN envoys said in war zones. She finished by ordering me to find time to visit Suffolk. I promised I would, soonest. We said 'goodbye'.

I rang Helen on the loaner mobile. Asked if May had called. She said no. I told her I'd be away for a couple of days but I'd stay in contact. She mumbled her thanks and we ended the call.

I drove to Chris Gould's shop, picked up the iPad and returned it to Bridget, as promised. She asked if it had been useful. I said yes. She asked me what the next step was. I said two days on Jersey and wished her luck with the receivers.

Back home, I pulled a brown holdall out from the bottom of my wardrobe and considered what to pack for a trip to Jersey in the last week in April. I had a range of clothing all over the bed when Mr Earl rang. He told me the Healey was running like the well-oiled machine she was built to be, and volunteered to drive her up to my house. Twenty minutes later he pulled up in the street. I saw him arrive and opened the front door. He ambled up the path. I asked him if wanted a drink. He said 'no thank you'. I conducted him through the house, out the back door and across the garden to the garage. He climbed into the Defender, turned on the ignition, dipped the accelerator pedal a couple of times, found first gear, swung into the lane and headed for the main road. I watched until he disappeared, then went back into the house and called George Hood's mobile.

"Hell, Jack, I'm watching *Final Score*."

"May is missing now," I said.

There was a moment's pause, then Hood asked, "Since when?"

"Maybe as much as thirty-six hours. And this is more than run of the mill."

"Yes," he said. "It is. I'll see what I can do. Call me if you find out anything your end. Otherwise, we'll meet on Monday."

"Can't do that I'm afraid. I'm in Jersey."

"So you are taking a spring break while I do your leg work?"

"No. I'm checking on Walter Cobb's business dealings. He has money over there. I'll only be a couple of days."

"For God's sake don't do anything we're all going to be sorry for. And call me as soon as you get back."

"Thanks, George."

"As I said, I like May."

* * *

There was no word from Helen or Hood the following morning – Sunday. Linda and I flew across the Channel mid-afternoon. After spending almost twice the flight time standing in a queue at Bristol Airport, checking in, waiting in the lounge at Gate 16 and taking a bus ride to the plane.

We got out of the taxi at the eastern end of St Clement Bay.

"I'm not getting any French vibe yet," I said.

The taxi driver pulled away. Linda stared at me.

"Hell, Jack, when are you going to stop moaning?" she hissed. "The only Jersey soil you've touched, is the thirty yards between the plane and the arrivals lounge, and the square foot you're standing on right now."

She led the way into the hotel lobby.

"I suppose, eventually, I will get round to being pleased you talked me into this."

The Hotel de Bretagne has an unimpeachable French name, some of the building is art deco, and the interior has a resolutely old fashioned feel. The big bonus is, the front door is not much further than a triple jump from the beach.

I introduced myself to Meg, the lady behind the reception desk with her name pinned on to her jacket collar. She had an expensive, flowing, haircut and was extremely beautiful. She asked if I had been to Jersey before. I admitted I hadn't. She smiled at me.

"I'm sure you will fall in love with the place."

Linda and I filled in the registration forms. Meg handed me a room key.

"Room 216," she said. "At the front, facing the sea. Do you want a hand with your luggage?"

"No thanks."

She pointed across the lobby. "The lifts are over there, Mr Shepherd. Enjoy your stay in the island."

Linda and I were the only people to step into the lift. She pressed the second floor button. The doors closed. There was a rumble and a slight jerk and the lift began to rise.

"You were ogling her," Linda said.

"What?"

"Meg. You were ogling her."

"I do not ogle," I protested. "I've never ogled in my life. Well, except a time or to at Emily. And now you. I'm allowed to ogle you."

She looked at me dead centre. I wavered a bit.

"Well erm..."

Fortunately, the lift came to a stop and the doors opened. I gave Linda the room key, picked up the bags and stepped into the second floor corridor.

216 had a no nonsense sea view. And French windows and a balcony from where we could see the whole of St Clement Bay. I was swiftly warming to the place. Linda tested the bed by lying on it and bouncing up and down. Then she lay back, raised her arms, put them behind her head and relaxed. Poetry in motion.

"I'm ogling now," I confessed.

"So show me how ogling transfers into action," she said.

* * *

We were out of bed, showered and changed in time to go to dinner. Linda ate fruits de mer, I had pork and beans. The dessert was no contest. I had éclairs and Linda chose tarte au citron. By the time we were sitting in the lounge drinking coffee, the French vibe had arrived.

And so had the sunset.

The tide was out and we walked along the beach. Hand in hand, like teenagers in a stolen moment.

"I hate to break the mood," Linda said. "But what's the MO for tomorrow?"

We stopped walking and turned and stood shoulder to shoulder. Looking at the horizon slowly morphing from orange into magenta.

"We'll begin by finding the beating heart of the Walter Cobb empire and then we'll pay a visit."

We lapsed into silence again. Walked a little further. The magenta sky was navy blue now. And the temperature had dropped. We shivered in turn.

"Back to the hotel for Ovaltine," Linda said.

What we actually did was have brandies in the lounge, sitting in two wing backed chairs by a fire blazing in a big granite fireplace. Close by, on a sofa table, there was the usual clutter of 'things to do' information leaflets and 'lifestyle' magazines. Linda got up out of her chair to root around in the publications. She came back with one of them.

"Did you notice that the first advertising hoardings we encountered in the arrivals lounge at the airport concerned finance?" she said, waving the magazine at me. "Well, there's the same mantra in here. Promising 'tax advice', 'wealth management' and 'asset protection'. This is Jersey's headline act. And look at that."

A half page advert from a company called *Westcountry Offshore*. I stared at it. Linda leaned against the chair and looked over my shoulder.

"See what this company does? It buys Jersey and Guernsey businesses and sells them to buyers in the UK, who continue to have them registered here."

I scanned the advertising copy. The company was currently looking for property within a price range of one million pounds to five and a half, to convert to a health spa. Apparently there were UK buyers lining up to shell out for such.

"Nothing wrong with that, in essence," Linda said. "But the system is ripe for exploitation. Especially as both buyers and sellers know that Jersey corporations enjoy zero percent tax and no inheritance or capital gains taxes."

Upstairs in 216, I checked my mobile inbox. There were two recorded calls. Hood said he had made no progress. Helen said May hadn't been in contact. I threw the phone onto the bed.

"Is this par for the course?" Linda asked. "This frustration."

"The major part of any investigation is spent in thinking and asking questions. Or the other way round."

"And the rest of it?"

"Leaping into action. Well, sometimes."

In no time at all, the wonderful evening had lost its mojo.

Chapter Nineteen

The following morning, the hire car, a Ford Fiesta, arrived at the hotel as we finished breakfast. We drove into St Helier and found the island Archive. We were in and out in twenty-five minutes. *Cobb CI* was indeed registered in the island, its major business listed as care homes. We looked up *Westcountry Offshore*. Its business was investment. And there was a bonus prize. The CEO was one H.W.Cobb.

"Has to be him, doesn't it?" Linda said. "It's time you got lucky."

We left with two printouts and took a walk around the harbour.

"Walter Cobb and concern for the elderly," Linda said. She considered the proposition for a moment. "No no. Let's face it. No one could accuse him of being concerned about anybody."

"Both Adam and Bridget cautioned me not to be deceived by his south Bristol wide boy act. Said he was capable of playing several ends against a pile of middles. Not in the same league as Freddie Settle, but still devious and clever."

"Okay," Linda said. "But care homes...?"

"It's the perfect front, for just about anything nefarious," I said. "Totally straight arrow."

"Perhaps, deep down in Walter's black soul, there lurks a caged philanthropist."

"Well, when we get him cornered, we'll put that to him."

"So we have a plan do we?" Linda asked.

"I don't know what I've said to give you that impression."

"I know we just got lucky, but I had assumed that your investigations were driven by theories rather than guided by serendipity."

I looked at her. "All investigations have a story arc and one discovery leads to another. And if the sleuth is on form, he makes the right connections."

Back at the car, Linda studied the map the hotel had given us. *Channel Skies*, had a Corbière address.

"South west corner of the island," she said. "Where the land sort of sticks out into the channel. There's a lighthouse."

"Okay, got that."

Linda looked at me. "Why are there question marks in your eyes?"

"*Channel Skies* will be exclusive," I suggested. "But it can't be making Walter millions."

"We are in Jersey," she said. "And presumably, multi-millionaires can afford to pay top whack for care. I doubt it's another... what was the Bristol place?"

"Winterbourne View."

"I bet the old folk hereabouts sleep in satin sheets," Linda went on. "And every room has a balcony and satellite TV. Whatever, there's also *Westcountry Offshore*. Based at an address on the north coast."

"Let's go and visit the senior citizens first," I said.

We drove the nine and a half miles to Corbière in no time at all.

Channel Skies was a hotel conversion. An enormous Victorian place, with a semi-circle of mixed woodland and expensive landscaping bordering the landward side. The big, carved, cast iron gates were open. I pulled up so that we could read the sign at the edge of the drive. The words of welcome made the place sound only a little short of paradise. Which, on reflection, is no more than any care home resident deserves. Along with millions of others I watched the *Panorama* exposé of Winterbourne and followed the subsequent revelations in Lancashire and Croydon. I have a choice as to where I live, as do most of the people in Jersey. I retain most of my faculties. And I'm not at the mercy of the staff at some under-funded bin of a place who don't give a toss about the people for whom they have a duty of care.

It took us an age to cruise up the drive. I parked the Fiesta in the visitors' car park, bounded by shrubs and small trees. At that moment, the clouds rolled by and the sun came out. Linda looked up at the sky.

"An omen," she said. "How can we fail on such a bright, bright, sunshiny day?"

I looked at the front of the building, a bit gothic but welcoming enough. The entrance was arched, ten or twelve feet high, with two sculpted oak doors which were open. We stepped inside and onto a flag-stoned floor. Ahead of us was a wide stone stairway, which rose to a landing, then split left and right and continued up to the first floor. There was a solid oak stair rail on the left – a relic from the hotel days I guessed. The right hand side had been re-structured to take the weight of a stair lift. There were big rooms on both sides of the hall with big doorways. We stood and marvelled.

"Crikey," Linda said. Her voice hushed and soft.

I looked at her. "Crikey?"

"I didn't want to swear. It feels a bit like being in church."

A lady rose from a chair to our right, circumnavigated an oval mahogany table and stepped towards us. She had short brown hair, sculpted around her face and brown eyes to match. She smiled.

"May I help you?" she asked. "I'm Sophie James, the Deputy Manager."

Her suit was made to fit. She looked smart and stately and welcoming.

"My name is Jack Sanderson and this is my wife Linda," I said.

We shook hands with Sophie, who asked how she could help us.

"We live and work in Bristol. My mother is getting older and a little unsteady. She has few friends now. She talks about Jersey more and more as the weeks go by. Her mother, my grandmother, was born in the island." Sophie smiled at my correct use of the participle. "And although my mother has the best of day care in her house, she doesn't get to see enough of us. To put it simply, she wants to come home. This place was recommended to us by a friend of the man who owns the business, Mr Cobb."

Sophie smiled again. Genuine and unforced.

"Yes," she said. "Mr Cobb is a real ambassador for the work we do here."

Tricky moment over, I tried to keep a straight face. Sophie, now in full public relations mode, asked us what we would like to know.

Linda spoke up. "Jack and I would like a tour of the home if that's possible. It's important that my mother in law should like this place one hundred percent. I don't want to go back to Bristol with any reservations."

"Of course not," Sophie said. "So if you would both follow me..."

We toured the ground floor. The living room first, with big windows and big comfortable chairs, a high ceiling and plenty of light. All the residents in the room seemed to be occupied; reading, talking – there was a heated debate going on around a table under one of the windows – playing bridge and chess. No one was lolling comatose in a chair, or staring mournfully into the middle distance.

Sophie spoke softly. "As you can see, no one is left in this room on their own to cater for their own discomfort. We have brilliant staff who keep a close eye on the residents but never get in their way. That's the secret to this work."

The reading room and library had bookshelves around all four walls, sofas to sit on and read, desks to write at. The dining room was neatly furnished and the tables laid with some care. It wouldn't have disgraced the Dorchester. The kitchen, a modern, gleaming stainless steel workshop, had a chef, a sous chef and two assistants, who were preparing lunch. But the room with the most going for it, at the rear of the house, was a projects room.

"We can organise all sorts of stuff in here," Sophie said. "Visits by guest speakers, drawing and painting, sculpting, aerobics and workouts, music, and even our own little bits of theatre."

She crossed the room and we followed, towards what felt like the rear of the building. She opened the venetian blinds across two windows and revealed an indoor swimming pool, stretching into the garden. A man and a woman were in the water; not floating about relaxing, but swimming lengths with some determination.

"Colin and Esther," Sophie said with some pride. "The over 60s Island Champions. There is a competition every year."

She guided us back into the hall and we began to climb the stairs. Linda asked Sophie how many people lived in *Channel Skies*.

"We have thirty-four residents currently," she said. "We can take up to thirty-eight." She paused on the first floor landing. "Six of the care staff are residents too, living in converted apartments in the stable block. We have a doctor on call 24/7." She pointed ahead. "The second suite on the left is not occupied at the moment."

Sophie unlocked the door, made way for us, and we stepped inside.

"Take a look around," she said. "Close the door behind you and come downstairs when you've done."

The suite had a bathroom, a bedroom, and a living room complete with flat screen TV, CD and DVD player. The room was comfortable and spotless. We sat down in two armchairs.

"Nothing wrong with these facilities," Linda suggested.

All that a wealthy senior citizen could wish for. But it was difficult to see what Walter Cobb could possibly squeeze out of this place, other than the average yearly stipend of an up market business person. *Channel Skies* wasn't going to get him into the super-tax bracket. He had to have some other scheme working alongside the respectability the care home gave him. Presumably *Westcountry Offshore* was it.

Downstairs, Sophie was back where she had been stationed as we came in. She picked up some leaflets from the table and offered them to us.

"Take these away," she said. "Read them. I'm sure they will provoke lots of questions. So please do call me. And thank you for visiting."

She shepherded us to the front door.

I sat in the Fiesta staring through the windscreen, Linda in the passenger seat perusing the literature.

"You have to be King Midas to live here," she said. "Still, a Jersey millionaire must be able to afford these prices for his old mum."

"The ultimate respectable front as I said. Here's Walter posing as Albert Schweitzer. I tell you he's at it. Getting away with murder."

"Not actually, we hope," Linda said.

"You can tour the shops in St Helier," I said, "while I drive up to St John's and knock on Walter Cobb's door."

I switched on the ignition. Linda looked at me, malice in her eyes.

"Oh right. Women shop while men go hunting."

"What?"

"If Adam were here you would—"

"If Adam were here, I'd be telling him the same thing."

"Oh yeah?

"Yeah. I'm paid to get beaten up and shot at. You two aren't. Besides..."

I was about to say something else incendiary, so I stopped. Linda picked up her cue however.

"Besides what?"

"Nothing. It won't come out right and it'll sound condescending."

"Spit it out, Shepherd."

"Alright. I might have enough on my plate without worrying about a sidekick as well. And that's not just because you're a female sidekick."

She paid me the compliment of considering that, but stayed resolute.

"No no," she insisted. "We drive up together. If Walter is at home, we will have achieved our object. You can do the testosterone fuelled macho PI bit, after which we can spend the rest of the day as tourists."

"What I meant in all seriousness was, if Walter is at home, there may be some unpleasantness. In which case I'd rather you weren't there."

"I shop as infrequently as possible. And I can be as unpleasant as the next person."

I gave in.

"Okay swop seats. Drive us there, but please stay in the car. This must be one to one. I want Cobb to deal with me, not both of us."

She relented. "Yes, okay. I get that. Just keep your mobile on. And shout if you get into trouble."

La Greve House sat on the seaward side of the road into St John's Bay. There was a pull-in twenty yards or so beyond the drive gates. They were electronically operated and they were closed. I didn't want to announce myself, so I set off on a recce of the boundary wall. The western side, running inland, was lined with trees and screened the wall from the house. I went over it, dropped into the garden behind a substantial ash tree well into late spring foliage, and looked at the house across God knows how many square yards of lawn. Granite, but in the style of one of the later French Louis. Three floors, with a line of dormer windows along the roof. Six bedrooms at least. Hell of a place for a bloke with no money.

I decided that if I kept behind the trees I had a reasonable chance of getting around the side of the house without being seen. I accomplished that bit. At the corner where the western and southern walls met, the trees were barely ten paces from the house. There was an art nouveau style glass covered terrace running the length of the south side. And at this end, a door which looked like it opened into the kitchen.

So what next? Climbing, creeping and running was not the sensible way to do this. Having got beyond the front gate and into the grounds without anyone in the house knowing, the obvious ploy was simply to knock on the front door.

I rang the doorbell. Walter Cobb opened the door and stared at me.

"Fucking hell," he said.

"May I come in?"

"No. Fuck off."

He tried to close the door and I stuck my foot in the way. This is never the best move to make. The brutal sandwiching of a soft soled size nine, between a seven foot high hardwood door and the door frame, hurts like nobody's business. But what it does do, is give the person closing the door a moment when he has to decide what to do next, and the same moment for the putative entrant to take action. With my left foot in agony, I leaned my shoulder against the door and shoved hard. It opened and Cobb staggered back into his hall. I hobbled through the gap and closed the door behind me. Leaned back against it and tried to ignore the pain in my foot.

Even in the hall, I could see that this house was as wonderful as the mock Tudor riot in Bristol was hideous. This was the home of someone with taste and understated style.

"You didn't have to scale the wall," Cobb said. "You only had to buzz at the gate."

"Would you have let me in?" I asked.

"Probably not. How did you find me?"

"Courtesy of your old iPad," I said. "Bridget discovered it."

"Clever girl. Which is why I hired her."

"She sends her regards."

"No she doesn't." He smiled at me. "So... Would you care for a drink?"

"A bit early for me."

He asked me if I'd had lunch. I said that was the next item on my agenda. He asked me where I was staying. I told him. He said the Hotel de Bretagne was okay for a mid-list sort of place and suggested I should have phoned him for a recommendation. He was cool and charming and welcoming. Then I remembered what Adam had said. I was supposed to fall for his schtick, but underneath that...

"Coffee then."

"That would be nice."

He led the way into the kitchen, fifteen feet square or thereabouts, fitted with stuff that was custom made. And in residence, here was Walter Cobb – stoked with bonhomie underneath all the bluster and bollocks. Which meant, like Freddie, that he was not to be underestimated. As he made coffee he told me about the house.

"It's Louis the Sixteenth. Built by a rich French merchant, Henri Carpentier, in 1778. A bit of a pirate by all accounts. He came to live here in 1784 at the height of *The Terror*, intending to go back to Paris after Robespierre's enemies had dealt with him. He did go back for a while, until he discovered he didn't like Napoleon either. So he returned, and lived here until he died in 1826. Another Frenchman, Philippe Giraud – engaged in the slavery business I'm afraid – bought the house, added this space and what is now the laundry and the garden room. He lived to be 85 and died up there above us in what was then the master bedroom, in 1879. His son continued to live here, and he managed to move most of his family into the house during the Great War. They all went back to France in 1919... Black or white?"

I was so engrossed in the tale I didn't know what he meant. He pointed at the coffee machine.

"Oh, white. No sugar."

He began to pour the coffee.

"The place was empty during the 1920s. Until it was bought by a hard case Yorkshireman called Edward Blagrove. He had a factory making grommets, which in turn made him a fortune. I bought the house six years ago from his granddaughter. Thought we might enjoy family holidays here."

"But you didn't?"

Cobb shook his head, and went on without any obvious sentiment. "One of my daughters died of a drugs overdose in 2010. The other two left. And shortly afterwards, Claudie moved out."

"Your wife?"

"Yes."

I muttered something about not knowing. He said the cold hearted bitch could go fuck herself – that was the Walter I expected – then transferred the coffees to the breakfast bar. We sat on stools on opposite sides. I wondered why I was getting all this guff, but I decided that while he wasn't threatening my life and limbs I'd let him go on. He had finished however. He picked up his coffee mug and drank from it.

"Mmnn, that's good."

I drank in response. And it was good. He looked at me without blinking for several seconds, then asked what I thought was going to happen next.

"I mean, is this a visit to catch up? Do you want to prise something out of me, or have you a firmer purpose?"

"Where's Bill Marsh?" I asked.

He didn't pause. "I don't know."

"Where is May?"

"At home I guess."

"No, she's missing too."

He seemed genuinely disturbed by that news.

"Visiting someone perhaps," he suggested.

He didn't believe that any more than I did.

"No," I said. "Missing. As in lost, gone, disappeared."

"She can't be. She has nothing to do with this."

"With what?"

Cobb put his mug down on the polished teak, got up from his stool, turned and moved to the window overlooking the terrace. He was not going to tell me, so I changed the subject.

"Did you kill Len Coleman?" I asked.

I couldn't see him smiling, but I'm sure he was.

"I didn't know he was dead."

This conversation was likely to go on as long as we could both draw breath. So I drank some more coffee, and when I looked up again, Cobb had turned round, silhouetted against the sunlight bouncing in from the glassed-over terrace, and inviting the next question.

So I asked it. "What pays for all this? It can't be *Channel Skies*."

That surprised him a little. He shifted his weight from one hip to the other.

"Maybe it's *Westcountry Offshore*," I said.

He didn't answer. So I offered the proposition again. He looked at me with some determination.

"And what's all this cloak and dagger stuff with Arnold Faversham. I've seen some of your budgeting. £15,000 for 'flowers', ridiculous amounts for 'materials'. And then 'disbursements', 'cleaning', 'coffin lids' and all the other shite. How long did it take you to come up with all that?"

"It actually works well, as long as you remember what everything fucking means."

I stared at him waiting for him to continue. He did.

"That's enough, Jack. Drink your coffee and go."

We had come to the point at last. And having made the journey from England's western shore, it would be a waste to return uninformed. I put the mug down on the teak and slid it away from me. He took that business for the statement it was intended to be and took a couple of steps towards me. Now no longer silhouetted, I could see his face. He had almost morphed back into the Walter Cobb on the Bedminster bog wall.

"How do you manage this Jekyll and Hyde thing?" I asked. "Switching from charmless buffoon on the mainland, to laid back businessman here?"

"It's never going to come up again. I'm going to stay here. I'm not going back to Bristol. At least not permanently. Just long enough to put the house in Moorend on the market and pick up anything I need. Like to buy it? I'll knock down the price for a quick cash sale."

I stared at him. He grinned.

"You're way out of you depth, Jack, did you but know it."

He was undoubtedly right, but I wasn't going to give him the satisfaction of agreeing with him.

"Walter, I have spent almost a week on this adventure. Lost contact with everyone except for you, been thumped around by a couple of Freddie Settle's employees, and had a close encounter with the corpse of Len Coleman. I'm now running with a very short fuse. I'm not leaving here without learning something."

"Okay. So what are you going to do? Beat it out of me? Go on." He opened his arms wide. "You don't want to go home wondering what I'm going to do next. Give it your best shot."

Cobb was a truly infuriating bastard. And I suddenly realised what Adam had been talking about. Schtick or no schtick, Cobb was unassailable. He was Mr Punch. Boss of his own crazy world, the hangman his only foe. He wasn't frightened of me at all. It would have been easier if he had been pointing a gun at me, or wielding the living room poker. I was simply never going to get him worked up.

"I mean look," he said. "I can just stay here. And you could spend a fortune – in your terms that is – on bed and breakfast at the Hotel de Bretagne, and we could sit it out. Eventually one of us would crack but by then we'd both be too old to care. So, Jack, just go home. I have nothing to hide here in Jersey."

He made a great show of pondering for a while. Then he snapped the fingers of his right hand, as though he'd just had a fabulous idea.

"Do you play golf?"

I stared at him. He went on.

"No? Pity. Tomorrow I'm playing eighteen holes with my bank manager. Then I'm hosting lunch in the club house. Had you been a golfer you could have joined us."

This self-congratulatory bollocks was not going to stop until I left the house. I moved to the kitchen door.

"Turn right into the hall," he said. "Excuse me if I don't show you out."

At the end of the drive, I stepped through the gates, which opened as I reached them. I looked back at the house. Cobb waved at me from the front doorstep. The gates closed like a fadeout in a movie, with him waving still.

* * *

We had dinner at a fish restaurant at the western end of St Helier promenade. Along with a bottle of Muscadet – Brittany's contribution to the great French wine list, especially good with oysters. The sun went down again, as it had the evening before. We were just a bit gloomier the second time around.

"You're better than this," Linda said over the dessert.

I looked at her, not sure what she meant.

"A better detective you mean? In which case that's a 'must try harder' in the report."

"No, I mean you're tougher and more resolute," she said.

"This is some distance to come, not to be so."

"Jack, I'll help you with this. So will Chrissie and Adam. And we will find Bill and May."

We finished our meal. I paid the bill and Linda drove us back to the Hotel de Bretagne. We were booked on the 7.45 flight the next morning. I re-filled the Fiesta's petrol tank, called the Hertz hire desk and reminded them to pick up the car from the hotel. We checked out before we went to bed, paid the bill, booked an early alarm call and a taxi for 6.15.

Chapter Twenty

"I apologise for asking this of you," the cab driver said. He was a little overweight, with a round face and round eyes and a round posture. But for the latter he would have been all of five nine or ten.

"Do you mind if my brother-in-law rides with us? He's catching the same plane as you. He will pay his share of the fare."

He pointed to a long, thin nosed man with a razor haircut standing a few yards away, holding a small suitcase. It was a twelve minute drive to the airport. Hardly the journey of a lifetime. I consulted Linda.

She shrugged. "Why not?"

The thin nosed man said 'thank you' and introduced himself as Eddie.

Linda and I introduced ourselves to him. The cab driver loaded Eddie's suitcase into the boot of the Vauxhall, along with ours.

We cleared St Helier a few minutes later. Then the driver turned the car north, pressed a rocker switch to his right and locked all the doors. Eddie reached inside his jacket and produced a revolver. He turned in his seat and raised the gun so Linda and I could see it clearly. A compact, snub nosed .32. The driver called over his shoulder.

"As you see, we're not going to the airport. We are driving north east."

"Courtesy of whom?" I asked. "Walter Cobb?"

Neither of the men in the front seats responded to that.

Linda weighed in with, "We have a flight to catch. When the check-in desk realises we're not getting on the plane they'll inform the police."

"Have you any idea how long it will take them to consider where you might be?" the driver said. "And then to check all the hotels in the island until they find your registration. Or, alternatively, how soon the real cab driver is discovered."

"He's tied up in a skip," Eddie the gunman said.

The driver summed up. "By the time everybody involved starts chasing around, you two will be dead, the car will be parked in a St Helier back street, and Eddie and I will be on the ferry to St Malo."

That was all clear. I could feel Linda next to me on the seat, shaking.

I began to think. Eddie wasn't going to shoot us sitting here in the back. And out of the car we might have an opportunity to do something about the situation. At which point I noticed both men were wearing gloves. That should have registered with me before we got into the cab.

Linda looked straight into my eyes. She mouthed 'what do we do?' I raised my right hand in what I hoped was a clear 'don't worry' gesture. She sat back in the seat and stared out of the side window. We were now travelling along a lane with grass growing up the middle and pointing straight at the sea. The driver pulled up. I looked around, trying to get the lie of the land. The place was less busy than a hermit's cave at bedtime.

"Nobody lives in this part of the valley," Eddie said. "There's no decent path down to the beach and we've driven the only road to get here."

The driver unlocked the car doors. Eddie was out double quick. He opened the door at Linda's elbow and waved the gun at her. Suddenly he seemed impatient. Or maybe nervous...

"Out this side," he said. "Both of you."

He stepped back a pace or two. Linda got out of the car. I slid across the seat and followed her. The driver slid out from behind the wheel, walked around the car, shut all the doors and looked at Eddie, who gestured towards the cliffs dropping down to the sea.

"Now, here's how we do this," he said. "You go first, followed by Nick." He nodded in the direction of the driver. "He knows the way down. You will move as he tells you." He waved the .32 at Linda. "She will follow you, with me behind pointing the gun at her back. Any fucking about and I'll shoot her. Off you go."

Nick stepped up close. "Turn round." I did. "Move to the edge." I did that too. And looked down thirty yards of cliff side to a small beach.

The tide rippled gently below. There was a rib at the water's edge, with an outboard on the back. Out in the bay, a trawler yacht was riding at anchor. The way down to the beach looked like an animal track – made by goats or sheep perhaps – sand studded with small stones.

"That's it." Nick said. "I'm right behind you."

I was wearing a pair of soft soled shoes. Linda was wearing jeans, but her knee length boots with stacked heels were not designed for an exercise like this.

Eddie read the look on her face. "So take them off," he said. Linda decided not to. Eddie pointed the .32 towards the cliff edge. "Let's do this then."

The track wasn't impassable. But it was easy to see why, in spite of its location, this little bay was well off the tourist trail. It took us ten minutes to get down to the beach. Linda slipped a couple of times, and was hauled to her feet by Eddie without much ceremony. At the foot of the cliff, Nick walked to the water's edge, pushed the rib clear of the sand, unlocked the outboard and let the propeller drop into the sea. Eddie rotated his wrist and waggled the revolver again. Linda and I walked to the rib.

"Sit side by side at the front," he said.

All of us got our trousers soaked moving between the water's edge and the rib. Eddie sat in the centre of the boat, facing us. Behind him, Nick pulled the starter. The outboard fired up the second time. We skimmed the surface of the water away from the beach. I realised how substantial the trawler yacht was, as Nick cut the outboard and slid alongside the swim platform at the stern. He reached out, grabbed the platform and held the rib steady. Eddie pointed the .32 at Linda.

"First again," he said and jerked the thumb of his free hand. "Up there."

Linda shuffled upright, stepped onto the swim platform and then up onto the stern deck.

Eddie stood up. "I'm next. You follow when I say so."

A couple of minutes later, Linda and I were sitting on the stern deck. Eddie was looking steadfastly at us from a padded bench seat backed by the stern rail. Nick had disappeared into the lounge behind us. I don't know a great deal about boats. I tried to look around, but the field of view is limited when you can't swivel. Eddie provided the specifications.

"The master bedroom is underneath you," he said. "There are two more towards the front. A bathroom, a galley, and right behind you the lounge and the bridge. I happen to know it's up for sale. You can buy it for three quarters of a million, or thereabouts."

"From whom?" I asked.

Eddie grinned at me, and shifted emphasis. "Not that you'll be in any position to do that, because you'll be roped and weighted and a fathom or two down."

He looked beyond me and shouted for his associate. Nick said he needed a minute. So Eddie pressed on.

"Basically, we're just going to drop you into the sea."

He paused for that note of doom to sink in. Linda, remarkably in control, swallowed and looked down at the deck.

"Teak," Eddie informed her. "And we don't want blood stains on that, or the crushed mulberry furnishings."

Nick stepped out of the cabin behind us, hove into view, hands full of a circular steel object about nine inches across, with spokes like an alloy car wheel.

"Christ, this is heavy," he said. He put it down on the deck, managing to avoid crushing his fingers before letting go. "The spare. The other one's at the front."

He walked around me and out of vision again.

"It's a mud weight," Eddie said. "Stainless steel. Twenty kilos. You use it for inland waterways, instead of the sea anchor."

"You know about boats then?" I asked. Hoping to keep him talking long enough to consider how to get Linda and me out of this.

"Just what I need to know," he said.

Like stuff about mud weights for instance. Nick came trundling back with the other one. He bent over and put it down. As he straightened up he yelled out and grabbed at the small of his back.

"Oh fuck!..."

He was directly between Eddie and me. I leaned forward onto my hands, swung my feet out from under me launched myself at him. I hit the side of his rib cage and propelled him sideways into Eddie – at that point rising from his seat and attempting to sight the .32. Eddie fell back onto the seat, hit the steel railing behind him and joined in the chorus of pain. Nick hit the floor, I stepped over him. Eddie was sprawled against the stern rail, his arms and feet splayed out like a starfish, still holding on to the gun. I grabbed his right forearm and smashed his wrist down onto the rail. I heard a crunch of bone, he yelled again, and the .32 spiralled up and away and overboard into the sea. I hauled Eddie to his feet and jammed my right elbow into his throat. He gurgled, choked, reached for the source of the pain with both hands and sank to his knees. Behind me, Nick yelled again. I turned just in time to see Linda bounce his forehead off the teak. She stood up. I heaved Eddie across the deck and dropped him on top of Nick. Linda offered a high five. We smashed the palms of our hands together.

"Find a knife," I said. "Must be one on the bridge somewhere."

"Aye aye, Captain."

She went into the lounge and moved on towards the bridge. Nick was unconscious. Eddie rolled off him onto the deck. He lay on his back, moaning and trying to take in huge chunks of air. I looked down at the mud weights.

Linda came back holding a chunky steel knife with all the bells and whistles – blades, files, screwdriver, corkscrew, bottle opener, scissors, pliers and the thing for cleaning out horse's hooves.

The rear mooring rope was coiled neatly under the stern rail.

"Cut a couple of three feet lengths off that," I said.

We double wrapped each length of rope around Nick and Eddie's wrists and tied them to the mud weights. Then we moved into the lounge and raided the cocktail cabinet.

After the second brandy, Linda suggested we go back to St Helier in style, and asked if I knew anything about boats.

"Not much. Enough to drive I guess."

We moved onto the bridge. The key was in the ignition. Twin lever throttles meant twin engines. I switched on the ignition. The heavy marine diesels roared into life and began throbbing away under our feet.

"Er Captain..." Linda said. I looked at her. "We won't go anywhere unless we weigh anchor."

She left the bridge and moved out on the foredeck. Looked down at the steel casing covering the anchor hawser. She turned a switch on the casing and the anchor rose swiftly and quietly. I felt the boat stir as she became free of the sea bed. Linda returned to the bridge. I pulled back the left engine lever and pushed the right. The boat turned through one hundred and eighty degrees and pointed towards St Helier. I pulled both throttles back to neutral, then gently eased them forwards together. I offered Linda the controls, walked to the stern to check on the contractors, found my mobile, and called 999.

* * *

There was a polite knock on the interrogation room door. The PC stationed at the door, opened it, and another PC ferried a tray of coffee and sandwiches to the table. He put the tray down, nodded at us, and left the way he had come in. The room PC ensured the door was closed again.

Linda and I had been guests of the Jersey Constabulary for an hour and a half. We had been questioned separately, and now we were in the same room, about to have lunch.

Detective Sergeant Ayres came into the room and motioned the PC outside. A smart, dark haired, five feet six, she looked as if she worked out. She began by addressing me."

"I have just spent ten minutes talking with Superintendent Harvey Butler. He says that despite being a dipped in bronze pain in the arse, you were once a hell of a Detective Sergeant. And though you now ply your trade as a private detective – a breed he has no time for on the whole – he does nevertheless vouchsafe that what you are telling us is more likely than not, to be the truth."

I felt I ought to say something. Ayres held up a warning hand. She took in both of us.

"The airline has confirmed your arrival on Sunday afternoon. The taxi company recorded the ride to the Hotel Bretagne, and confirmed this morning's booking. We found the taxi where you said it would be. The hotel agrees that you stayed two nights and checked out earlier. The Deputy Director of *Channel Skies* confirmed your visit to the home, albeit under aliases. And thirty-five minutes ago we located today's bona fide taxi driver, in a skip. Apart from the bump on his head and the pervading smell of wet cardboard and rotten veg, he's not much the worse for his ordeal. You may now leave the building and book yourselves on the next flight out of the island."

The look in her eyes said 'don't hurry back if this is the way you intend to behave'. Then she remembered something else.

"Oh yes. Superintendent Butler also asked me to convey to you the news that Dylan Thomas is dead. Does that mean something?"

I breathed in and out. "Unfortunately, yes. Did he say anything about Gareth Thomas?"

Ayres thought I was taking the piss. She opened her mouth to say something but I managed to get to the point first, and explained. Ayres decided to believe the tale.

"Finish your lunch and leave," she said.

"I think that Nick is a Jersey resident," I added. "He talked about being 'in' the island and not on it. And he drove us from the hotel to where we got out of the car like he did it every day. No map, and no pausing at any moment to figure out where he was."

"Okay. Thanks."

"Is there any sign of Walter Cobb?"

"No."

"Do you think he's left the island?"

"Looks very much like it. Do you want me to show you out?"

* * *

We managed to book ourselves on to the 4.25 flight to Bristol. The Jersey Constabulary gave us back our suitcases, and we lumbered them to the nearest quayside bar.

"I've never seen you in action before," Linda said.

"It's not a regular part of any day's work."

"No. But it comes up, doesn't it?"

I paused, small glass of beer in hand. "You're beginning to sound like Chrissie."

"Only because we both care about you."

I put the glass down again.

"What I do is..." I began. Then tried to sort out what I really meant to say. "I liked being a cop. It may not seem so now, but I did. You get massive highs, like when a court convicts someone you've put in long days and sleepless nights to arrest. And bloody awful lows, like..."

I paused. Linda looked at me.

"Like when you shot that seventeen year old kid," she said.

"Yes. Like that. And it's what makes me do what I do now. On good days I make things right."

"And is that enough?" Linda asked.

"Not yet. But I'm hoping someday it might be."

She reached across the table and laid her right hand over my left.

"You're a good man, Shepherd. But there are times when you sound as if you're on a mission. It's right that you care about what you do, but..."

She didn't finish the sentence. Instead, she sat back and sipped at her Chardonnay. I waited.

"Oh shit, I'll just mind my own business," she said. "It's probably old ground anyway."

"Probably," I said. "But go over it if you want."

"No," she said. "It's clear we both know what I mean." She raised her glass of wine again. "Actually, it's been an exciting couple of days. So cheers."

Chapter Twenty-One

Chrissie and Sam picked us up from the airport and we drove to Redland making a detour via Linda's house. At 7 o'clock, we were sitting in the living room catching up. Sam was lying across the doorway into the hall, snoring. Adam was working late and due to knock on the door within the next half hour.

"The point is," Chrissie said, "are you any further forward?"

"Not much," I said. "I've no idea which side anybody is on. And I won't improve the shining hour until I find someone who will confess."

The phone rang. I picked it up from the coffee table. George Hood was on the other end of the line. He said he had something to impart.

"The Murder Team duty DC has just received the answer to something I asked him to check over the weekend. Arnold Faversham, wherever he is, is not really Arnold Faversham. He is in fact, Mr Andrew Featherstone. Once a consultant surgeon in the city, and by all accounts, one of the best in the trade. But no longer. Now disgraced and struck off the medical register."

"Because...?"

"Under the influence of drink, he cocked up a bowel operation and his patient died."

I asked the obvious question. "Why didn't someone notice he was drunk?"

"First, he kept his drinking under wraps," Hood said. "Secondly, operating theatre staff question the consulting surgeon at their peril. He is the man in charge and his word is law. And thirdly, the Registrar assisting Featherstone during the operation and the only person who knew about his drinking problem, was a close friend."

"Was?"

"She is now a GP in the Orkneys."

"So Featherstone re-invented himself as an undertaker. That has a certain neatness about it."

"Still not part of my brief," Hood said. "Yet. But if you are to pursue your own investigation into comings and goings at the funeral parlour, I'd appreciate you keeping me in the loop. There may be nothing nefarious going on at all. Faversham may have changed his name simply to put the disgrace behind him. And kept the initials to match his monogrammed shirts and suitcases."

"On the other hand..."

"There is that," Hood said.

"Thank you, George," I said.

He wished me a good night and ended the call. I put the phone receiver back on the coffee table. Chrissie looked at me.

"Well...?"

I didn't say anything.

"Come on," she said. "Give."

Impossible to believe, but we had a lead. After eight days of getting nowhere. I must have been grinning from ear to ear. Chrissie looked at me.

"Are you alright, Dad?"

Out of nowhere it seemed, a light had come on. Low wattage maybe. But now I had choices.

Adam arrived twenty minutes later. Sam woke up and went barmy for a minute until the novelty wore off. We went through the obligatory 'what did you do in Jersey?' stuff and then I asked Adam if he knew anything about Andrew Featherstone.

He thought about that for a few seconds.

"Yes, a bit, yes. Surgeon who lost his job after being drunk in charge of an operation."

"Do you remember any more?"

"No, but the *Post* archive will. I'll get my pc out of the car."

"Use mine." I pointed to the ceiling. "In my office."

He stepped over Sam who was lying in the doorway again. The dog got to his feet, excited because Adam seemed to be going to the front door. When it turned out that he was doing no more than going upstairs, Sam's interest waned. He lay down again and sighed.

Two minutes later Adam called from the office.

"Hey guys, come and look at this."

Chrissie and I stepped over Sam. He looked up, realised that something was happening upstairs which might, after all, hold something of interest to him. And being the optimist he is, he decided to follow. All four of us crowded into what was once the third bedroom. Adam gestured at the screen.

"This was a big story in December 2011. Ran for days and days, as stuff came tumbling out of the closet."

Andrew Featherstone's life appeared to be a bed of roses. Just about to turn 50, living in a mansion facing the Downs built by a slave master in 1802. With a stunning looking wife who did more good works than Mother Theresa. One daughter reading Classics at Brasenose College, Oxford, the other at Durham University reading Earth Sciences. Featherstone was consultant to a European heart charity, a non-executive director of two hospital trusts in Switzerland, and masterminding research into new lung treatments for cystic fibrosis, with a huge grant from the US drugs company attempting to persuade the NHS to buy in. No one in any position of importance in these organisations, realised he had a drinking problem. His wife wondered if perhaps he had, but couldn't be sure. The person who knew he had, was his long time extra-marital partner, 46 years old hospital registrar Joanna Harper – the aforementioned GP in Kirkwall.

Five days before Christmas, a car overturned on the iced up A36, south of Bradford on Avon. The 22 year old driver died on a trolley on his way into A&E. His donor card authorised doctors to harvest any, or all of his organs, suitable for transplant. Featherstone was consulted. He ordered a test on both lungs, for a potential cystic fibrosis recipient, a kidney test for a patient who was not going to see Christmas without two new ones, handed over the rest of the decisions to the in-house Head of Surgery and washed and scrubbed up. The bowel transplant didn't work, and throughout it, some members of the theatre staff wondered about Featherstone's concentration. There were several moments when the Registrar was forced to intervene. Moments when it appeared that Featherstone was about to do something inadvisable.

There was an internal enquiry two days later. Journalists were barred from that, so they sought out the car driver's parents, looking for an angle. The day after Boxing Day, the back story began to leak out. By New Year's Eve, the surgeon was under siege, his drinking and his relationship with Joanna Harper headline news. There were public cries for justice from the driver's parents. Ultimately Featherstone was deemed culpable, disgraced and dismissed. He was sentenced to fifteen months in a low security establishment in Wiltshire. By which time, Joanna Harper had resigned and was speeding on her way to the far north.

"Featherstone dried out in prison," Adam said. "He was released after nine months and no longer news. There's no coverage of that. But there was a temporary unpleasantness, when the next door neighbour revealed that Mrs Featherstone was now living in the Loire Valley and the mansion had been sold."

"And the trail ends there?" I asked.

"Effectively."

Chrissie offered a question to the room. "And so... what now?"

Adam nodded in my direction. "He's the sleuth."

He and Chrissie and Sam stared at me. I picked up the ball.

"I may," I said, "have to do a little bit of breaking and entering."

All three looked alarmed. Sam barked and shook his head. Chrissie asked what I was going to do.

"You don't need to know. So it's best if I don't tell you."

After some objections and a little dog wrangling, I escorted all three of them to the front door.

* * *

The accomplice I needed was a retired safe breaker, appropriately named Joe Locke. His mother had named him Joseph after her favourite singer, the great Irish tenor – he of *Galway Bay*, *Hear My Song*, and *I'll Take You Home Again Kathleen* fame – and Inland Revenue fugitive.

The Joe Locke I knew was in his 60s and overqualified for the work he was doing as a part time locksmith. Among all the con artists, blackmailers, burglars, enforcers, murderers, adulterers and pornographers I have met in the course of twenty one years as a detective, few have driven me to grudging moments of admiration. Joseph Locke was one of them. A man with a heart bigger than a circus tent. A gentleman, a scholar and a skilled professional.

I considered calling him on the loaner phone, then decided this next conversation should be done face to face.

"Jack Shepherd," he said. "By all that's wonderful."

We swapped catch-up stories for a minute or two, then he asked me why I was visiting. I told him some of the story and gave him time to respond.

"Is the man who runs the place good people or bad people?"

"Bad people."

"Mmm. Which helps us to justify this breaking and entering?"

"Correct."

"Okay, Jack."

It was my turn to be silent for a while. This was a huge favour to ask of a man who had resolved, twenty-five years ago, never to risk going back to prison. So I told him the whole story. He listened without interrupting. And when I had finished, he took time to ponder.

"So we need to get into his emporium, without being apprehended, and dig around until we find... whatever it is?"

"Yes."

"And the aforementioned premises, is likely to be alarmed."

"Certain to be, but not linked to a police station," I suggested.

Joe picked that up. "Because if this Faversham bloke is a felon, the last thing he will want, in whatever emergency, is to have a bunch of coppers tramping round his property and peering into things. So the proposition is...?"

"You need to visit the place during business hours," I suggested. "Give Mr Berling, the senior undertaker, a false name and address. Tell him a relative of yours is nearing his end and only the best will do. Ask him to show you round, and recce the locks and the alarms."

"Okay," Joe said. "When do you want me to visit?"

"Tomorrow morning," I said. "Then call me afterwards."

Chapter Twenty-Two

I remember when I was toying with the idea of becoming an English teacher, I wrote an essay on Shakespeare's obsession with the curative powers of sleep. I think I discovered about a dozen references in the plays and son nets I read. And now, during the course of a long night, I re-acquainted myself with all the similes I could recall – from *nature's soft nurse* to knitting up *the ravelled sleeve of care.*

I set my alarm for 8 o'clock, lay back and waited for the mattress and the lateness of the hour to take over. But thoughts of tomorrow night's barmy scheme crept into my head and stuck there. I drifted in and out of sleep, checking the time with the bedside clock twice an hour it seemed. Nature's Soft Nurse gave me no more than a cursory examination and went off to find a paid up member of BUPA. I was still punching the pillow at 3 am. Then after what seemed mere seconds, I was rewarded with the ringing in of the new day.

It was some time before I worked out where I was, and that I had stuff to do – if only I could figure out what that might be. I clambered out of bed, crossed to the window, drew back the curtains and squinted into the sunlight. I put on a dressing gown and sat in the kitchen drinking coffee, while outside, the sun tried to warm up the garden. I went back upstairs, showered and shaved and returned to the kitchen. After toast, two eggs and more coffee, I retired to the living room sofa to think. My mobile rang.

"Your friend Molly is here," Jason said from his desk in the lobby. "She wants to speak to you. I'll hand her the phone."

There was a silence, then a rustle, and then Molly's voice. She apologised for interrupting what I was doing.

"Not at all," I said.

"Do you think it would be possible for Don and me to see Martin? Assuming he hasn't been... erm..."

I remembered I had promised to help find where he was.

"I imagine he's still in the city morgue. I'll find him and organise a visit."

"If you could."

"Of course. I'll get back to you later today. Where will you be?"

"There's no place like home," she said.

"Give me back to Jason."

Another rustle, the Jason's voice again. "Mr Shepherd..."

I asked him if he would be in a position to take a message across the road later. He said that would be no problem. I wished him 'good day' and ended the call.

I got on to Irving again. This time, the body in question was in cold storage in front of him.

"Will Molly and Don be able to give us some information about their friend?" he asked.

"Maybe," I said.

"The Coroner's Office and the police are checking databases, records and census info. But nothing has surfaced so far."

"How much more time will they spend on this," I asked.

"Perhaps another week," Irving said. "In which case, your friends should visit soonest. I'll find a space in the diary and call you back."

I thanked Irving. He told me it was a pleasure.

So, next?

The weather forecast was good, why not go out for the day? In fact, why not go and see James Warburton, the man with

1800 acres on the top of Mendip and interest in his welfare from Freddie Settle?

The Mendips are not very high. Really not much more than a wide ridge along hills running across north Somerset. The *High Combe Estate* sits between the villages of Priddy and Charterhouse. A piece of land given to a Warburton ancestor, the adjutant to General Lord Thomas Fairfax, after his troops had lifted the siege of Bristol in September 1646.

Old property and old money have always been the backbone of the English aristocracy. Recalling the photograph taken with Freddie and letting supposition run free, it seemed James Warburton might be close to losing both. And his backbone too, come to think of it. He was in hock to the worst person he could have chosen. Perhaps he hadn't yet come to realise what he'd done, or felt the noose of Freddie's real scheme – whatever that was – tightening around his neck.

I googled *The High Combe Estate*. The centrepiece was still the manor house, sitting inside its own twelve hectares of Capability Brown magic. It had been a number of years since those lawns and gardens had played host to an event. Although it was said that James Warburton would be only too happy to run out his collection of sports cars and play host to all who bought a ticket. I spent an hour cleaning and polishing the Healey, which I hoped would be the star attraction in the fantasy I was about to propose.

I used the loaner phone to ring the *High Combe Estate*, and got through to the Estate Manager, Arthur Mayfield. I told him the details of the proposition I had rehearsed and he asked me to hold. The line clicked and buzzed and clicked again and rang twice.

"James Warburton..." the man said.

His voice sounded efficient, if a bit weary; but neither overbearing nor pompous. I repeated what I had just said to the Estate Manager. Warburton's voice cheered up. Of course he was interested, he said. I asked him if he had anything special in the diary today. He said absolutely not, we could have the place to ourselves, and yes why didn't I drive up to see him straight away? He would make sure there was someone at the gates to meet me.

I put on the best countryside visiting clothes I could muster and climbed into the beautiful, shiny Healey. I took the old coach road out of the city and drove up the Wellsway onto the top of the Mendip ridge. I parked outside the double wrought iron gates at the main entrance to the estate and buzzed the intercom. Warburton drove his Range Rover down the drive to collect me. He smiled when he saw the Healey.

"1968 is it?" he asked.

"66."

"Well you really have looked after her, Mr Shepherd."

We shook hands. I told him to call me Jack. He suggested in that case I call him James. He looked at the Healey again and asked me to follow him up to the house. The mixed woodland on both sides of the drive was dense. Even in late April, with the deciduous trees between the conifers just greening, the impression was that once you got forty or fifty yards into the wood, closed your eyes and spun round twice, you would have no idea which way was out.

The manor house, shaped like two 'Ls' lying down and meeting at the heads of the letters, sat in a huge bowl in the landscape. The front door, protected by a substantial porch, sat in the middle of the centre section. The house was three storeys high, the two wings had tall leaded windows, and the whole effect oozed solidity and a sense of permanence. It looked stunning, with the morning sunshine warming the stone. I pulled the Healey up behind the Ranger Rover, got out and looked around. The landscaping made the setting work brilliantly.

"Done by Capability Brown," Warburton said at my shoulder. "During the 1760s. Beautiful, don't you think?"

"Absolutely," I said.

"We keep it up as well as we can with three members of staff, the Estate Manager, a Gamekeeper, and an Arborealist. We hire in tree surgeons, planters and labourers on contract when we need to."

Warburton waited while I drank in the view.

"Enjoy that for as long as you wish," he said. "I'll go and put the kettle on. When you come into the great hall, shout and I'll hear you."

He walked to the porch, swung open the ancient wooden front door and disappeared into the house.

Lancelot 'Capability' Brown needs no testimonials from me. He re-designed and re-shaped hectare after hectare of rural England during the mid-eighteenth century. He re-built mansion gardens, dug valleys and moved hills, made lakes and serpentine rivers, and planted hundreds of trees which still flourish in all their massive grandeur today. He had two simple rules for his kind of landscaping. Everything should work seamlessly, nothing should star in the design; and all of the estate should serve the needs of the house.

Oh to be in England, now that April's there...

Browning may have gone to Italy because his wife was consumptive and because that's what romantic poets did, but *Home Thoughts From Abroad* betrays his longing for the English countryside.

The lowest boughs and the brushwood sheaf
Round the elm tree bole are in tiny leaf,
While the chaffinch sings on the orchard bough
In England – now!

Those words are simple, the cadence is light but the imagery shimmers. There is a suddenness about the arrival of April, a great surge in nature, and within days it seems, the countryside begins to turn green. Capability Brown's art was Browning's verse made flesh. Both men get my vote.

The Great Hall had a flagstone floor and massive stone fireplace. And it was cold enough to warrant two vests and a thick jacket. The centrepiece was a long oak refectory table with eight, thick cabriole style, turned legs. I counted fourteen dining chairs, actually arranged around the walls, rather than the table. There was no other furniture in the room; the table and chairs a token of what there once was, or, in the best of all possible worlds, what there could be again.

Warburton re-appeared before I had to shout; carrying a tray with teapot, cups and saucers, milk and sugar. He put the tray down on the table. I asked him how old it was.

"All of thirty-five years," he said.

I stared at him, then back at the table. He explained.

"Made for us by John Makepeace. At a time when the family had money to burn. Now there is enough furniture left to eat in the kitchen, relax in the drawing room, sit down in the library and sleep in three bedrooms. Although we are doing something about that – the bedrooms I mean." He looked round the hall. "I'm sorry it's cold in here. It costs a fortune to heat the place. I switch off the central heating at the beginning of April and on again on October 10th."

"That's very precise," I suggested.

"My birthday," he said. "And my present to myself. Warmth."

All of which explained why he was wearing a thick sweater under his Harris Tweed jacket.

"I'm sorry, I should have warned you to wrap up."

I studied him properly for the first time. Early 40s probably. He looked like I expected a countryman to look. Warm working clothes, albeit properly tailored. Probably expensive when they were bought, just a little shabby now. He was taller than me. Well over six feet, he had a graceful smile and an easy manner. The thick brown hair was complemented by wide brown eyes. But there were dark bags under the eyes, and the lines across his forehead seemed to suggest he frowned a lot.

He picked up the milk jug and looked at me.

"Yes please," I said. "No sugar."

"It's just plain old Earl Grey I'm afraid." He nodded across the hall. "Pull up a couple of those chairs."

I gathered two chairs and placed them at a table corner. Warburton poured out cups of tea for both of us then pushed a saucer to me across the beaten oak. We sat down. He began the conversation by asking me where I lived and what I worked at. I was honest about the first matter but I lied about the second.

"I live in Bristol, in Redland. I work at a bookshop in Clifton."

I was on relatively safe ground there. A friend of mine is the owner of a small independent bookshop, and if the occasion demands, can act as my answering service and business filter.

"So what's this plan you have for a classic car weekend?"

I lied to him again. "I belong to a car club. And we're looking for somewhere to hold a gathering in mid-September. The landscape outside the front door with the house as a background would be terrific."

Warburton nodded. "Yes it would. And maybe we can open the old stable block Tea Room again. Like old times."

This was hurting. Firing bullshit at a man I'd only known ten minutes, but who had struck me as genuinely likeable. However, I had started so I had to finish.

"I guess you've done this sort of thing in the past," I said.

"Oh yes," he said. "In the good old days." He looked away from me and smiled as he recollected better times. Then he came back to me, brisk now. "Drink your tea and I'll give you the one guinea tour."

He began by escorting me round the house, which was no National Trust re-furb. The place was old and venerable and looked like it – in some sections more so than others. Warburton had managed to find money over the past few years to restore the drawing room and the library to their former glory. He had patched up the dining room to a degree and the kitchen worked, but the other rooms downstairs were in the grip of rising damp, dry rot and wet rot. The main staircase from the great hall to the first floor, had been re-built by a decent craftsman and the landing floor re-laid. But there, the money and the work had run out. There were five bedrooms on the first floor. Three of them were furnished, the other two looked like their counterparts downstairs – damp wallpaper, peeling plaster, rotten floorboards and leaking windows. We didn't explore any further. Warburton said the rooms above weren't safe.

After which cheery note, he offered me a tour of the estate, and led me into the old stable yard. We climbed into a battered Toyota pickup.

The woodland was fabulous, as thick and flourishing as the house was disintegrating. We travelled a hundred yards down one track, turned left on to another, then two hundred yards later right again. Warburton pulled up and we got out of the Toyota.

It was amazingly quiet. There was some birdsong, from where I couldn't tell, and some rustling in the undergrowth to our right. The surrounding woodland looked impenetrable, but beautiful.

"You may think there's nothing going on here," Warburton said. "But I can assure you there is. It takes a lot of work to keep woodland looking like this. Not quite as nature intends perhaps, because we can't allow her to run riot, but we do enough to make sure she stays strong and well."

"Don't you ever get lost among all this?" I asked.

"Sometimes I have to think about where I am," he said. "A little test for you. Can you point in the direction of the house?"

I looked around me. Tried to recall the lefts and rights we had just taken.

"Okay," I said. "That way."

Warburton grinned at me. "You're almost one hundred and eighty degrees out."

I turned round. "You mean it's that way?"

"Or thereabouts."

We climbed back into the Toyota and moved on. We spent the best part of an hour, trundling around the tracks in the woods. Warburton told me how to recognise beech trees and birch and ash and oak and sycamore. And spruce and larch and a host of pine trees. He was clearly passionate about what his father had bequeathed him, along with the death duties and the unpaid bills.

Which made me think about Freddie Settle.

"All this must cost a bob or two," I said.

He looked glum. "Indeed. We have grants from central and regional government. This quango and that. But it's hell of a struggle to make ends meet. All the money goes into these woodland schemes of course. So the house is left... well you've seen it."

"What about Westcountry businesses? Have you tried mining that source of supply?"

"We're beginning to, yes. In fact, among them we have hooked quite a substantial donor."

"And who's that?" I asked.

"I can't tell you I'm afraid. The person wishes to remain anonymous."

Assuming that person was Freddie, I wondered why – considering all the posing outside the hospital wing. So I asked

Warburton what his donors got out of the deal. He happily warmed to the subject.

"Depends how much they offer. The donor we're talking about is given exclusive access to the estate every Sunday"

"To do what?"

"Whatever he likes. As long as he doesn't uproot the trees or shoot the wild life. Orienteering, paint balling, clay shooting... that sort of thing."

"And you just leave this person to it?"

"Yes. I usually take a train to London and visit my daughter."

Suddenly it felt like I was asking too many questions. I apologised.

"Not at all," he said. "Would you like to stay for lunch? I've got some pork pie and a bottle or two of cider. And we can talk about your proposal."

Probably not a good idea. Especially as I was being so disingenuous. I looked at my watch and told him I had taken up too much of his time. I suggested I give him my phone numbers and that we swop email addresses.

"I will relay all we've talked about to the club committee and get back to you soonest."

He said that would be fine. We were about to climb into the Toyota, when my mobile rang – the contract one. I apologised to Warburton, turned away from him and pressed the receive key. Irving, offered ten minutes at 8.30 the following morning. I thanked him and called Jason, asking him to tell Molly and Don I'd pick them up at 8.15.

In front of the house once again, Warburton and I shook hands.

"The drive gates open automatically from this side," Warburton said. "I look forward to seeing you again."

I drove away from him and the house, feeling like my head should be cut off and spiked on the gates. I liked James

Warburton, and I was concerned that he seemed to know nothing about what Freddie and her mates got up to every Sunday. As the gates closed behind me I reflected that I didn't either. And I was the detective.

* * *

I drove through Chew Valley and over Dundry Hill into south Bristol. I called at *The Junction Retail Park*, bought a chicken mayonnaise baguette in one of the cafés and sat down to eat. As I looked out of the window across the mega-car park, it began to rain. Stair rods, bouncing off the tarmac. The Healey was all of a hundred yards away and if I left my seat I'd be soaked within feet of the café doorway. I decided to have another coffee and wait to see if the rain eased.

It didn't. In fact, the sky darkened like a November dusk and the steady, demoralising downpour went on. In the end, I bowed to the inevitable and ran for my car. It wasn't where I thought it would be. I checked the next parking lane and the one parallel to that. Then back-tracked to beyond where I'd started looking, and found it. By which time my jacket was soaked, rain was seeping down my neck behind the collar, my country-casual-look trousers were glued to my thighs and my hair was plastered flat. Inside the Healey, the windows were steamed up. I turned the engine on and switched the blower to full. The initial blast of cold air just made the damp and the visibility worse. I struggled out of my jacket, threw it over my shoulder, then leaned back in the driver's seat which was coated with damp from the jacket, and soaked the back of my shirt. The windscreen began to clear and I switched on the wipers. The blade directly in front of me, juddered across the screen, swung back in the opposite direction, then began to squeak.

When I pulled into the office car park, I was still cold and the wiper blade squeak had morphed into an insistent scraping noise. Jason respectfully refrained from making any comment on the soaking apparition that dripped its way across the lobby to his desk. He handed over my post and wished me a good afternoon.

There was a spare shirt in the office, on a hanger on the door. I collected it, walked along the corridor to the third floor shower room, took off the shirt I was wearing and towelled the bits of me still wet. It didn't really improve matters, because I had no trousers to change into. What the hell... I took them off, dried my legs, put on the replacement shirt, stuck my head out of the shower room, ascertained the corridor was empty, then strolled back nonchalantly to my office door, as if I swanned around the building without trousers on a regular basis.

Going into the office this time, I noticed the note on the carpet which had been pushed under the door. I picked it up and dropped it on the desk. I turned the thermostat up, draped my trousers over the radiator under the window and sat behind my desk in my underpants. I opened the note.

Linda had written *Knock on my door when you get in*. I had done the trouser-less in the corridor bit, so I rang next door. There was no response. So I sat in my chair thinking, hoping for inspiration to strike, waiting for the phone to ring and my trousers to dry. They were still steaming on the radiator when Linda opened the door and walked in half an hour later. I rose from behind my desk, stepped to my right and posed for effect in my socks.

She didn't blink. Began by staring at my socks, then worked upwards to my shirt.

"It's a new, casual office look I'm trialling," I said.

"I hope so," she said. "Because if it's an attempt at some sort of foreplay statement, it's not working."

I gestured in the direction of the radiator. "I got soaked."

"Sit down again for God's sake," Linda said.

I did. She asked if I'd had lunch. I said, if I hadn't paused to do so, I wouldn't have been soaked. She asked if I wanted something to drink. The clock on the wall said 2.30. It was too early to raid the bottle of Laphroaig in the bottom of the filing cabinet.

"Coffee," I said.

"Coming up," Linda said.

She took the cafetière from the top of the filing cabinet and left for the kitchen along the landing.

There is not a lot you can do without your trousers. Well that's not true; you can do most things you normally do. I'm speaking here of comfort and confidence. Even in quarantine behind my desk, the thought of picking up the phone and talking to a client, whilst trouser-less, was unsettling.

Linda returned with the cafetière, two mugs, and a milk jug on a tray. She looked in the direction of the radiator.

"How long do you estimate this no-trousers interregnum will be?" she asked.

I looked behind me. The trousers were still steaming, though less than earlier. I stood up, moved to the radiator and turned them over. Linda averted her eyes.

"I'm not sure how soon our relationship will recover from this," she said.

I turned to face her and posed proudly. She put the tray on the desk.

"It's the socks, Jack. No trousers is a little alarming, but socks on regardless, is no look at all."

We sat down; Linda in one of the client chairs, me back behind the desk, visible only from the waist up – if you discounted the view between the desk pedestals. She poured the coffee and sat back in her chair, cradling her coffee mug.

Joe Locke knocked on the office door and walked in. He looked at Linda, switched his gaze to the view between the pedestals, took a beat, then apologised for intruding.

"You're not," Linda said.

She got to her feet, explained that she occupied the office next door, said she had a thing about knees, and that I often helped her indulge in this minor fetish during the course of a wet afternoon. She bade us both 'goodbye' and took her coffee with her.

I pointed to my trousers. "I've been out in the rain."

"I've been to the funeral parlour," Joe said. "Piece of cake."

"Even the alarm system?"

"That's the easiest bit. Do you want to do this tonight?"

"Err..." That needed a simple straightforward 'yes'. But without my trousers on, all confidence in breaking and entering had evaporated.

"There is a way into the place from the back of the car park," Joe went on. "Hidden from Rycroft Road."

He paused, waiting for a response. In my mind I was now putting my trousers on.

"Jack..."

Suddenly my trousers were on again, and I was aglow with confidence.

"How did you get on with Mr Berling?" I asked.

"He rather over-does the smooth bit. More smarm than charm."

"Probably a side effect of the job," I said.

Joe went back to the point. "Well? Do you want to do this tonight?"

"Tonight, yes. What time?"

"I'll pick you up at midnight. We'll go in my car. Wear dark clothes."

"And a black ski mask and brothel creepers?"

Joe laughed. "Brothel creepers. Haven't heard that for decades. Later, Jack." He nodded at the radiator. "But not in those trousers."

He left the office. A couple of minutes later, Linda returned.

"Are you free tonight?" she asked. "With or without trousers. Depends if we're at the pictures or in my house."

I swallowed a mouthful of coffee. "Actually I'm not free."

Not exactly true that. But if we spent the early part of the evening together I'd have to dodge questions about why I was off to work when sensible people were on their way to bed.

"Why aren't you free? What have you got to do?"

"I can't tell you."

Linda stared at me. Then shrugged. "Okay. Later?"

"Err no... What I'm doing will go on until much later than that."

She thought about that for a moment or two. "This is something I shouldn't be asking you about, isn't it?"

"Afraid so."

She sighed.

"I'm sorry," I said. "Are you alright with this?"

Linda nodded.

"Are you sure?"

She smiled. "Yes, I'm fine."

"Because this is what I do."

Well not breaking and entering. At least not often. Linda sipped her coffee. Unease was stalking the office like a caged leopard. Neither of us spoke.

* * *

I called at the *Cotham Fish Bar* on the way home. I checked there were no messages on the answering machine, left it in answer mode and ate my fish and chips at the kitchen table. I washed the plate and cutlery in the sink.

The clock on the wall said 7.30.

I made coffee, took it into the lounge and sat down on the sofa. Leaned forward and picked up the TV remote. Did the round of channels and decided I didn't fancy anything on offer. I searched the DVD collection and found a copy of the re-mastered version of *Farewell My Lovely*. One time hoofer Dick Powell was Hollywood's first Philip Marlowe. A rendering of the character three years before Bogart's and still a defining piece of work. But even this seminal slice of noir, which always seems fresh and exciting, couldn't hold my attention. I switched off the DVD player and took myself for a walk.

I began to think about Emily.

I do so at some point most evenings when I'm alone. The human mind has an eject button, of sorts. And if you possess a kind of super resolve, you can use it in moments of regret and pain and anger. Until you discover it's not really what you want after all. Because you still pick up the photograph and choose to remember the moment it was taken, or listen to the song and reap the memories it evokes. That time was over. I could handle all the 'once were' moments now, without too much hurt. Able to go back through the photo albums, share the memories of Emily with others. She would have hated what Joe and I were about to do.

So I switched to thinking about body parts. Given up, like Martin in the old privy and perhaps Don's friend Ted, and Alice Davis and Brian Watson and Lily. All this operating – it was beginning to sound too fantastical – would need a top surgeon. So enter, one of the best. Now disgraced, desperate for money and unable to practice the skills he was so proud of. Slightly more plausible than the return of Doctor Frankenstein. And if there was the remotest chance...

I went back home to wait out the hour and a half until Joe arrived.

Chapter Twenty-Three

Joe knocked on the front door at 11.45, in tracksuit and sneakers, looking like he was about to visit the gym. Except everything he wore was black, including a woolly hat covering his bald head. I was in dark blue jeans, a black high necked sweat shirt and black soft soled shoes. Joe looked me up and down.

"You'll do," he said.

I held up my hands. "No gloves."

"We can solve that," he said.

I closed the front door and followed him to his car, a five year old silver grey Volvo. He pointed his key fob at the front door and the warning lights flashed. We climbed in. Joe went through a check list.

"Mobile phone?"

"No."

"Money in your pocket?"

"No."

"Nothing else on your person that jangles?"

"Ah... house keys."

"Put them in the glove compartment." I leaned forward and did as I was told. "No identification of any sort – wallet, credit cards, driving licence?"

"No."

He handed me two pairs of white surgical gloves. "Put those on when I tell you to."

"Both pairs?"

"Yes. To be sure. You can't do the fiddly stuff with leather gloves. And woolly ones can be too slippery."

He reached out, turned on the car ignition, depressed the clutch and engaged first gear. He took a deep breath.

"Okay," he said. "Here we go."

Suddenly I broke out into a sweat. And grew more and more nervous, street by street, as we drove northeast across the city. Joe recognised the symptoms.

"Talking sometimes helps," he said.

I picked up my cue. "What did you say to Mr Berling?"

"I told him all about my Aunt Edna," he said.

"Your Aunt Edna has been dead for over ten years."

Joe glanced across the car at me.

"I told Berling I wanted the best he could provide. He gave me a brochure. The superior deluxe service offers an exotic hardwood coffin with satin interiors and gold plated handles, two limousines and four members of staff on the day. There's a long list of other stuff before we get to that. Disbursement costs they're called – death certificate documents, preparation of the body, announcements and invitations, burial or cremation fees, minister or celebrant fees, flowers... Even an online memorial, costing eleven hundred quid. Everything but a gilded carriage and four black horses with plumes."

"And what does Berling charge for all that?"

"Fourteen thousand pounds."

I stared across the car at Joe.

"Of course you can have it done by the Co-op, with all due care and attention, for around three and a half. I've got that."

I was still staring at him

"Best to get your affairs in order when you're as stricken in years as me. Have you made a will?"

I was about to tell him I had, when he swung the Volvo in to the western end of Rycroft Road. He pulled into the pavement, midway between two street lamps and shadowed by a tall hedge in a front garden. The funeral parlour was fifty or sixty yards ahead of us. Joe switched off the ignition.

"Put your gloves on," he said.

A bit of a palaver at the best of times, surgical gloves. It took me a while. Joe waited patiently. I raised my hands for his inspection.

"Got all the wrinkles out?"

"Yes."

"Okay. This is what we do. There's a small gate at the back of the car park. Padlocked. It should take thirty seconds. Don't get out of the car until that's done."

"How will I know when it's done?"

"Watch me move along the street. As soon as I step into the car park and disappear from view, start counting. Then get out of the Volvo. Lock it with the key, don't alarm it. Then follow me, at a reasonable walking pace. Turn left, go through the gate and close it behind you. By the time you join me, I'll be ready to open the funeral parlour side door. I'll tell you about the next bit then."

"Okay."

He opened the car door.

"Remember, softly softly. Don't rush. If anybody sees us, we're just a couple of blokes a bit late getting home."

He reached into the back seat, picked up a small black shoulder bag. He took the key out of the ignition and handed it to me, eased himself out from under the steering wheel, got out of the Volvo, closed the driver's door gently, leaned against it to ensure it was shut tight, then set off along the pavement.

I watched him with my heart thumping. He disappeared. I started counting. I got out of the Volvo, closed the passenger door carefully, walked round the car, locked the driver's door and followed Joe.

The car park gate was slightly ajar. I pushed it open and closed it behind me. The fifteen feet square yard was dark. The side wall of the funeral parlour cut out direct light from the street. Two black limousines were parked in the yard; the hearse was obviously quartered elsewhere. Joe and I were standing in the corner of an L created by the main building and an extension I hadn't expected to be there. I tried to recall the geography I had logged on my visit to the place with George Hood. The inside layout didn't match with the view from the yard I was getting now. Joe was at the side door – solid with no windows. I joined him. We talked in stage whispers.

"This door opens to the left," Joe said. "The alarm box is on the wall to the right." He handed me a torch. "When we get in, close the door and point that, at eye level, to the wall on your right. You'll light up the box. It'll be ringing like all buggery but don't let that get to you. I'll have it disabled in less than a minute. Once that's done, we'll take a rest and have a cup of tea."

"Have a what?"

"Never mind. Ready?"

I grunted. My mouth was so dry I couldn't actually speak. Bill's shoulder bag was on the ground at his feet. He took a small pencil torch out of the bag, clamped it between his teeth and started to work on the deadlock. I couldn't see what he was doing. I couldn't hear anything but the sound of distant late night traffic. And all I could feel was the thumping in my chest. Suddenly the door alarm burst into life. At a thousand decibels it seemed, the noise hurting my ears. Joe opened the door. I followed him into the building, closed the door and lit my torch. Joe took his torch out of his mouth. I counted the seconds, helpless and unable to do anything else. By forty-two, Joe had the alarm casing off and thirteen seconds later had disconnected the battery.

And then there was silence. Deep and dark and the most welcoming I had ever heard. Joe exhaled loudly – as if he had been holding his breath – turned and slid down the wall, his knees up against his chest. I sat down next to him. He turned his head and grinned at me.

"Tea now," he said. "Point the torch this way."

And, amazingly, tea it was. He took a small vacuum flask out of his bag. Unscrewed the cap, handed it to me, and produced another small plastic beaker.

"I hope you like tea with milk and no sugar," he said. "Not the place for milk jugs and sugar bowls."

I managed to find my voice. "That'll be fine."

I put the torch on the floor in front of us, pointed it at our feet, and we drank our tea. The only sounds were of Joe and me sipping and swallowing. I felt like William Hartnell's character in *The Yangtze Incident*. In peril and under fire, Leading Seaman Frank is handed a cup of tea. He drinks and says *Bloody Lovely!!*

"There are no windows in this lobby," Joe said. "The light switch at this end is just above your head. I'll check the other end."

He picked up the torch. Navigated his way along the lobby, checking for places light could leak out. The door at the other end was closed. He leaned to his left and flicked a switch. The sudden shock of light made my eyeballs dance. Spots flickered in front of my eyes like shapes changing in a kaleidoscope. I closed them, re-opened them slowly and got to my feet.

Joe walked back to me. "So far so good," he said. "Finish your tea."

I did. He gathered the flask, the cap and the beaker, put them into his bag and we moved to the door which led into the body of the building. Joe half opened it, told me to stay where I was, and stepped through the gap into the hall where PC Laker had been stationed. I waited.

I heard him say, "Keep the torch beam low, come into the hall and close the lobby door behind you."

We both checked where we were and which direction we were facing.

"Front door behind us," Joe said, "to our right, the waiting room and secretary's office. In front of us, to the left, is Berling's office. The two doors at the end of the hall lead to the preparation room and the resting room. The first door on our left is er..."

He paused to think.

"The storeroom," I said.

Joe turned to face me. Shone the torch at me, just below my eye line.

"So go back to the 'L' shape," he said. "Question one... If we have the geography right, and that door opens into the storeroom. And if we accept the evidence of our eyes which tell us it's little more than twelve feet square, then what takes up the rest of that bit of the 'L'?"

"And question two," I said. "How does one get into that space, whatever it is?"

Joe added question three. "And finally, why does the alarm system control operate from the yard door and not the front door?"

I began thinking about that. Joe continued, answering his own question.

"Because," he said, "most of the traffic into the building comes that way."

I considered that. "Hardly a surprise though. It's the work access. More discreet than hauling corpses across the front door threshold."

"And also handy for other discreet bits of business," Joe said.

He unlocked the Yale on the storeroom door in moments. We moved into the room, found the light switch and flicked it on. It was mainly as I remembered it. Full of stuff but with an avenue of space running across the room.

Joe pointed along it. "There has to be something behind that back wall."

We inspected the shelving system. I began from the left, Joe from the right and we worked towards each other.

Joe suddenly said, "Bingo. Take a look at this."

I moved to his shoulder. He was standing in front of a shelf section, three feet wide, separated ceiling to floor from the shelves on each side, by a gap he could slide his fingers into.

"I think this is a door," Joe said. "I bet you this section swings open somehow. You take a look at that side."

Joe handed me the big torch, fished inside his jacket for his, switched it on, stuck it between his teeth and peered into the gap in front of him. I started from the top on the left and worked down. The torch didn't help much. The beam was too wide and bouncing reflections back at me from the steel edged frames. I turned off the torch, twisted my wrist, held my left palm and fingers vertical and reached inside the gap until I touched the wall. I drew my hand downwards. Then at eye level, my little finger came up against a horizontal piece of steel.

"I've got something here, Joe. Some kind of catch."

"Press it, or twist, or jiggle it a bit," he said.

I tried all three, but couldn't apply enough force with the ends of my fingers. I took my hand out of the gap.

"We need a tommy bar or a narrow tyre lever."

Joe dug into his bag and produced exactly that. I stared at him.

"Normally the work I do is more subtle than this. But when brute force and ignorance are required..."

I took the lever from him, held on to the curved end and slotted the other into the gap. I slid the lever downwards until

I felt it reach the piece of steel. Raised it an inch or two, then struck down onto the steel catch. Nothing happened beyond sending a shock wave through my wrist and along my right arm.

"Shit!"

I hauled the lever out of the gap, dropped it and massaged my elbow. Joe picked up the lever.

"I'll do it." he said.

I stepped back to give him room.

"That was from the top," I said. "Try underneath."

Joe did. Slid the lever under the catch and moved it upwards. There was a double click. The steel catch responded to the pressure. It lifted. Joe took hold of a shelf and pulled. The whole thing swung open from the left to the right. Like Joe had suggested, it was a door.

There was another one behind it and another deadlock. This one tougher than the last, and taking a minute of Joe's time to crack open. He looked at me.

"Okay... If this room is blacked out, as it appears to be from the yard, then you can switch the light on. On the other hand you might do that and light up the yard and the whole side of the building. But what the hell..."

I pushed the door open, reached round the left hand side of the door frame, located a light switch, and clicked it down. The room lit up like the lobby had done a few minutes earlier.

I stepped into the room. Joe followed, stepped to my right shoulder.

There was a long silence, eventually broken by Joe.

"Jesus Christ," he whispered.

We were standing inside an operating theatre.

"Is this...?" He couldn't finish the sentence.

I have never been in an operating theatre. But it looked like all the places I'd seen on TV and at the movies. Even in this state, under what must have been the general purpose working lights, the cupboards and storage units around the walls gleamed in polished, stainless steel brilliance. And right in the middle sat an operating table, with above it, half a dozen concentrated beam, high-wattage lights.

I began to walk around.

"Don't touch anything," Joe said. "Even with the gloves on."

There were TV monitors, boxes of electronic gizmos, trays of implements – straight and curved, bent and shaped – cupboards with words on them I couldn't read and wouldn't be able to remember. At which point, I realised they were written in German.

Joe summed up what we were both thinking.

"Where the hell did he buy this stuff?"

"All these bits and pieces are German," I said. "Or maybe Austrian. Or Swiss. Yes, that's it Swiss." I faced Joe across the operating table. "In the good old, rich old days, Andrew Featherstone was a senior UK consultant to a couple of Swiss health trusts."

"So when he set this place up he pulled some strings?"

"Looks like it," I said.

I looked round once more. Joe asked me if I had seen enough. I said I had. We turned out the lights and left. Joe checked that both doors were locked. In the storeroom, he re-assembled all his gear, made sure he wasn't missing anything. We skirted the stuff in the room, opened the door into the hall, put out the lights and closed the door behind us. Both of us were breathing more easily now. Joe locked the door. Minutes later, we were back in the street and walking towards the Volvo.

Chapter Twenty-Four

"Is this your friend?" Irving asked Molly and Don.

Molly nodded. Don said, "Yes it is."

We were standing in a squeaky clean air conditioned room with rows of cold stores along the walls. Don put his left arm around Molly's shoulder. She turned her face to his. Don asked when Martin was likely to be buried.

"Cremated actually," Irving said. "We have done all the work we can. We have determined the cause of death and the coroner has agreed with us. We will hand Martin over to the undertaker once the police are satisfied there are no next of kin to find. At which point, under the terms of the 1984 Public Health Act, the city will pay for a pauper's funeral. Not much grandeur in that I'm afraid. A basic coffin, transportation to the South Bristol Crematorium, a short service and committal, then Martin's ashes scattered in the adjacent Memorial Garden."

"And when is that likely to be?" Molly asked.

"Perhaps in a few days. I will make sure Mr Shepherd is told, so that he can pass on the details to you, and anyone else you would like to inform."

Molly looked down at Martin again, letting the tears flow now. Irving tapped my shoulder and pointed towards his office door. I nodded and he moved away from us. Don turned to me.

"Do you think one of us would be allowed to say something about Martin, on the day?"

"I'm sure," I said. "And I'll drive you to the crematorium."

"Thank you, Jack."

He pulled Molly closer to him. I took a last look at Martin. Although he looked older, he had made perhaps half of his three score years and ten. Whatever he had been paid for giving up his lung had been spent or lost. A street person, with no connection to anything remotely close to a dignified life, he had died cold and alone, lying on a pile of cardboard boxes in a back street toilet. It was a dismissive 'fuck off' from the world of plenty around him. A brutal and monumental injustice.

I moved around the trolley, covered Martin's face again, pushed the trolley back into the fridge and closed the door.

I took Molly and Don back to what passed for their home. I didn't want to go into the office. Instead I drove to Redland, working on a solution to the question on my mind. To tell, or not to tell the police about the funeral parlour operating room.

I could imagine Harvey Butler's reaction as I offered him my version of the discovery. Currently, this wasn't of any concern to MIT. On the other hand, George Hood had told me to keep him in the picture. He could be the bloke to call, in order to avoid the inevitable 'go home and stay there' tirade from Harvey.

Only enter the battles you can win. I decided to talk it through with Adam. He was at his office desk.

"I have something I'd like to discuss," I said. "Are you busy? Can we meet?"

"No I'm not and yes I can. At the new café in Clifton. The place in Caledonia Road. Do you know it?"

"Yes."

"Give me half an hour to clear my emails and get through the traffic."

I sat in the kitchen. Thinking about May. I needed to know how the Missing Persons investigation was going. I decided to ring George Hood about that. He wasn't at Trinity Road. The obliging DC Holmes put me through to Harvey before I could rehearse what I wanted to say. Harvey came on to the line. I began by asking him about Hood's promotion. He snorted.

"George was offered it. But not within MIT. No money to replace the previous DI here. The powers that be asked him if he would like to go to Vice. They have money left over in the budget from some initiative they canned because it wasn't working. Vice, for fuck's sake... It's a bargain basement job. Crap hours, investigations that take weeks to get anywhere, moody clientele, pimps with short tempers, massive egos and BMWs..."

"So George is staying with MIT?"

"About which I'm immensely pleased. But he could be somewhere else, enjoying a serious pay hike. He won't give the squad any less than his best. Which only makes it worse."

He decided we had done enough by way of intro chat and changed the subject.

"Are you making any progress in your hunt for Bill?"

"No. I'm thinking of hiring Bear Grylls to find him."

"And May?"

"No. Missing Persons is supposed to be on to that."

Harvey grunted. "Stay on the line. I'll put this phone on speaker."

There were a series of button tones, then a voice said, "Missing Persons. DC Hitchens. Can I help you?"

Harvey introduced himself and told Hitchens to put the boss, whoever he was, on the line. There was a click, twenty seconds of mild static, then another click.

"DCI Waverley," a new voice said. "Can I help, you Super?"

I've heard some utterly useless conversations in my years as a detective, but what followed was an award winner. It took several minutes of rigmarole from DCI Waverley to reveal that

225

Missing Persons had no idea where May was. Harvey ended the call, only just in control of his temper.

"Tosser," he said. "Jack, you have carte blanche."

"As in, whatever I need to do to find her I can do?"

"Anything short of violence or murder. Just keep me posted."

* * *

I met Adam fifteen minutes later.

"About that little bit of breaking and entering I mentioned the other day. Actually, there wasn't any breaking involved."

"Only entering then," he said. "No less a charge unfortunately."

I ploughed on. "The disgraced, former consultant surgeon Andrew Featherstone, is now running a state of the art, illegal operating theatre, out of a room at the rear of his premises."

Adam processed that information.

"Jesus Christ. How do you know that?"

"Because I've seen it," I said.

The tone of his voice changed from astonished to wary.

"What the hell are you getting into now?"

I took a piece of paper out of my pocket and passed it to him. It's a list of names."

He looked at it.

Bill Marsh, May Marsh, Walter Cobb, Brian Watson, Alice Davis, Ted Harris, Arnold Faversham, James Warburton, the Thomas Brothers, Freddie Settle, Len Coleman (deceased).

Adam studied the list. A waitress brought us coffee and croissants. Adam handed the list back to me. He said 'thank you' to the waitress. She gave him a gigawatt smile, said it was her pleasure and moved away.

"The first seven of those people are missing," I said. "Bill, May and Cobb are probably still alive. Faversham has some connection with Bill, and perhaps with May and Cobb also. Brian, Alice and Ted – connected with the Drop In Centre –

are probably dead. Freddie has James Warburton in virtual chains, but I'm sure he doesn't realise that. And as we speak, I have no idea what Freddie is engaged in, and how far up her hit list I am."

"Close to the top would be my assessment," Adam said. "Dylan Thomas died a couple of nights ago. Gareth is out of IC but still pissing blood. Freddie knows what they were supposed to be doing; and, therefore, will be in no doubt as to who was responsible for the Audi hurtling backwards into the road."

"In which case, why hasn't she been in touch?"

I bit into a croissant and took a drink of coffee.

"Have you considered that the Jersey excitement may have been Freddie's work, not Walter's? She told you she would stay on your case."

I sucked at the residue of croissant stuck behind a molar.

"Have you any notion of Walter's current whereabouts?" Adam asked.

I freed the piece of croissant and swallowed it.

"He did say something about coming back to Bristol to put his house on the market. But er..."

"You're not betting on it," Adam said. "And meanwhile, Freddie is keeping her powder dry until she can make you an offer you can't refuse"

He swallowed the last of his coffee and put down his mug. I asked him if he wanted another. He said no, and offered up a completely new idea.

"What if all the elements in this scenario are orbiting around Walter, and not Freddie? Could it be that everybody concerned with this grim narrative is waiting for Cobb to do... whatever he intends to do? Maybe you have to re-arrange the motives and the relationships. You said yourself that someone has spent hundreds of thousands on Faversham's operating theatre. And Cobb's resurrection men are kidnapping to order."

I guided another piece of croissant into my mouth. Adam continued with his analysis.

"So considering the money invested, there has to be a full schedule of operations and not just the odd weekend gig. Which, given the evidence, would be in the hands of whom?"

"Bill Marsh or Walter Cobb," I said. "Or maybe the deceased Len Coleman."

"And not Freddie's?"

"It's the sort of thing she could mastermind, yes. It's a high risk activity, with a lot of people on the payroll come operations time. It's extremely lucrative. Big fees are paid by the recipients of black market hearts and lungs and livers and kidneys. But Freddie talks about her aspirations for the Settle firm like it was some major public company. Somehow I don't think illegal transplants would fit the portfolio."

"But they would fit Cobb's?"

"He's confident and sneaky, but not top banana material. That's why I've got him pasted to this body parts business. And we do have evidence, of sorts – a Transit van and the results of an illegal visit to a funeral parlour."

"Which you can take to George Hood," Adam said. "He'll get a warrant, on the grounds of something or other, and discover the place for himself. You may get your knuckles wrapped, but you're unlikely to have the book thrown at you."

That sounded dangerously simple.

"Suppose the police find Faversham and his associates," I said. "But not Walter or Freddie. Thus leaving my clients still deep in the clarts."

Adam leaned across the table top.

"Jack... The longer you hang on to this, the more the odds shorten on the bad guys finding out what you know. Faversham and his mates have been doing their Sweeney Todd thing under the radar. They could all go to jail for a long time if discovered. So they must have an exit strategy. Which might involve getting rid of the person who discovers what they are up to."

Adam looked at me, dead centre. I stared at him, frustration boiling over.

"I haven't a clue where this is going. I've lost my client, the person my client hired me to find, and the man who owes money to the person I'm trying to find. Who, it turns out, could probably pay the debt several times over."

"Go to George Hood, Jack."

"No. Only as a last resort."

"And you're not there yet?"

"I hope not."

"I think you might be, Jack. Sitting on a towel on the beach, waiting for the tide to come in."

He stared at me. I tried to look resolute. He went on.

"Okay... How rich is Bill?"

"I don't know. I don't think May knows either."

"Why did he call you from Faversham's operating theatre? Is he in cahoots with Walter? Is he helping to bank-roll the business?"

"Why not? Anything's possible in this spellbinding miasma."

"And could Walter be blackmailing him? Or Faversham? Or both of them?"

My mobile rang from my jacket which was clothing the back of the chair. I found it and pressed the answer button. Freddie Settle picked out the noise in the background. Asked if I was alone. I said I was in a café. She said I should go to my office and ring her from there soonest, and ended the call. I put the mobile down onto the table in front of me.

"Your face has gone grey," Adam said.

Not surprising. I could feel the blood draining from it. I took a huge deep breath.

"Freddie Settle wants me to call."

"In person?"

"No. By phone. From the office. She wants me to be alone."

"Why?"

"I don't know. Maybe it's a flair for the dramatic."

"I'll come with you if you like."

"No. Let's obey orders for now."

"Get going then. I'll pay the bill."

I stood up and shrugged into my jacket. Adam told me to take care. I promised I would and, in return, he promised not to tell Chrissie what I was doing. I walked out of the café, into the sunshine and towards the Healey.

Chapter Twenty-Five

The quickest route from Clifton to my office is to cross the Gorge on the suspension bridge and drop down to the Cumberland Basin. But on this occasion I reckoned without the zeal of a road gang who had closed the slip road to the basin swing bridge. The 'diversion' pointed me in the opposite direction. If I'd spent less time thumping the steering wheel and swearing at the incompetent bastards who had devised this method of jamming up traffic into the city, my senses would have been ordered and in the right place. As it was, Freddie's ploy caught me out.

I sat imprisoned in gridlock for twenty minutes. To my right, less than one hundred and fifty yards as the crow files, I could see my office window. Eventually I managed to turn on to the exit road, coast down and around, and into the turning circle in front of the office. I barely noticed the dark blue Mercedes parked outside the entrance with its engine idling. I rounded the building and drove along the riverside to the car park. At which point I realised the Mercedes was behind me, driving in my wheel tracks. I turned into the car park. The Mercedes stopped at the entrance. I was boxed in.

To my right, a man heaved himself out of a silver Audi; a match for the one destroyed in the road accident. He was a giant; as wide as he was tall, with more chins than the Hong Kong telephone directory. I stopped the Healey. The Giant waddled towards me. I sat in the car, waiting for whatever this was about to be, to get under way. He came to a standstill six feet in front of the car, reached inside his jacket – who the hell made clothes that big? – and produced what appeared to be a .38 magnum semi-automatic.

Another man stepped out from behind the Giant. It looked like a stage reveal. He was slimmer than the Giant and substantially more agile. He moved to the Healey passenger door, opened it and slid into the car. He closed the door and nodded at me.

"Mr Shepherd. My name is Robert."

He had the shoulders of a hammer thrower and hands that could pull bolts out of gate posts. Not a man to argue with. Under any circumstances.

"The Mercedes behind us will now turn around," he said. His voice was soft and his manner impeccable. "When that is done, you will do the same thing and then follow the Mercedes. The Audi will follow us."

The Giant waddled his way to the Mercedes. I followed instructions to the letter. All the way to Walter Cobb's warehouse in Avonmouth.

The Mercedes pulled up on the forecourt, facing the warehouse door. I pulled up alongside. The Audi slid into position to my right. I noticed it had tinted side and rear windows. The Mercedes driver got out of his car and stood up. He was another big man. Robert nodded at me again.

"If you please, Mr Shepherd..."

We got out of the Healey. The Audi driver materialised, shorter than the rest of the coterie and wearing a chauffeur's uniform. He moved to the rear door on his side and opened it. Freddie got out, straightened up, looked at me, and delivered her fabulous smile.

"Jack! How are you?"

I managed to tell her I was okay. The Mercedes Driver circumnavigated all three cars and opened the side door into the warehouse. He stepped back out of the way, and the rest of us crocodiled inside.

It was maybe forty feet long and thirty wide. With what passed for a mezzanine floor at the far end, which looked like it housed a couple of offices, a small kitchen space and a toilet. Running from the mezzanine back to the front door on each side, were landings ten feet or so deep. There were two long, oblong skylights set into the opposing slopes of the roof. The place was empty. Except for two stacks of wooden pallets, a pile of large cardboard boxes with something I couldn't read stamped on the sides. And two men sitting in wheelchairs underneath the mezzanine, flanked by two more burly flat-nosed types. The whole set up looked like a scene from *The Rockford Files*.

The man in the chair on the left was Gareth Thomas. His right arm was in a sling and he had a bandage around his left wrist. He was wearing a kind of skull cap on his head and a whiplash collar round his neck. He wasn't moving. Just staring straight at me. Walter Cobb sat in the other wheelchair. He wasn't bandaged, but looked like he needed to be. His face was a mess and his torn shirt was streaked with blood. His head lolled back on his neck, as if it has slipped out of place.

The Giant pointed at the lower pallet stack, and asked to me to sit. I did. My toes just managed to reach the floor. This was intended as a serious confrontation and Freddie wasn't smiling any more. But she did look a million dollars in a tailored charcoal grey Armani suit.

"You're a menace, Jack," she began.

I sat up as straight as I could.

"I'll take that as a compliment, Freddie," I replied.

"I'm sorry about the welcoming committee," she said. "But I knew you wouldn't come without a formal invitation. I gave orders that you weren't to be hurt."

I dipped my head in acknowledgement of her courtesy.

"We have to talk, Jack."

A masterpiece of précis that. A euphemism for 'answer my questions to my complete satisfaction, before I hand you over to my associates for a trip to the grinder'.

"Talk away, Freddie," I said. "I'm listening."

She looked at me with some regret.

"We have a problem, you and I. Basically I believe it's a lack of understanding. From your direction that is, not mine. We both know I have been providing all the good will. You have responded by refusing to co-operate, by wrecking an expensive piece of machinery, by sending Dylan to the morgue and Gareth," – she nodded in his direction – "to intensive care. That is poor reward for the interest I have shown in your health and welfare."

It was an irredeemable load of crap, but she was dishing it out with some urbanity. It didn't merit much of a response as yet, so I simply shrugged my shoulders and looked down at the floor. Freddie accepted the gesture as an invitation to carry on.

"I'll get to the point shall I?"

She stepped close, folded her arms, tapped the floor a couple of times with an expensive Italian shoe and went on.

"I am a business woman, Jack..."

"No Freddie," I said. "You're scum in a fifteen hundred quid suit."

That did it. Freddie's cool evaporated in an instant. She moved her right arm across her chest, adjusted the huge diamond on her third finger, then swung the back of her hand across my face. The ring tore some skin out of my cheek and I yelled in pain. Blood ran into my mouth. I licked at it, then raised my right arm and dabbed at my cheek with the back of my hand. God it hurt.

Then calm once more, Freddie continued.

"I control a large organisation. I employ a considerable number of people. And in normal circumstances, the business runs very smoothly indeed. However, there are some..." she searched for the right word... "interests, which I can't afford to disclose. You are with me, yes?"

I licked my lip again. "So far, Freddie..."

She stepped back a pace. "Where is Bill Marsh?"

"I don't know," I said. "Where is May?"

"That's for later. Do you know who killed Len Coleman?"

"I thought you did." I looked towards Thomas. "Or rather he did, under orders from you."

Freddie nodded at the Giant. He moved to me, hauled me to my feet, executed an effortless full nelson and presented me to my co-driver Robert, who squared up to me.

"A thousand apologies, Mr Shepherd," he said.

He shifted slightly to his right and slammed his right fist into the pit of my stomach. My whole body seemed to go into spasm. The pain spread to my chest. I choked, gasped for breath and immediately wanted to be sick. The Giant released me and I pitched forward onto my face. It was some time before the nausea subsided. No one in the warehouse moved or spoke. I managed to get to my knees. The Giant picked me up and sat me back on the pallets.

Freddie weighed in again, with another morsel of advice.

"This is no way to carry on, Jack. It's not sensible to be so obstructive. You will only get seriously hurt."

I was hurting so much I couldn't frame a reply. Freddie pointed to Cobb.

"He is responsible for all this." She opened her arms wide to include all those present. "We caught up with him on his way to the airport."

"Must have been after the meeting with his estate agent," I offered.

Freddie gave me an old fashioned look. Which morphed into deeply suspicious. I dredged up something else to say.

"Is he alright?"

"I hope not," she said. "Apparently, he's not broke at all. He has a lot of money in Jersey. And a fine house, I understand."

"Yes," I said. "I've been there."

Freddie kept her surprise to a minimum. "Oh, I didn't know that."

"Louis the Sixteenth vernacular. Built by some French pirate in 1778."

If this was news to Freddie, it could only mean that our tourist guides in Jersey were a pair of cut price enforcers hired by Walter. One question answered then.

Freddie turned her face and looked at him again.

"Did he offer you any other kind of hospitality?" she asked.

"We didn't get on." I looked at Walter too. "Did he tell you much?"

Freddie shook her head. "Unfortunately, no. That's why he's in such a state."

"Did you ask him if he killed Len Coleman?"

"Of course."

"And what did he say?"

Freddie shrugged. We were approaching the end of the conversation, so I asked a final question.

"Why are you looking for Bill Marsh?"

"We have important matters to discuss," Freddie said. "We need to set some boundaries, Bill and I. Get a few things straight."

"About what?"

She looked deep into my eyes. Hers were beautiful. But not at all friendly, and contemplating something or other. She called up to the mezzanine.

"Lester. Bring her out."

There was the sound of chairs scraping on wood. One of the office doors opened. A man in his 30s with a bad haircut and a cheap suit, ushered May out on to the mezzanine. I stared up at her. She tried to smile at me.

I launched myself at Freddie. I was barely upright before arms came from nowhere and encircled me. I jabbed my right elbow backwards and made satisfactory contact with a ribcage. I was rewarded with a vicious punch to the kidneys. My knees buckled and I slid to the floor again. I rolled over onto my back and looked up. Freddie stepped forward, hitched up the knees of her expensive trousers and crouched beside me. She pasted on her megawatt smile side

"Find Bill Marsh for me," she said. "I'll give you forty-eight hours."

She stood up. The Giant hauled me back onto my feet. I shook off his arms and stared at Freddie. The smile stayed fixed.

"Take Mr Shepherd back to his car," she said.

The Giant stepped towards me. I waved him away, took a couple of steps to test my equilibrium, straightened as much as I could, and looked up at May again.

"I'm fine, Jack," she said; her voice strong and her body language resolute.

I turned away and walked slowly towards the side door. Robert and the Giant followed me outside to the Healey. They waited patiently while I eased myself into the driver's seat and fumbled at the keys still in the ignition. When the engine fired, they walked back into the warehouse.

It was a long and extremely painful journey home.

* * *

An hour later, I lay soaking in the bath. I let the heat work on the bruises, my anger cool and my pulse rate slow down. Encased in the cocoon of water, I did some thinking. May was the only concern – at least for now. But I had learned something earlier in the evening. Heroic though my quest was, I needed help. Not just ordinary help. I needed muscle.

But not tonight. Tonight... phones disconnected, one drink with a light supper and early to bed. I eased under the duvet just after 9 o'clock, took a while to discover the least painful sleeping position, then mercifully, the light went out.

Chapter Twenty-Six

I woke up at twenty-five minutes past eight, and a split second later discovered I was hurting all over. At least it seemed that way. I rolled over without thinking and the bruises caught me out. I levered myself upright, swung my feet to the carpet and stood up. That wasn't too painful. In the bathroom, I looked at my face in the mirror. The damage Freddie had done to my cheek looked as bad as it felt, but I concluded I could do without stitches.

I called Harvey to ask if he had time to see me. He asked me if it was urgent. I told him it was bloody serious.

The extremely polite PC De'Ath, was back on the gate. He refrained from commenting on my face, wished me good morning and said Superintendent Butler was expecting me. I parked the Healey in the same place as last time and walked across the car park. Harvey was in the lobby, glaring at me and all but stamping his feet.

"Who did that to your face?"

"I had a meeting with Freddie Settle in Avonmouth."

Harvey raised his arms in despair.

"Now don't get cross," I said. "It wasn't my idea. I was press-ganged."

"Do you want us to check the place out?"

"No point. They'll be long gone by now. But for your information, it was the warehouse owned by Walter Cobb."

"Was he there as well?"

"Yes. A bit under the weather though."

Harvey pointed along the corridor to his left. He didn't say another word until we got into his office. Then he pointed me to a chair.

"Sit down."

I did. Slowly and carefully, all the while trying to look like a man about to offer up a great idea.

"So now what?" Harvey asked.

I looked across the desk at him. I still hadn't sorted out the best place to begin. Harvey waited.

"I need to give you the whole story, I guess."

"Always best," he said. "Although I'm never convinced that's what I get from you."

"Okay..."

I began with Mr Berling and the funeral parlour. Two sentences in, Harvey held up his right hand.

"Hang on. Let's get George in here. Save a second trip to the well."

He picked up his mobile. Pressed two buttons and waited.

"George," he said. "Where are you?" He listened for a second or two. "Okay. Within five minutes. Siren and blues and twos." He glared across the desk at me. "Yes, he's here too."

He ended the call, laid his mobile on the desk, re-adjusted his position in his chair and folded his arms.

"You said Walter Cobb was under the weather."

"Just a bit. His face looked like a yard of bad road, and there was blood all over his shirt."

"So he doesn't know where Bill Marsh is either."

"If he does, he's taken a hell of a beating to keep it secret."

We talked about odds and sods until George Hood walked into the office. Harvey looked at his watch.

"That was bloody quick."

"Blues and twos you said. That's carte blanche."

"He gave that to me too," I said.

George sat in the other chair. Reached out and shook my hand. "Okay, Jack?"

Harvey grunted. "When you two have finished..."

He looked at me with barely suppressed ire, in spite of carte blanche.

Hood knew the beginning of the story. He nodded two or three times as I began to tell it. Then I cleared my throat and launched into a slightly edited version of the stuff he and Harvey didn't know – from the funeral parlour recce, through the break in and the search, to the discovery. I avoided mentioning Joe's name, maintaining I had found a way into the place through a rear window that wasn't alarmed. Both detectives knew that bit was a distortion of the truth, but sensibly chose not to pry. Hood came to the same conclusion as I had done about the interior space.

I wound up. "I looked round the room. I didn't contaminate a potential crime scene. I wore gloves and I didn't touch a thing, except the door handle. I went out the way I got in. You can raid the place acting on information received. Which you can't disclose at this time, as doing so might damage an ongoing investigation."

I gave Harvey my best 'over to you' look.

"Okay," he said. "You want us to bring Mr Berling in here. Then let George and Sherlock play good cop and bad cop, until he folds under the strain and tells us all about the illegal operations. Maybe he genuinely doesn't know anything about them." Harvey sat back in his chair, snorted and opened his arms wide. "In any case, it's not MIT business."

"Hood looked at me. "Do you still think that Bill Marsh called you from inside the funeral parlour?"

"Yes."

"And you don't believe he was there on behalf of a dying friend or relative?"

"No. I think he is part of Faversham's set up."

"Which part?" Harvey asked. "Bill's clearly not qualified for cutting and sewing."

"Bill has money," I said. "And I believe that, for reasons we will not know until we find him and ask him what they are, he helped finance the initiative."

Hood shook his head. Harvey asked why he would do that.

"I don't know," I said. "That's why we need to find him."

"And you think Berling may be a person who knows where Bill is?"

"He's the only person we can ask," I said.

Hood seemed to agree with that assessment. I pressed on.

"You two have the badges and the warrants and the weight of the law to hand. I would have to beat the information out of him."

"Heaven forbid," Harvey said. He pushed his chair back a bit. "You still haven't heard from May?"

I sat up straighter in my chair. Cleared my throat and explained.

"Freddie Settle has her. She was in Cobb's warehouse too."

Harvey rocked forwards and laid his elbows on his desk.

"Was she hurt?" Hood asked

"Didn't seem to be. She actually said she was fine."

"Freddie hadn't harmed her."

"Not as far as I could tell."

Harvey rubbed his eye sockets. "So you're about to suggest that we send the ACC's designer commandos to the rescue."

"Hell no! If you do that, May and whatever this is all about, could perish together."

Hood and Harvey exchanged glances.

"May's a prosecution witness," I offered.

"To what?" Harvey grumbled. "A story that Freddie will deny with such outrage, the echoes won't die away for weeks... May isn't hurt, so there's no evidence of intimidation or violence."

"So long as we get her back. Christ, Harvey..."

He glared at me. "Righteous indignation won't work either."

He was close to throwing me out of the building. I had to be very careful.

"Freddie hoped May would lead her to Bill," I said. "I don't think May knows where he is. So the task has fallen to me, knowing that I'll move heaven and earth to make sure May isn't harmed. I have been given forty-eight hours."

"So the intention is, to get on with the crime chief's recommendations while ignoring intelligent suggestions from the proper guardians of law and order."

I didn't say anything

Harvey put his elbows back on the desk. He lifted his right hand to his face and supported his chin. He mumbled into the palm of his hand, looked down at his desk, then up again at his sergeant, decision made.

"Okay, George. Get up to the funeral parlour and scare the living shite of out this Berling bloke."

"I want to go," I said.

Harvey nodded at Hood. "Take Don Quixote too."

Chapter Twenty-Seven

I sat in the front passenger seat of Hood's Vauxhall in the car park. He had four uniformed PCs corralled a few yards away. He spent five minutes briefing them. I watched a lot of ndding. Then Hood joined me. The constables got into a patrol car and followed us out of the car park.

The first ten minutes of our journey were made in silence. Hood stared in front of him, concentrating on navigating his way through the late afternoon traffic. As we drove up Stokes Croft, he opened the conversation.

"How the hell has Faversham been getting away with this?"

"It's one hell of a secret business," I said. "I mean you and I paid a visit, got the conducted tour and we didn't notice a thing."

"But you said it's a state of the art operating theatre. With big bits of kit I should imagine. Must have taken some getting in."

"Sure. But with the bits in crates and boxes, who would know? It went in at the side of the building from the back of the car park, not through the front door. If it was delivered in a hearse, who would take a second look? And apparently you don't need a lot of stuff for routine organ surgery. It's a 'carve up, take out and put back' exercise according to a surgeon friend of Adam. As long as the new organ has been properly harvested and stored, and you join up everything with due care and attention, it works. It's not keyhole or brain surgery, doesn't need expensive hardware. It's all down to the skill of the surgeon. And we know that before his drink problem, Featherstone was considered one of the best."

"Okay. What about the cost?"

"Obviously he was bank-rolled in the beginning. But he is serving an elite client base. You need to be earning close to a six figure salary to afford a black market lung, or heart, or bowel. A bit less for a liver or a kidney. So if he's been at this for two or three years..."

"He has probably paid back whoever it was financed the setup," Hood said.

"A friend of Chrissie has a brother with cystic fibrosis," I said. "He's nineteen. He needs two new lungs. He may get them before he dies, but it's a long shot. His mother was recently heard to say she would do absolutely anything for two lungs."

Hood glanced at me. I went on.

"Supposing you had a spare twenty thousand, and the person dearest to you desperately needed it, would you hand it over?"

"Probably."

"And if it was a matter of life and death? An operation or a trip to the morgue? Would that be any different?"

"Probably not."

"And if the only way for this to happen was to pay Featherstone to do it?"

"Well that's the point," Hood said. "Paying Featherstone. He's making a fortune by trading on people's misery. You're not going to tell me that twenty grand is the real cost. I mean what's his mark up?"

"Sixty percent at least, I should think. But if the recipient's family has the money to pay..."

"Okay. But the bottom line is, the organ will have been harvested illegally and such an operation is against the law."

"And that's all that concerns you?"

"There's no moral issue here, Jack. Featherstone is indulging in stuff for which he can, and should, go to prison. And if, as we suspect, Walter Cobb's men with the Transit are on the payroll, there's a shed load of other wrong doing to add to the crime sheet as well." He turned his head and stared at me. "You're not trying to tell me there's a plus in this?"

"Watch the road."

He turned back to look ahead. He hit the horn, pulled across the road to his right and switched lanes. "Answer the question," he muttered.

"Of courses there's a plus," I said. "The family and loved ones of the recipient get exactly what they stump up for, and are rendered deliriously happy."

"After paying through the nose for something one hundred percent illegal," he said. "The law is the law, and if you break it by indulging in criminal activities you have to be stopped. Featherstone or Faversham or whatever the hell he calls himself, is pond scum."

No denying that, but I couldn't leave the conversation unfinished.

"People living on the streets are there for all sorts of reasons," I said. "But the bottom line is, they have nothing to their name. Only the clothes they stand up in. So when someone appears and offers them more money than they've seen in years, the choice is a no-brainer. If the harvesting goes wrong, or it turns out the organs aren't any use, what the hell? It's just the end of a long story of pain and misery. And who's going to miss them?"

Hood stayed resolute. "We, the police, the people paid to protect and serve, can't do much to reverse these injustices, but we get paid to try."

* * *

At the funeral parlour, Berling began with the knee-jerk response.

"Have you got a warrant for this search?"

Hood responded with, "Would you like to come to Trinity Road and answer my questions there?"

Berling looked alarmed. Hood ploughed on.

"And in the meantime we'll get our warrant and the four police officers out in the lobby will begin the search. Everyone on the premises will be held here until all questions are answered. At least, everyone who can talk."

Berling was in no state to find that funny. The colour had drained from his face. Hood finished what he had to say.

"Which could take most of the evening. And you could end up in a police cell overnight."

Hood waited for the emphasis he put on the last few words to hit the mark. Berling said nothing.

"So do you want to make a drama out of this," Hood went on. "Or would you rather it was low key?"

Berling found his voice again. "What grounds do you have for being here?"

"We're acting on information received," Hood said.

Berling shifted his position in his chair. As squirms go it was a small one, but a squirm it was nonetheless. Now he looked glum. Hood moved to the office door and opened it. He called for one of the uniforms, who arrived and took up position in the doorway.

"This is Police Constable Merrill," Hood said. "He and his fellow officers will escort you to the police station." He took a breath. "Mr Berling, I am asking you to come with us, to answer questions concerning the disappearance of Bill and May Marsh, and the murder of Leonard Coleman."

Berling stood up behind his desk.

"I have absolutely no idea what you are referring to. Search the place. Go on. Please do."

Hood turned to Merrill.

"Officer... Will you keep this gentleman here please?"

Berling sat down again. Hood and I left the office. Merrill closed the door. In the lobby, Hood pointed to a chair.

"Sit there," he ordered. "The rest of this is by the book." Then he lowered his voice. "I don't want you anywhere near the discovery. Let us find the door to the operating theatre and then pretend to be surprised and excited."

He turned to the other PCs. "Wareham, you come with me. We'll work this side of the lobby. Green and Arnold, you start with the storeroom."

Hood and the PCs set to work. Ten minutes later Hood re-joined me. We waited another four or five minutes. Wareham came back and stood next to us. Then PC Green stepped back into the lobby.

"Sergeant. We've found a door at the back of the storeroom. We got it open, but behind it, there's another door with a deadlock."

"Go and ask Mr Berling for the key," Hood ordered.

Green walked the length of the lobby, opened the office door and stepped inside. I looked at my watch. Monitored the seconds. Just short of a minute later, PC Green stepped back into the lobby.

"Mr Berling insists he doesn't know what I am talking about."

Hood got to his feet muttering. "What a fucking pantomime... Bring him out here."

Mr Berling was retrieved from his office, then escorted into the storeroom followed by Hood. I hovered in the doorway. Berling seemed genuinely disturbed by what he was looking at. He insisted he had no idea what was behind the locked door, and as this was the first time he had seen it, how the hell could he have a key for it? Hood stepped back into the hall, asking PC Wareham to join him.

"Have you got an enforcer ram in the car?"

"Yes."

"Go and get it. Then smash your way into the room and introduce Mr Berling to whatever's hidden in there."

Wareham went out the front door. Hood dug into a trouser pocket, found his car keys, took them out and turned to me.

"Go outside for a walk. Get off the premises until we've done this. Wait in the Vauxhall if you like."

I did as I was ordered. Walked up to the eastern end of Rycroft Road, bought a KitKat in the newsagent's on the corner, and walked back to the Vauxhall. I unlocked the car and returned to the passenger seat. I unwrapped the KitKat and ate it.

Moments later, PCs Green, Arnold and Wareham emerged with Berling and escorted him to the patrol car. I watched the car drive away. Hood and PC Merrill stepped into the street. There was a brief conversation, then Merrill went back into the building and Hood walked towards the Vauxhall. He got into the driver's seat and I handed him the key. I asked him if Berling had said anything of significance.

"He moaned about the amount of work he was having to get through without Faversham being in the building. Then he said something about a bloke with a name like a venereal disease. Syfy something."

"Sisyphus," I said. "A Greek. He was punished by the gods for his sins, by having to push a huge boulder up a hill forever."

"Ancient Greek you mean?"

"It's a metaphor for any age. Sisyphus was a great ruler, until his businesses began to make a fortune. At which point he couldn't resist creaming off more than his share. He got rid of anybody who suspected what he was up to, and continued to fleece traders who passed through his land."

"Did he get to the top of his hill?"

"As he tired, the boulder got the better of him. Rolled back to the bottom and he had to start again."

"Sisy who?"

"Sisyphus," I said and spelled it out for him.

"I'll try and remember that."

He turned on the ignition.

"Is that all?" I asked

"The gist... I did ask him where the operating staff came from. He simply continued to insist the business had nothing to do with him. He had no idea it was going on. And you know what? I'm beginning to believe him."

He looked into the rear view mirror and pulled out into the road.

* * *

I picked up the Healey and drove back to my office. There was another note under my door. *Why don't you keep your mobile switched on? I'm having dinner with someone whose business I'm trying to hook. But I can be all yours from 9.30 or so. I'll call you.*

I looked at the clock on the wall. Forty-eight hours Freddie had offered. It was now forty-four and at breakfast tomorrow, it would be thirty-six.

Harvey called me. I asked him if Hood was making progress.

"Not much. And Berling's lawyer will have him out of here by supper time."

"Has he coughed up anything about Bill? Anything at all?"

"Sorry, Jack. And now the bottom line is..." He paused to put the right words together. "Arnold Faversham and his business are no longer of interest to MIT. Unless he re-surfaces as part of our investigation into the murder of Len Coleman, which seems unlikely. We are no longer tapping your phones."

He apologised again and ended the call.

"Shit, shit shit shit shit."

I threw the phone receiver across the room. Mercifully, the office door was open and it sailed out into the corridor. It was collected by the heavy curtains lining the window opposite and it dropped on to the carpet. I leaned back in my chair and stared up at the point above the door where the office wall met the ceiling. There was a plaster crack I hadn't seen before, running along the join. I got out of my chair and collected the phone. It seemed none the worse for its flight though the air. Then I came up with an idea.

I called Adam with the store bought mobile. He picked up the call at home.

"Is our no-reply email address still in existence?"

"Yes. I told Chris to hang onto it. Thought it might come in handy again."

"Can we send out a blog this evening?"

"I'll ask him."

* * *

We met in Chris Gould's workshop at 9 o'clock. I gave him back the loaner phone and thanked him. He left a key with us and told us to lock up when we had finished. Adam and I drafted a piece of text designed to provoke a response from Bill.

The Bristol private eye who was left staring down at a pool of blood on his client's parquet floor, has compounded his misfortune. There is still no sign of the AB negative's owner and now, to add to his miseries, his client has gone missing too. The victim perhaps, of a kidnapping by seriously dangerous people. This private investigator clearly needs help. Call him. Somebody.

"We've passed the copy deadline for tomorrow morning's *Western Daily Press*," Adam said. "But I can get a response to the blog into the early edition of the *Post*. From which I can then quote, questioning the way fools and fetishists misuse the power of the world- wide-web. Which will leave you with twenty-four hours before Freddie makes her next move."

This really was close to conspiracy – Leveson could certainly make something out of a journalist writing a blog and then responding to it in the newspaper he works for – but we had nothing left in our armoury. Somehow, and sometime soon, Bill had to read the blog and the headlines and put two and two together.

Chapter Twenty-Eight

I spent the following morning, the second Saturday on the case, finding things to do.

I woke up at half past seven. Checked the landline by picking up the receiver in the hall and listening to the dial tone. Checked that my mobile had enough juice in the battery. Made coffee, and ate two slices of toast.

I looked at the kitchen wall clock. 7.48.

Upstairs in my study, I fired up the laptop and googled the local section of the newsdot website. Our email was first up and writ large.

The sun was hard at work outside and tomorrow was May Day. I opened the kitchen door and stepped out to test the temperature. Warm enough for a bit of light exercise. I put on an old pair of jeans, took all the phone receivers into the back garden, and spent an hour tidying up the beds around the lawn. But my heart wasn't in it. I looked at my watch. 8.55.

Back in the kitchen I made and drank another cup of coffee. Checked the wall clock again. 9.03.

I realised what I had been putting off. I called Linda's mobile. No reply – something of a relief. I called her office number. Same again. I left a message. *I'm really sorry about last night. I'll explain when I can. I'm stuck at home this morning. Expecting a package I have to sign for. Catch up with you later.*

I sat down in the living room. Put my mobile and my landline receiver on the coffee table in front of me. Stared at them with some malice. Switched the television set on. Looked through the electronic guides of as many channels as my patience would allow, then gave it up when I discovered I had seen all the westerns on offer.

I looked at the clock above the fireplace. 9.40.

Adam rang. I asked him where he was. At home he said, and asked me if I had looked at the newsdot bollocks upload. I told him I had. He said he'd be at home all morning if I had anything to impart. I asked about Chrissie and Sam. Adam said Sam was stretched out on the floor by his desk, and Chrissie was working through her tutor's reaction to her latest assignment. At which point we agreed we ought to keep the line clear and ended the call. I put the receiver back on the coffee table and stared at it again.

I looked at my watch. Wishing time away. 9.46.

What would I normally be doing if at home and at leisure? I decided to update my notes on this case and took the phones upstairs. Not that there was much to write, apart from *The cops have no idea where Faversham-Featherstone could be. I still have no idea where Bill is. Freddie Settle is extraordinarily pissed off and has May as a hostage.*

I leaned back in my chair and gazed at the laptop screen. So much for eleven days work. The clock in the bottom right hand corner of the screen read 10.15.

My mobile rang. I grabbed it and pressed the green button. It was some pillock from my mobile phone provider asking me how I was today and if I'd like to enhance my total mobile experience. I closed the line.

I got to my feet, moved to the master bedroom window and looked out. The bay window, matching the one down below in the living room, gave a widescreen view of the street. I looked across the hedges on both sides. There was no car in the street I didn't recognise. No silver Audis to be seen.

There was a cupboard on the landing, full of cardboard boxes which had been on my list to sort for months – most of them from eons ago, which I thought might come in useful someday if I decided to move. It's amazing how long you can hang on to this concept once it takes root. There was a monster box in which a huge, fat, analogue TV set had been delivered back in the 90s, full of bits of polystyrene and bubble wrap. I burst a few bubbles but got no thrill out of the exercise and gave it up. There was an equally large box which had arrived with a fitted kitchen oven (more polystyrene), a big old VHS recorder box (empty), two old DVD player boxes (empty), two satellite receiver boxes (empty also), a wide slim-line box in which the current TV set had been delivered (more bubble wrap), a small fat box (polystyrene again) in which the microwave had arrived, and a solid looking box which had delivered something from Ikea (God knows why, I wasn't aware I'd bought anything from Ikea).

So now I had a pile of boxes on the landing. I hauled them downstairs and re-piled them in the hall, beside the front door; working on the assumption that falling over them five or six times would drive the message home, and I would take them to the Recycling Centre.

The living room clock said 10.50.

Then I remembered something that would help. *The Strange World of Gurney Slade*. A TV series from the early 1960s, starring the late, great, Anthony Newley, which I had first discovered in cult re-runs when I was a student. About an actor who walks off the set of a sitcom which is failing to provoke laughs from the studio audience, and into a world entirely of his own devising. At his own pace, he wanders through the countryside; bringing to life objects and people on advertising hoardings, passing the time of the day with plants and trees, discussing matters of great import with dogs and farmyard animals, and creating a whole new way of taking on the pressures of the world. Only six episodes were made, inventing absurd TV comedy long before the Pythons and Vic Reeves. Like Gurney Slade, I had time on my hands and an overwhelming need to make the world work my way, at least for the next twenty-four hours.

I found the DVD and sat back on the sofa. I was halfway through episode three when my mobile rang. I stared at it buzzing and vibrating on the coffee table. I picked it up and pressed the call receive button.

"I get the message, Jack," Bill said.

I grabbed the TV remote and hit the 'mute' button. Then Bill and I were talking, if not in the same place, at least in the same conversation.

"We need to talk, Bill," I said.

"How is May?"

I ignored the question. "Face to face, Bill, and within the next hour. I'll come to you."

"No don't do that." He offered an arrangement he'd obviously rehearsed. "Meet me in the M4 Services café at Aust. You know it?"

"Yes. This side of the old bridge crossing."

I looked at my watch again, this time with some purpose. 12.40. I could be there in less than half an hour. But better to add a minute or two.

"Quarter past one," I said. "Be there whatever happens, Bill."

"Slit my throat and hope to die, Jack."

The line went dead. I leant back into the sofa cushions and breathed as if the breaths I were taking were my last. A pulse in my left temple was throbbing, my heart was racing.

Something to do. Finally.

* * *

Now cheerfully re-named *Severn View*, the services area at Aust is accessed from the northern side of the east bound carriageway. It's less tatty than it used to be. The old trucker's café has had a makeover and boasts a new entrance beneath the coffee and burger signs.

The car park was sparsely populated. I arrived ahead of time. Sat in the Healey for a couple of minutes thinking about stuff, and hoping that Bill had enough guts for what was going to play out.

He was already in the café. In a hell of a state. Hugging himself and visibly shaking. He had chosen a table by the panoramic window with a view of the channel looking north. But he wasn't enjoying the view. He was staring down at the table top. As I reached him, he looked up and tried to smile.

"Hello, Jack."

"You haven't got a drink," I said. "Would you like one?"

Bill shook his head.

"Well I would."

I re-located to the coffee shop. It took five minutes to get in line, shuffle forwards, order an 'Americano', and take it back to the table. During that time, Bill stared out of the window, only turning to look at me when I sat down. I took a sip of coffee and burned the roof of my mouth. I put the mug to one side, rested my elbows on the table and leaned forwards. Bill was still shaking.

"Where is May?" he asked.

"She is currently enjoying the hospitality of one, Freddie Settle," I said.

There was a beat rest, then Bill groaned and thumped the table. I ploughed on.

"Who has given me until 5 o'clock this afternoon – that's five and a half hours from now – to find you and swap you for your wife. Are you getting all this?"

257

"Yes. Yes I am. Oh Jesus..."

"I've had a crap twenty hours or so," I said. "And I've got enough adrenalin inside me to bottle and sell to hospitals. So let's make this simple. Where have you been?"

"In a caravan at Severn Beach," he said.

Possibly the best corner of the Westcountry in which to get lost. If there was one place nobody would dream of hiding in, it was Severn Beach. Which meant that it was exactly the place to do so.

"Do you remember Libby Mason?" Bill asked. "It belongs to her."

I remembered Libby. A veteran sex worker, with pretend red hair, a second hand tan and a lumpy face. Bill had gone to her rescue a number of times over the years. Now, she was apparently paying her dues.

"The caravan looks out over the mud flats to the channel," Bill said. "It's rusted to buggery, needs a coat of paint, and a new bedroom window. But it's anonymous."

Bill didn't have to paint a picture. One hundred battered brown and white caravans on the banks of the Severn Estuary was a low rent destination.

Bill went back to the beginning of the conversation

"Is May alright?" he asked.

I gave him a précis of yesterday's trip to Cobb's warehouse. He looked more hollow-eyed, if that was possible, by the time I had finished.

"But May's alright isn't she?" he asked again.

"She was then."

"You see, Freddie doesn't know."

"Know what?"

"If she did, she wouldn't harm her."

"Know what, Bill?"

He took his time to say the next four words. Like a cheap actor in a bad whodunit, he gave each one equal emphasis.

"Freddie is May's daughter."

I reached for the mug of coffee and swallowed a mouthful that scorched all the way down. I gasped. Bill thought it was because of the information he had just offered. He asked if I was alright. I nodded as the heat began to dissolve in my chest. He went on with the story.

"Freddie and Lisa, and May and I, sort of grew up together. We all lived in Bedminster, went to the same junior school. We lost touch as the years went by. Until May and I met again. I was working for Uncle Jimmy by then and—"

I interrupted him. "Were you married to May when this happened?"

Bill looked at me, the expression on his face half surprise at the suggestion I had just made and half apology for not explaining properly.

"No. We, we were engaged."

He took time to sort out the next bit of narrative. I waited.

"Back in the day," Bill went on, "Uncle Jimmy was killed by one of Freddie's employees, working for himself on the boss's time. The situation was dealt with, the bloke disappeared, and Freddie put some money into my new business. He looked after me. I knew everything there was to know about the betting shops, but nothing about the vultures that were circling. Freddie made it clear my business was a no go area and they stayed away. May came back to Bristol around that time, and all four of us, Freddie and Lisa and May and I, hooked up again. Freddie married Lisa, because he loved her to bits and was desperate for an heir. They discovered Lisa was infertile. IVF was still a bit science fiction in the 1970s. Freddie spent a fortune on experts and treatments. Until Lisa, broken by disappointment, called a halt. So, he and May..." He offered me a 'you know what I'm saying' gesture. "And Freddie got an heiress. Prematurely. Because the pregnancy didn't go well and May—"

I interrupted him. "Hang on. Wait a minute. What was this? Some kind of deal?"

"Yes... No, not really," he said.

"Did Lisa know about it?"

"Yes. We all did. We were all part of it."

It was my turn to stare out of the window. I was the most not-knowing detective in the Westcountry until this moment. And now... Freddie Settle, May's daughter. The Freddie who had threatened my life, who had Walter Cobb beaten to within an inch of his, and who was now menacing the woman who had kept this secret for over thirty years.

"May only just survived the birth," Bill explained. "Almost bled to death. She convalesced in a very expensive private hospital, and Freddie paid all the bills. She was told she couldn't have any more children. We got married five months later, in September 1982."

"Didn't you want kids?"

"I was in love with May. I never thought about kids."

"And Lisa?"

"She accepted the arrangement from day one. Freddie doted on the baby. And, some years later, when I told him May was opening the shop and the Drop In Centre, Freddie insisted he help out."

I could imagine that. And the unblinking eyes and infamous fixed smile, which settled every dispute.

"He paid the set up costs of both places," Bill said. "He still helps to fund the Centre."

Bill fell silent. He looked down at the table again, as if the answers to all questions lay enshrined in the laminate.

"So when did everything begin falling to bits?" I asked.

"When I helped out Walter Cobb," Bill said. "Four years ago. I paid his debt to Freddie."

"Fifty-six thousand pounds."

"No, he owed Freddie forty-two. The fifty-six was something else."

"What else?"

"I'll get to that," he said.

"Was any of it on the books?"

Bill shook his head. "No."

I picked up the mug, blew on the coffee and drank some more. It gave Bill time to get the next bit of the story in order.

"I've known Walter since we were in the Scouts. I was patrol leader of the Kestrels when he joined the 10th Bristol Troop. He's six years younger than me."

The Scouts...?

It took me a while to get across that idea. My astonishment must have been stencilled on my face, because Bill waved a hand at me.

"Every schoolboy joined the Scouts back in the early 60s." He took a deep breath. "Walter was always a chancer. By the time he left the 10th Bristol, he was running all sorts of mini rackets. And he did alright. A score here, a profit there... He was a hell of a poker player. And one Sunday night, in a motel out on the A38, he won a bundle and the scrap business, in a game of Five Card Draw. At a stroke he was rich. He parleyed that into a bigger chunk of money and set about behaving like a winner. Which I guess he was, for a while. He survived all the fiscal nonsense of 2008. Seemed to be immune. Then he started borrowing. Big sums of money. For another year or two it looked like he was managing to service his debts. Then suddenly, he was on his arse. Broke."

I couldn't let this down and out and bust story go further without adding my quid's worth. I interrupted the flow.

"Sorry to jump in here," I said. "But you do know about *Cobb CI*, and Walter's Jersey endeavours?"

Bill looked genuinely puzzled. "Jersey? No. What do you mean?"

First Freddie, and now Bill. I told him the story of my recent two days in the island. His eyes got wider as we got closer to the reveal.

"So Jersey is where he stashed all his money," Bill said.

"I think he was working up to a carefully planned exit from the UK," I said. "It was his version of the long con. His kipper-tied buffoon thing was brilliant. He'd worked on it for years."

"And he's not broke?"

I flashed back to the warehouse, to his broken looking body.

"Not in financial terms."

"Fucking hell..."

Bill paused for a moment or two. I asked my next question.

"Did Walter organise the Drop In Centre break in?"

"Yes. He needed to find more potential down and outs"

"Why didn't you stop him?"

"I didn't know he was doing it?"

I sat back in the seat. "Oh, Bill, please..."

"I didn't," he insisted.

I bowled him one on the stumps.

"I need the truth, the whole truth and nothing but the truth. And I need you sound and resolute. Whatever happens. Okay?"

He nodded. I asked him where he had spent the last few days. Most of the time at Severn Beach, he said. Then I asked him what he was doing in Arnold Faversham's funeral parlour.

"I wanted to find out where he'd gone." He sat up straight. "How did you know I was there?"

"You rang me. The police were tapping my phones at the time."

"Ah..."

"So where is Faversham?"

"I've no idea."

Of course not. He had disappeared, like every other member of the supporting cast. And I was racking up 'I've no ideas' like meat pies on an assembly line.

Bill sat back again and seemed to relax a little. He was wearing a comfortable old jacket, a light brown shirt and dark brown trousers. He hadn't shaved for a day or two. That was unlike him. Bill was always clean shaven. I looked into his eyes. They were blue, but seemed darker under the shadows produced by the café lights above us. Deep purple rings around them – the proverbial piss holes in the snow. He had lost some weight since I last saw him. And the stress of the past ten days had probably peeled off a bit more.

"Okay," I said. "The blood on the parquet floor?"

"It wasn't mine," he said. "The same blood group though; that was the point. Andrew provided it."

Of course he did. That should have occurred to me. Where else was Bill to get a pint of AB negative?"

"What was this for? To add a bit of drama to the disappearance?"

"I wanted people to think I was dead."

"Including May?"

"Only until I was clear of Freddie Settle."

"Which is why left your laptop and mobile behind. To help with the idea that something serious and un-planned had happened to you."

Bill nodded. "A bit of a risk I know. I did consider that May might hire you."

I reached for the mug. The coffee was a bit cooler suddenly.

"I need a real drink," Bill said. "Let's go to the pub."

I looked at my watch. 1.40. I drained the coffee mug, stood up and followed Bill out into the car park. He unlocked a battered Renault Megane.

"My loaner," he said. "It's Libby's."

263

Five minutes later, we were sitting in the lounge of *The Boar's Head* in Aust village, two pints of Butcombe Gold on the table between us.

"Why did you lend Walter Cobb fifty-six thousand pounds?" I asked.

Bill looked uncomfortable again. I kept at him.

"I need to know, Bill."

He swallowed a mouthful of beer, then put his glass down.

"Okay. It wasn't actually a loan. It was a payment."

"What for?"

"You know May has a twin sister?"

I did know that. She lived in Piraeus. Married to some ex-pat Dutchman. And this seemed miles off the point. Bill assured me it wasn't, then did another long think. Finally he put the words together.

"It's where the whole business began really. With Jenny. She and May are very close, even though Jenny moved to Greece in 1998. Five or six years ago she developed the symptoms of chronic kidney disease. Got on to the donor list, and she and Hugo waited. Eighteen months down the line a kidney became available, but something went wrong, and the operation never happened."

"Did Cobb know about this?"

"Yes. I told him one night, in the *Silver Star*. Around the time he and Andrew were in the process of organising their new business. They met on Jersey late autumn 2012. Andrew had fallen off the wagon after leaving prison and had been drying out in a clinic. His wife and kids had left him by then, but he still had the house around the corner from me. Walter stumbled across him on a beach, recognised him, and they got talking. It was a moment of... synergy... is that the word?"

"Yes."

"Andrew uses it a lot. Well, to cut the story to the bones... Walter made a great show of sympathising with Andrew.

They spent three or four days together and at some point, the subject of what Andrew was going to do next came up. Between them, they dreamed up the operating room scheme. I think even then, Walter was imagining their first patient – Jenny. And back in Bristol they set it up. Andrew ordered all the gear through his Swiss health trust connections. Between them they spent just a bit short of quarter of a million."

"And it wasn't quite enough."

"That's what they said."

"So you offered a little top up finance and Jenny got her transplant."

"That's right. Andrew did the harvesting and the operations."

"And where did the kidneys come from. Who was the donor?"

Bill took a drink, put the glass back on the table and wiped the corners of his mouth with his left thumb and forefinger.

"I don't know," he said. "It's like that in the real world too. The only people fully in the know are the administrators who sign the papers. Donors aren't told where the organs are going and the recipients don't get to know where they come from. Sometimes the surgeons who do the harvesting have no idea who the donor is."

I took a drink too. Bill was slouching again. Not the Bill I knew, not even the Bill I thought I knew. This was a sad, frightened, defeated old man.

"And Walter Cobb found this person?"

Bill nodded. His mouth made the shape of 'yes' but no sound came out.

"Would you have stopped this, had you known what was to follow?"

"But I didn't."

"Not the answer Bill."

He shook his head again. He looked up at me. We stared at each other as if we had forever. Question answered, so I moved the conversation along.

"Why did you have to disappear?"

Bill sighed, ran his fingers through his hair and sighed again. "Do you want another drink?"

I looked at my watch. Three minutes after 2 o'clock. We had time for another half.

Bill got up and moved to the bar. I watched him. He seemed to shuffle, rather than walk. The core of this bloody narrative, in which he was a leading player, was careless, ruthless and shameful. Events rolling on like a soap storyline; as the actors dropped in and out of episodes which spiralled into darker and darker material as the story progressed. Bill came back, put my glass on the table in front of me, and sat down again in front of his. Shrouded in gloom, he stared into his glass as if looking at his reflection in the beer.

"So how did we get to the present crisis?" I asked.

He looked up at me. "Old man Freddie was ill. He'd tripped and fallen down the stairs at home. He had compressed two discs in his back and trapped a series of nerves in the wrong place. It hurt like hell just to turn over in bed. He needed an operation."

"But that wasn't a problem was it?"

"Not in terms of cost," Bill said. "Freddie could afford any bed in the poshest of clinics. The problem was, this city has armies of people who'd love to take over Freddie's business. And word that he was out of sorts, in any way, would be enough to make them start planning. And he knew that checking into a hospital, in this neck of the woods, however private, was a huge risk. Someone was bound to find out."

"So why didn't he charter a Lear Jet and fly to some place in California?"

"He doesn't like America. He doesn't like abroad. He's never left this country at any time in his life. Hell, he hasn't been any farther north than Gloucester. He copes with south Wales, even though he hates the Welsh. Won't go to London on so much as a day trip. The op had to be done secretly, and swiftly. Even the most discreet of private clinics would have been bound to record what was happening. So Walter offered him a solution."

"Featherstone's operating room," I said.

"Andrew was terrified. He knew that the odds of the op being successful were long, and if it didn't work, Freddie might end up worse off. Getting bed baths, pissing and shitting into bags. Andrew told us spines weren't his speciality. But, if pushed, he knew a bloke who was shit hot. Freddie settled for that."

"And the operation went wrong."

"Nobody but the surgical team knows why – whoever and wherever they are. The last time I saw Andrew, must have been just before he disappeared. He was swearing on a stack of bibles he'd never met any of the team, apart from the surgeon. Who has gone on the run, along with everyone else."

"Where did Featherstone get his theatre staff from? Presumably he didn't advertise."

"Apparently there is no shortage of depressed and broke nurses and doctors, knackered after years working against the odds in the NHS."

"When was Freddie's op done?"

"Six days before I er... disappeared."

"And now he is totally incapacitated?"

"Yes."

"So, after announcing that her father had retired, daughter Freddie parachuted in to run the outfit. And set about contemplating what to do to you and Walter and all the rest."

Bill looked frightened again. "Yes. Freddie's not new to the business though. She's been her dad's right arm in the shadows for some time. She just came out into the light, that's all. On a mission."

"Alright," I said. "Freddie has Walter Cobb locked away somewhere, Len Coleman is dead, and you're here with me."

Bill reached for his beer glass, changed his mind, and rested his right arm across his knees. He was anticipating my next question. So I asked it.

"Do you know who killed Len?"

He looked up and stared straight into my eyes.

"Can this stay just between us?" he asked.

"Maybe."

Bill shook his head. "Not good enough, Jack. I need your word on this."

"Okay, you have it."

Bill swallowed. "It was me. I killed him."

This was a hurricane of a surprise. Bill's eyes were locked onto mine. He looked guilty, miserable and frightened; all at the same time.

"Back in the day, I caught up with Len after his last stretch in Horfield. He had money in the bank but you wouldn't know it to look at him. He lived in a—"

I interrupted him. "Yes I know, I've been there."

"Okay... Len didn't gamble much, mainly because when he did he lost. Though it seemed that Freddie senior liked him. Len was allowed to sit around in *The Silver Star* with a beer or two of an evening and enjoy the place, unmolested by staff, and without feeling he had to risk losing his money."

"Why?" I asked.

"I've no idea." He looked at my disbelieving face. "Seriously."

"So how did you really get on with old man Freddie?"

Bill looked surprised.

"Freddie bought my company when I sold up," he said. "Didn't you know? He always had first refusal. It was in the contract we signed. In the late 60s, when Freddie was making more than he could stash away, Uncle Jimmy helped him launder money through the betting shops. Not easy to do now, but then..."

"So, in the end, what went wrong?"

He looked at me. His body language now ferocious, anger in his eyes.

"Walter fucking Cobb. Again. He was a partner in one of the Settle business enterprises. And all was going smoothly. Until he began brown nosing selected *Silver Star* patrons. Cherry picking from Freddie's membership. Offering cut price deals for... well I don't know. I never knew. But Freddie found out."

"Which Freddie?"

"The daughter," Bill said. "As soon as she took the reins. A week before Walter announced he was bankrupt."

"So when he flew to Jersey after I met him, he didn't know what Freddie was contemplating?"

"I guess that would be right."

We sipped our beers. Then I asked about the burnt papers in the fire grate.

"Hard copy of all the recent emails and dealings between me and Len and Walter and Andrew. Freddie was closing in, and I had killed Len. So I was stuck with a double whammy. I got the blood from Andrew, who handed it over without asking questions. I guess he figured that what he didn't know couldn't backfire on him."

We both drank in silence for a while. Then Bill rounded off the dismal narrative.

"So, I shacked up in the caravan with a pile of books and an old laptop which just about got onto the net, via the site owner's wi-fi. And I stayed there, to sit out the days until I dared to get in touch with May."

I stared at him. He read my mind.

"Yes I know," he said. "Not the most well thought out plan in the world. No sensible er... what do they call it...? Exit strategy."

I turned to the sentence with the big question mark.

"Why did you kill Len?" I asked.

Bill sighed, took a deep breath and answered the question.

"I asked him for help. We had been friends a long time. He knew the Settle clan well. He said I should throw myself on Freddie's tender mercies. That might have worked with her Dad, but there was no chance of a result from the new regime. As the hours and days went by, Len became more and more agitated. He asked me to meet him in his flat. He began begging me to face her. We had a hell of a row, which ended up with him threatening to go directly to Freddie."

"Did you believe him?"

"Yes." He grimaced. "That's why I hit him with the candlestick."

"Two or three times," I suggested.

"I had to make sure," he said, suddenly without a trace of emotion in his voice.

"Where is it now? The candlestick."

"As far into the channel as I could throw it from Severn Beach," he said. "It's buried out in the mud somewhere."

Behind me, our host called 'last orders'.

"Dick doesn't like working afternoons," Bill explained. "So he sticks to old fashioned hours. Everybody out by 2.30 on a weekend."

He picked up his beer glass and drained it.

We had to plan the rescue of May out in the car park. The Renault interior smelled like a refuse skip; so we talked in the Healey until we had something half arsed worked out.

Chapter Twenty-Nine

I called Harvey Butler's mobile. He told me he was in his office; reading the paperwork he hadn't had time to read Monday to Friday. George Hood was there too, attempting to explain what the short-hand references and the typos were meant to convey.

Bill and I stood in front of Harvey's desk, actually and metaphorically on the carpet. Harvey stared at Bill, radiating some degree of impatience and not a little menace. I fed the story to him bit by bit, beginning with the more palatable stuff and working up to the complications of the current situation. Under orders from me, Bill didn't speak until he was spoken to. Eventually Harvey did that.

"This is something of an ice cream sandwich, don't you think?"

George Hood came back into the office with a tray. He had been for some coffee. He put the tray down on Harvey's desk.

"Go and get another chair, George." He addressed Bill and me again. "No mention of Len Coleman in all that."

I looked straight into Harvey's eyes, not daring to look at Bill, and hoping he was staring at the carpet.

"Len Coleman's murder is an MIT investigation," I said.

Neither of us blinked. Hood came back into the office with another chair. He sat down next to Bill, the three of us making a small crescent in front of Harvey's desk. He remained looking at me.

"So... As usual, you've shown a remarkable disregard for the methods of those of us who strive for the common weal."

The tricky moment had passed and we were now on familiar ground.

"We haven't got time for satire, Harvey," I said. "I need to talk to Freddie within the hour. If that doesn't happen, May will be killed."

Bill spoke for the first time. "The thing is, Freddie is May's daughter. Only she doesn't know it."

Harvey stared at him.

"The result of er..." Bill faded into silence and looked down at the carpet again.

Harvey chewed over that morsel of information. He looked at his sergeant. Hood shrugged in response. Harvey sat back in his chair.

"May is a prosecution witness," I offered hopefully.

"To what?" Harvey grumbled. "A story that Freddie will deny with such outrage, the echoes will reverberate for weeks. And if whatever we decide to do turns into a dog's breakfast, we could end up with no witnesses at all."

Hood joined the conversation. "Is May hurt?"

"She wasn't when I saw her," I said.

"So no evidence of intimidation or violence," Harvey said.

"So long as we get her back. Christ, Harvey..."

He glared at me. "Indignation won't work either."

He was close to throwing us out. I had to be very careful.

"Look, Harvey, I'm not in denial here. I know that my life won't be worth the price of a taxi ride to the coast once I agree to meet Freddie."

"No question. You may get in to wherever you're going to meet, but you won't get out."

I persisted. "Freddie will let May go as soon as she sees Bill. We can stage manage the handover. And with a little help from you, Bill and I can get out from under as well."

Harvey was listening, but not agreeing yet. I looked at Hood for signs of encouragement. No evidence of any. I turned back to Harvey, who straightened up in his chair, decision made.

"Okay. George. Call in surveillance and get this lunatic wired up."

"Now?" he asked. "Saturday evening? They won't like it."

"*We're* fucking working." He pushed the phone across his desk to me. "Call Freddie. Get her out from wherever she is to somewhere we can get to you when it all goes tits up."

Hood left the office. I called Freddie at *The Silver Star*. She was on the line within seconds.

"Jack..."

I could picture the smile.

"Freddie. I've got Bill. Let's meet."

"Put him on the line."

I handed the phone receiver to Bill. He put it to his right ear and said 'hello'. He asked after May. There was a pause, then Bill became animated.

"Are you alright?" he asked

He listened for a few seconds more then shouted, "May, May..." There was another pause. Bill nodded into the phone. "Yes, understood, yes."

He handed the receiver back to me.

"Where are you both?" Freddie asked.

"We'll meet somewhere neutral," I said.

The location took time to negotiate. We ended up agreeing to meet at 6.30, in a redundant church hall in Barton Hill. A place Freddie had recently bought, apparently. East of Trinity Road and a ten minute drive away. I put the receiver down. Hood had come back into the office and caught the end of the conversation.

"There's a surveillance team on the way," he said. "DCI MacIntosh asked who was going to pay for it."

Harvey nodded at me. "He is."

There was no ceremony attached to being wired up. I was followed into the nearest toilet by the surveillance team radio operator – a man with a close resemblance to Les Dawson. I took my trousers and pants off. The radio man offered me a razor and shaving soap. He stood out in the corridor while I shaved off a chunk of pubic hair. I called him back. He taped a tiny transmitter onto my skin and a microphone behind my jacket collar. He asked me to put my pants back on and scrutinised the effect. Then he said I could put my trousers on too.

"Comfortable?" he asked.

Surprisingly so, considering.

We assembled in the car park. A posse, consisting of DC Holmes and two other DCs in an un-marked car; PCs Laker and De'Ath and another three uniforms in two patrol cars; the radio operator in a Ford Galaxy with tinted windows; Hood, Harvey and me. He nodded towards the patrol cars.

"There's a narrow alley behind the church hall. We haven't had time to check if there is an exit into it. If we find one, the uniforms will cover it."

We moved to the Healey. Harvey reeled off the remaining instructions.

"Leave the car parked under a street light round the corner from the hall. As soon as you know May is fine, tell Freddie that Bill is sitting in your car, and hand over the keys. She'll send one of her broken noses to get him. We'll collar him, then we'll come to the party. You'll have a minute or so to improvise something. Just stay close to the door. If there's bother, I want you where those officers..." he pointed to the un-marked car "... can get to you. Is that clear?"

"Crystal," I said.

We left the station yard in convoy. As we drove into Barton Hill, I could see the Galaxy four or five cars behind me. The backup seemed to have disappeared. At 6.30, I turned into Cannon Street, drove past the church hall and parked round the corner in York Road. The Galaxy arrived and pulled up twenty yards away, at the head of the T.

"On my way, Harvey," I said.

The Galaxy sidelights flashed in acknowledgement and I climbed out of the Healey. Walked around the corner and covered the thirty or forty yards to the hall – set five paces back from the pavement and up half a dozen steps. Robert and the Giant were by the door. Robert smiled, with the enveloping politeness he had displayed last time we met.

"Good evening, Mr Shepherd."

He opened the door and waved me inside the hall. The Giant didn't move.

Freddie said, "Welcome, Jack."

She was standing in the centre of the hall, dressed in blue jeans, silk shirt and tailored red jacket. Her father sat in a wheelchair next to her, motionless. He was wearing a black suit. Two employees, one bald the other dark-haired, both in bespoke tailoring – presumably replacements for the Thomas twins – stood behind him. Freddie introduced them as Messrs Kane and Black. There was a plastic stacking chair with metal legs, six feet in front of the group.

Robert patted me down and stepped away. Changed his mind and stepped back to me. Reached out again, rummaged between my jacket collar and my neck and found the microphone. He held it up, shook his head, sighed, dropped the microphone on the floor and stamped on it. Then took up station to my right.

That bit of the plan wasn't going to work.

The church hall hadn't been used for years. Broken windows had been boarded up from the outside, damp patches discoloured the walls, there were chunks of plaster on the floors. The stage behind my hosts was missing its curtains and most of its wooden floor. Only half of the fluorescent lights in the ceiling were lit.

Freddie told me to sit down. I did so, eyes fixed on Settle père. He didn't look the man who had nodded at me and grinned 'Just you wait' from the dock fifteen years ago; the moment when Judge Alwyn told him he could leave the court, free and clear. Gangster, murderer, thief, extortionist... Now bogeyman turned basket case.

"Why the hell did you buy this place?" I asked.

The only response from him was a twitch of his bottom lip and a blaze of anger in his eyes. Now I could see what the failed op had done to him.

"My father can't speak," Freddie said. "But he can understand what we say. He doesn't go out any more, but he couldn't pass up this opportunity."

Her father's face twitched again. Freddie got down to business.

"Where is Bill Marsh?"

"Where's May?"

"Safe."

"So is Bill, until I know where May is."

Freddie looked beyond me and called out, "Lester..."

I swivelled around in the chair. Lester stepped into the light on the balcony above the door, May at his shoulder. I asked her if she was okay.

"Yes," she said in a hushed voice. The sound carried in the empty hall.

I told Freddie that Bill was sitting in my car. She raised her eyebrows. I told her where it was parked.

She nodded towards Robert. "Give the man the keys."

I stood up, fished them out of my pocket and handed them over. Robert left the hall and closed the door behind him.

Freddie looked up to the balcony again. "Bring the lady down."

May disappeared from view. I heard footsteps cross the balcony and descend the stairs. She was shepherded into view again.

"A few steps forward, May, if you please," Freddie said. "Stop. And now to your left please... Stop. Thank you."

She spoke to Lester again. "Outside please. Lock the door and wait."

Lester did as he was ordered. Freddie switched her attention back to me.

"So..." she began.

I was beginning to sweat. I found myself counting seconds. If the detective squad was on the ball, Robert wouldn't come back. Improvise Harvey had said.

"Why is your father here?" I asked. "If he doesn't get out any more."

This provoked a response from the wheelchair. Slowly Settle began to move his right arm towards his right jacket pocket, grunting with the effort. His daughter answered my question.

"He wanted to see you again."

I watched, fascinated and appalled, as with all the strength he could muster, Settle extracted a lightweight automatic from his pocket. He supported his arm on his right knee.

"Can he fire that?" I asked.

"I don't know. He hasn't tried," Freddie said.

She moved to her father, took the gun from him, released the safety catch and put it back into his hand. Then stepped away from him and looked at me.

"If he doesn't kill you, I will," she said.

Settle raised the gun in the slowest of slow motions, panting and grimacing. The gun wavered and moved to Settle's right, my left. He grunted and pulled the gun back into position. He fired. And missed. The bullet shot past my right elbow and thudded into the wall somewhere behind me.

I lunged at the wheelchair, grabbed the left footrest and hauled the chair upwards. Settle was launched over and back, the chair described a circle in the air and crashed onto its side. The gun slid across the floor. Freddie stuck out an expensive shoe, halted its progress, and picked it up. Kane and Black moved to help Settle. I moved back and to my left, intending to put myself in front of May. But she moved too. Freddie raised the gun and fired at me. The bullet tore the flesh of my left arm just below the shoulder, sped on in a straight line and into May's chest. She yelled out, staggered back under the force of the bullet, then crumpled to the floor. I turned and knelt down beside her. Blood was soaking the front of her blouse. I pulled off my jacket, unfastened the top two buttons on my shirt, and pulled it over my head. I wrapped the shirt into a hand sized bundle and pressed down hard on the wound. May's blood soaked it within seconds.

I sensed Freddie move up behind me. May struggled to stay awake, tried to focus on Freddie. Her mouth moved but no sound came. She managed to turn her head enough to look up at me.

"Jack," she whispered, and died.

I looked up at Freddie. Her face was a mask.

"Do know what you've done?" I asked.

A shot was fired outside. Followed by a wave of yelling. Across the hall, Kane had picked up Freddie Senior and slung him over his shoulder. Black was heading towards a door at the side of the stage. Freddie pointed the automatic at my forehead. She couldn't miss from eight feet. Outside, the yelling subsided. It was followed by a hefty bang on the door.

Then instead of shooting me, Freddie stepped back a pace and gestured at the door through which the others had disappeared.

"Follow them," she said.

There was a second bang on the front door.

Suddenly Freddie wanted me alive. So there seemed no point in getting shot right then – something she would surely get round to if I delayed her long enough. The part of the plan where I saved May had disintegrated into a million pieces. I stood up and looked down at her, all bled out.

There was a third bang on the door, accompanied this time by the sound of splintering wood.

Freddie tossed me my jacket. "Now," she said.

I turned and looked straight into her eyes.

"They who turn and run away..." she said.

I set off in the direction of the door. Beyond it, we followed a passage alongside the stage. Moved into the hall kitchen, smelling of damp, rubbish and rot. Crossed the room and left the building by an exit door held open by Black.

A Range Rover was standing in the lane, engine idling. No straight from the showroom model. It had jacked-up and re-built suspension with a kangaroo bar across the front of the radiator grill and wrapped around the lights. Kane was sitting behind the steering wheel. Settle was strapped into the front passenger seat, his chin down on his chest. Black slammed the hall exit door and caught up with Freddie and me. Freddie climbed into the back seat reached over the head rest in front of her to check on her father.

"I think he's okay," Kane said

Black pushed me into the back next to Freddie and climbed in after me. Kane slid the gear lever into drive and floored the accelerator pedal. We stormed down the lane towards the patrol car parked across the entrance. Slammed into it; driving it out into the cross traffic. I saw one startled face – PC De'Ath behind the steering wheel – then the Range Rover swung left and set off in the direction of the south circular ring road.

To my right, Black bent forward, head between his knees. From under the seat, he produced what looked like an old fashioned police truncheon. He raised it and slammed it down onto the side of my head. The interior of the car spun round before my eyes, my vision blurred, the light around me turned grey and then black.

Chapter Thirty

The world was still dark when I woke up, lying on a mattress on a stone floor; my hands across my stomach tied at the wrists. There was a six peal of bells ringing in my head. I reached for the source of the pain, managing to twist the ties so that the fingers on my right hand could locate the injury. No wound, but one hell of a bump. I tried to sit up, using my left elbow as a lever. Whereupon another helping of pain seeped from my upper arm into my shoulder. I could feel a bandage wrapped tight. I slumped back to the floor. I rolled to my left, and this time got up into a sitting position. I was wearing my jacket and my vest, but no shirt.

Then I remembered why.

And then I remembered re-gaining consciousness in the Range Rover with a sack over my head, travelling some distance in the dark and being bundled into a house. Somebody relieved me of the radio transmitter. Somebody else looked at my wound and bandaged it. Then I was dragged down steps, along a corridor, into this room, told to sit on the mattress and had the sack taken off my head. My escort left the room and locked the door.

It was pitch black in wherever I was. I decided not to blunder around in the dark and lay back on the mattress. After a while, I fell asleep.

When I woke up again the room was brighter. I looked around me, waiting for my eyes to adjust to the dark. Details of shapes brightened a bit and my eyes re-focused. I got to my knees and from there managed to stand up. I did a careful 360 degree turn and didn't trip over anything. There was a dim light source, above head level, on the wall I was facing. Some sort of reinforced glass window. I could now see across the floor. I took four steps towards the light and realised it was a grating, two feet above me at ground level. I could see weeds growing round the edge of it.

I was in a wine cellar; unfortunately without wine. The place was furnished with empty racks. Obviously, once upon a time, someone had a substantial collection of chateau bottled vintages.

The watch Emily bought me three Christmases ago is a retro design timepiece, with hands rather than digits and no button to press to light up the face. So no way to tell the time. I mooched around a bit and found a couple of wine boxes. I sat down on one and began to ponder. After a while, I realised that the light through the grating was brighter. Which gave some clue as to time. May Day. Dawn at what time? Five, five-thirty? I had stiffened up sitting on the box, so I got to my feet and began to walk backwards and forwards across the cellar. I found myself thinking of the great prisoners of literature – Edmond Dantès, the Man in the Iron Mask, the Birdman of Alcatraz. And my namesake, Jack Shepherd, an enterprising thief who had escaped from Newgate and other prisons on a regular basis, and even from the hangman at Tyburn once. That was four hundred years ago however, and the hangman did get him the second time.

The sound of footsteps approaching the door brought me back to reality. I stood in the centre of the floor. The door opened and Kane produced a serious piece of hardware from under his left arm. Not unlike the gun Dylan had used to blow holes in the Healey windows. He stood in the doorway, radiating 'Don't mess me with me pal'.

"Good morning," I said.

He waved me past him into a stone flagged corridor. "Don't rush. Turn to your left at the end."

We took another left, climbed a stone staircase, and emerged into James Warburton's Great Hall. Kane pointed towards the kitchen.

"That way."

I looked at my watch as we crossed the hall. 6.35.

Black and Freddie were sitting at the kitchen table. Freddie asked me if I knew where I was. I told her I had no idea. She chose to believe that, pulled out a chair from under the table and invited me to sit. Asked if I'd like some breakfast. I said eggs Benedict and caviar were a regular thing in my house. Black offered to punch my lights out. Freddie grinned and told me I'd have to work hard to keep my spirits up as the morning went on. I asked why someone had taken the trouble to bandage my arm. She said she had more substantial stuff scheduled for me than bleeding out on a cellar floor. Lodged in the back of my mind, currently un-retrievable, was something I'd been meaning to ask her.

* * *

An hour later the Great Hall had filled up. At least that's what it sounded like from my position in the kitchen, roped to a table leg and scowled at by Black. He was clearly miserable by nature and was wearing a deodorant I could smell from ten feet away.

At 7.45, Freddie materialised again, followed by Kane. All business now.

"Free him from the table."

She waited as Black set to work. Then I remembered the question I wanted to ask.

"What was so special about Len Coleman? I heard he was something of an insider. Never had to pay for his drinks."

Freddie thought about the question for a moment and decided to answer.

"Back in the midst of time, Coleman and my Dad had a thing going. Friends from the old hood. A kinship based on decades of deals, and growing up in the back street badlands. All the old tribal shite. Bollocks, all of it, but you know how it worked back then. Coleman traced the employee who ran over Jimmy Marsh. And my father, as lord of the manor, dealt with the matter. Coleman was loaned to Bill Marsh. Basically to keep an eye on him. The hospitality deal followed."

"So why terrorise Bill? He's not got a role in any of this." For a second, she was almost betrayed by the family smile. "Or has he?"

"He inherited the arrangement my father had with Uncle Jimmy. It worked, in the old backyard honour way. And Bill did well out of it. But in some misguided impulse, he paid off Walter Cobb's debt to the company, so that my father could cut him loose. I can't recall how much it was."

"Forty-two thousand pounds," I said.

Freddie took a couple of step across the kitchen, eyes suddenly blazing in anger.

"You know what, Jack? Bill just got in the fucking way... I'm tired of the old gangster network thing; a favour here, a drink there; you take south of the river, I'll take the north. I'm pissed off with handshakes and deals which are brokered on the basis of secret ambitions – you look after the bloke I'm chasing, I'll nail this miscreant to the warehouse floor. It means fuck all, Jack. It belongs back in the day, with the Krays and the Richardsons, the celebrity, the gang wars and the paranoia. Bill Marsh, Len Coleman, Walter Cobb, and the unwanted attention they bring to organised crime... They are all in the fucking way."

She looked at Black; the anger gone as quickly as it had appeared.

"Tie his wrists again, and bring him outside."

The Range Rover we had left the church hall in was parked alongside a Defender in the stable block yard. Three people I hadn't seen before – two men and one woman wearing moleskin trousers, boots and camouflage jackets – climbed in the Range Rover. Kane put the cloth sack over my head once more. I was shoved onto the rear seat of the Defender and joined by Black and his deodorant. Freddie got into the driver's seat. No Kane. He was obviously driving the other vehicle.

"Alright back there?"

"Fine," Black said.

Freddie turned on the ignition. And we began a trundle deep into eighteen hundred acres of Mendip forest. I tried to count the rights and lefts and estimate the distances between them, but it was an exercise of diminishing returns. The Defender leant over a number of times, dipped and bounced in and out of holes. I lost all sense of direction and time. Then we stopped, and Freddie cut off the engine. Black opened the passenger door on his side and heaved me out of my seat. I was escorted along a pathway, stumbling ankle deep into holes and tripping over tree roots. I began to feel sick, hoping it was only because of my companion's deodorant. He pulled me to a standstill. My wrists were freed and the sack pulled off my head.

The daylight was fierce. I closed my eyes, opened them again, massaged my eye sockets as much as my bound wrists would allow, and looked around me.

We were in a kind of glade; a small, moss coated amphitheatre, about twenty yards in diameter, surrounded by trees. I was standing in the centre, facing the camouflage jackets, all three now wearing baseball caps. Freddie was to my right, Kane and Black behind her.

She smiled, all welcoming bonhomie, and began to speak.

"Lady and gentlemen, welcome to our morning of sport. Your prey is a change from the person billed. A more formidable sample than you might have imagined. In a couple of minutes, each of you will be issued with a .357 light weight rifle, pre-loaded with ten rounds. Mr Shepherd here, will be set loose and given a ten minute start. You will then be free to hunt him down."

Absurdly, my first thought was 'Does James Warburton realise this is going on?' It was followed by a massive jolt of fear and now seriously growing nausea. Three hunters, three rifles and thirty rounds of ammunition. Freddie continued, holding up a circular object about the size of ten pence coin.

"One of these will be pinned on to your jackets. A wire-less transmitter which will enable us to track you, find you if you get lost, and pick you up when the hunt is over. Mr Shepherd will be wearing a monitoring tag, locked onto his right ankle. We will know where he is throughout the excitement. You will not."

It was small comfort that there appeared to be a uniform and rules to this exercise, one sided though it was.

Kane opened the wooden case at his feet. He took out three rifles and passed them to Freddie. She spoke to the man closest to her.

"Mr Lord... you prefer the lever action I understand. It's a Browning."

Lord stepped forward and took the rifle.

"Ms Baron. Lever action for you, too. A Winchester; it's lighter. And Mr Knight, you requested the pump action. A Remington."

Black pinned a transmitter to the jacket lapel of each hunter. Freddie ordered me to sit down, and Kane clipped a tracker onto my right ankle. I watched him closely, in case there was the remotest chance I'd be able to take it off. The strap was leather, and attached to the fabric of the transmitter case with leather rivets. Freddie told me to stand up. Kane cut the rope binding my wrists. Black climbed into the Range Rover. Moments later the tracker and the transmitters were activated.

Freddie stepped back a pace. "Good luck, Jack." For a moment I felt as if she actually meant it. "Make your choice. Any direction you'd like to take."

I looked around. The woodland was dense whichever way I faced. Freddie looked at the slim Rolex on her wrist. My heartbeat had risen into the hundreds. She lifted her head again and looked straight into my eyes.

"Go, Jack."

I looked at my watch and went. In what I hoped was a straight line.

Experts say that such a thing is an impossibility on terrain which doesn't vary and has no landmarks. They point to pictures of footprints in the desert which simply go round in circles. Apparently we lose all sense of direction when we have no idea where we are going. I looked at my watch. Two minutes gone, eight minutes to go. That was when I came up with a kind of plan. If I didn't know where I was, then there was no point in going anywhere. I decided I should leave the hunters to find me. What I was going to do at that point I had no idea. But hell, one step at a time.

I walked on for another five minutes, beating the undergrowth around me, crushing ferns and breaking low branches, leaving a trail to follow.

At zero plus seven, I stopped moving and found a shallow moss covered foxhole. It had a three hundred and sixty degree view. I collected clods of earth and ground covering plants, dragged branches to the hiding place, ringing it as best I could. The camouflage wouldn't have fooled Baden Powell, but it was probably enough for present circumstances. Most of the club sized pieces of wood I found were rotten and fell to bits in my hand. I did find one which seemed solid. I tested it by trying to break it over my knee. It didn't, and hurt my knee in the process. I dug a solid piece of stone out of the moss, small enough to hold in my hand, limped back to the foxhole and dropped down into it.

My shoulder began to hurt. The moss was soft to lie on. But I had to arrange myself into a position which I could hold without moving, and see around me at the same time. After another frantic minute or so, I managed to do that, favouring my shoulder in the process.

I waited. For minutes.

In a world of total silence. Apart from the odd rustle to my right and left. Soft and whisper loud. Small animals of some sort.

Then to my right, maybe thirty yards away – I couldn't pinpoint exactly where because I couldn't see anything without breaking cover – I heard the unmistakable noise of someone on two legs moving through undergrowth. He, or she, passed by, and my world fell silent again.

A minute or so later, the same noise seeped onto the soundtrack from somewhere dead ahead. I looked through the foliage around the rim of the foxhole. Mr Knight – he of the pump action Remington – appeared, stopped, and listened. Carefully, I took hold of one of the ground cover plants and I shook it; producing a sound just loud enough for him to hear. He looked around. I watched and waited. As he turned his head into my line of sight, I moved the plant a couple of inches to my left, wiggled it, then got down as low as I could. He raised his rifle and sighted it on the plant. He fired. I yelled out in response. I heard Knight pump the next bullet into the chamber. I groaned.

Then he was above me, leading with his left leg. I rose and swung the piece of wood in one motion. It slammed into his ankle. He over-balanced, fell sideways, and rolled on to his back still holding on to the Remington. It took him too long to realise what was happening. I was out of the foxhole and standing over him in tenths of a second. I stamped down hard on the wrist holding the rifle, dropped beside him and slammed the stone onto the bridge of his nose. He screamed. Blood poured from the wound. I prised the rifle out of his hand, tore the transmitter from his jacket, stood up and threw it as far as I could. Then turned away from the foxhole and threw up.

When I looked back at Knight, he was choking and crying in pain.

I'd only seen pump action guns in American TV series and Steven Seagal movies. The Remington was smaller than I had expected, with a custom made stock and a short barrel. I sighted on his right thigh and fired. He yelled once again and passed out. I pumped another bullet into the chamber, bent down, transferred the baseball cap from his head to mine, unbuttoned his jacket, turned him on to his face, pulled his arms back and up and hauled the jacket off him. I put it on, rolled him into the foxhole and dropped my own jacket on top of him.

Now what? I've never been a fan of TV survival shows. I began to wish I had paid more attention.

Someone was approaching from my right. I added Knight's baseball hat to my costume and turned my back. Stared down into the foxhole. Whoever was coming might believe, at least for a moment or two, that I was Knight. I listened to the footsteps. They stopped.

"Mr Knight..."

I turned round, and pointed the Remington at Ms Baron.

"There's a cartridge in the chamber," I said.

She stood still, the Winchester in her right hand pointing at the ground.

"Throw it over here," I said. The rifle landed at my feet. "Now lie down. On your face."

She did that.

The Remington had eight cartridges left. The lever action Winchester had ten. I now had more fire power than Mr Lord, but no one can fire two rifles at the same time. At least I can't. John Wayne could, but this wasn't *Rio Bravo*. And no time to dither.

I moved to Baron. Told her to roll onto her back. She did and looked up at me. She had looked tough when I first saw her in the stable block, but now I could see sweat on her forehead. I fired into the ground to the left of her. She flexed, as though I'd put a charge of electricity though her body. I asked her if she knew Knight and Lord. She shook her head.

"I met them for the first time, this morning."

"Have you got a mobile?" I asked.

She looked down the front of her jacket. "In the right hand pocket."

"Take it out."

She found it and clutched it tight.

"Unlock it please."

She looked at the phone. Perhaps working out the odds on me actually shooting her. I counted to five and fired again; this time to the right of her head. She dropped the mobile, scrabbled for it, found it and unlocked it. I pumped another cartridge. She stretched out her arm. I took the phone from her.

"Now roll over again. Back on to your face."

I called George Hood's mobile. It went to message.

"George," I said. "This a matter of life and death. I mean it. No exaggeration. Call me as soon as you get this."

I tried Harvey's mobile. That went straight to message also. I repeated what I had said to Hood. I stepped back a couple of paces, bent down, picked up the Winchester and ordered Baron to get to her feet. Waved her in the direction of the foxhole. She stood looking down at Knight, still unconscious.

"Next to him," I said. "Face down."

She got into the foxhole. Shuddered as she stretched out.

The mobile rang. I dropped the Winchester and answered the call.

"Where the hell are you?" Harvey asked.

"I'm on top of the Mendips on *The High Combe Estate*. You get to it from the road between Priddy and Charterhouse. I need your help. There is a manhunt going on. Freddie has a three people trying to kill me. And there are—"

"What?"

I thought I was being succinct enough. I began again. He interrupted.

"No Jack, I've got it. I just don't believe it."

"Jesus Christ, do you think I'd make up something like this? People are creeping around here in the woods with .357 rifles." I raised the Remington and fired it. "Hear that?"

"How do we find you?"

"God knows," I said. "Drive on to the estate with as many cars as you can muster, making as much noise as possible. Keep the sirens running. And bring something hefty to open the gates. They're probably locked. Big cast iron things. And get here bloody quickly. I'll keep this phone live."

I ended the call. Looked down into the foxhole again.

"Ms Baron, do you have a knife?"

She said no. I pumped a fifth cartridge into the Remington. Then I heard Lord shout. "Knight... Baron."

I pointed the Remington at Baron. "Don't say a word."

I stepped back a pace. Fired the Remington into the air. Shouted Lord's name. Pumped another cartridge into the chamber and shouted again. He shouted back. I located the direction of the sound. Moved around the foxhole and crouched into cover on the other side. Now I could hear him moving. He called again. I called back. Then I saw him, twenty yards from me, negotiating his way through a cluster of shrubs and young trees. Fifteen yards. Twelve. Ten... He stopped and shouted again. I stood up and pointed the Remington at his chest. He stared at me.

"Drop the Browning," I said.

He thought about it. I shifted the Remington a degree or two and fired. The bullet smacked into a tree trunk inches from his head. Bits of bark sprayed out. A piece went into his left eye. He flinched, yelled, dropped the Browning, and raised both hands to his eye. I re-loaded the Remington. Three shots left.

Lord was grunting and cursing. He stopped and squinted in my direction.

"Over here," I said.

He moved towards me, still fiddling with his eye. He tripped over an ant hill and fell on to his face.

"Stay where you are."

I moved back to the foxhole and ordered Baron to her feet. I pointed in Lord's direction.

"Over there."

She moved towards him. I stopped her a couple of strides short. I told Lord to sit up and unbutton his jacket. I asked if he had a knife. He mumbled. I pointed the Remington at his head. He said 'yes', fished around in his jacket pockets, found it and tossed it to me. It dropped to the ground a yard in front of me – a slim, stainless steel, short blade case knife. I looked back at Lord.

"Take your jacket off, but don't shift your arse." He shrugged out of it. "Give it to Baron." He stretched out his arm. She looked at me. "Take it from him." She collected it by a sleeve.

"Now take off your jacket, and tie the sleeve in your hand to one of yours. A reef knot. You know, right over left and under, left over right and under." She did that. "Now pull on both sleeves and check the knot is tight." She did, and it was. "Okay. Sit down, back to back with Lord." She sat down. "Keep the knotted sleeves in front of you and pass the two other jacket sleeves to Lord, left side and right." I crabbed sideways into Lord's line of sight. "Help her." Lord reached behind, groped about a bit, found both sleeve ends and pulled them around in front of his chest. I told Baron to slide her arms inside the ring of jackets and sleeves, and Lord to pull tighter. I stepped closer to Lord; still squinting and blinking. I told him to put his hands into his trouser pockets. He hesitated. I fired a shot over Baron's left shoulder. The Remington was angled down. The bullet ploughed into the ground two yards in front of Baron, kicking up grass and dirt. She yelled out. Lord stuffed his hands into his pockets. I knelt in front of him, laid the Remington down out of his reach, picked up the sleeve ends, linked them right over left and pulled tight. Baron yelled again. Lord arched his back as best he could and shouted, "Alright alright."

I completed the knot, picked up the Remington, walked back to the knife lying in the grass and collected it.

The odds against me getting to the end of the day had shortened considerably. Knight's transmitter was now part of the great outdoors. Baron and Lord were still wearing theirs. I was still wearing the tag. But we were all in the same place and not moving. So if Freddie, Kane and Black were awake, they'd realise that the wrong person was in charge. Waiting for the opposition to arrive had been successful so far. And when plan A works, don't invent a plan B. If I sat down beyond where Lord broke cover, I'd be facing the way the bad guys would come.

I dropped to my haunches in front of Baron. She stared at me. She had green eyes. I gestured behind me.

"I'm going over there. You two will be in my line of sight. If there is any commotion from you when our hosts arrive, I will shoot you."

It seemed she believed that. Behind her, Lord hadn't moved. I called to him. "Did you hear that?"

"Yes, yes."

I stepped back and sat down, opened Lord's knife, slid the blade under the leather sleeve of the tag, and began to saw. It took no time at all. The leather rivets popped and the tag fell off my ankle. I picked it up, got to my feet, swung round to face the other way and threw it as far as I could – my theory being, that if I appeared to be some distance beyond Lord and Baron, then our hosts would feel more inclined to break cover and go to the assistance of their clients. I was also working on the assumption that this kind of incident had not happened before. So telling myself I'd set this up as best I could, I moved into the bushes, picking up the Browning and the Winchester on the way.

There were two rounds left in the Remington and ten in the other rifles. I was the prey and I had done all the shooting, and so far, I hadn't killed anybody. I fervently hoped it would stay that way. *I'm A Detective Get Me Out Of Here...*

I looked at my watch again. Ten minutes since I had talked with Harvey. It would take another half hour at least, for a fast patrol car and the best of drivers to get here from Bristol. Perhaps twenty minutes from Wells. But convincing the Somerset Constabulary that this escapade was not someone's 'film of the day' fantasy, would have used up precious time.

The mobile rang again. I grabbed it.

"ETA twenty-five minutes," Harvey said.

I wanted him to say 'listen out for the sirens, we're tear-arsing down the drive'.

"There are two armed officers in this car, and two in the patrol car behind us. Hang on..."

The sound of detectives talking fast, underscored by a speeding car engine, was all I could hear for a few seconds. Then Harvey came back to me.

"And there's a posse on the way from Wells. The man in charge lives up on the Mendips. He knows the estate. ETA twelve minutes."

That sounded better.

Harvey ended the call. I switched the mobile to silent and put it in a trouser pocket where I'd feel it buzz against my skin.

And sat back in the undergrowth to wait.

Chapter Thirty-One

My shoulder was hurting again, but it didn't appear to be bleeding. I began to feel hungry; which I guessed was a good sign. But I was turning cold, in spite of being wrapped in the camouflage jacket. The sweat had dried on me, the overnight dew was soaking my backside. At least it was a bright morning. No cloud cover and no wind. You could hear a sparrow fart at twenty paces.

I couldn't help thinking what Emily would have made of this. I wondered what Chrissie and the household were doing now. I counted back over the hours. I hadn't see Linda for almost two days. If I wasn't sitting on my arse in the woods, I could be having breakfast with her.

And then I began wondering how good Kane and Black were at this revved up field craft. The manhunt business was clearly a regular thing. It had a uniform and rules of engagement. So where did the prey come from? I began thinking about Walter Cobb and his resurrection men. Cobb had clearly annoyed Freddie. Why else would he have been sitting on display in the warehouse, propped up like Billy Clanton in the undertaker's window in Tombstone. After all, you could say that Cobb was working in a related field. Maybe he was Freddie's prey supplier. And maybe she had decided Walter's moonlighting as a supplier of body parts for Faversham was a breach of security.

It wasn't a bad theory. It was just bloody aggravating to come up with it in the current circumstances. Cobb could be dead by now. He might be buried in these woods. Somewhere in the eighteen hundred acres along with the previously hunted.

I wondered how much Freddie charged these perverted rich folk with money and time on their hands. Ten, fifteen, twenty thousand per ticket? She didn't have any R&D to pay for and no overheads. The guns were good, but still not more than five or six hundred quid each. The ammunition was peanuts. The jackets were around what, thirty quid? In my next moment of boredom I could price up this endeavour and work out how much Freddie was making every Sunday.

There was a noise ahead of me, beyond the opposite side of the glade. I tightened my grip on the Remington. The noise died away. Kane and Black were listening for sounds ahead of them too. I sat still and waited. Looked at my watch. If the Wells team was on time, we should hear the sirens in a bit less than five minutes. The mobile vibrated in my pocket. I struggled to get at it, trying not to move and give away my position.

"Harvey," I hissed into the phone. "There are two men, maybe twenty-five yards away. They haven't seen me yet, but it's a matter of moments."

"You should hear the sirens in three or four minutes," he said, and rang off.

At least I didn't need to conduct the next piece. I was in charge of this situation as thoroughly as I could be. Just had to sit and wait for Kane and Black to break cover.

There was a rustle at eleven o'clock. The sound grew in volume. Kane came into focus. He stopped. Now he had a view across the glade. He could see Baron and Lord, tied back to back. Lord was shaking his head furiously bumping up and down on the moss. Tied to him, Baron was getting hurt in the process. Kane looked back over his left shoulder. There was more rustling, which grew in volume. Black appeared at one o'clock. I turned my head slightly and got both men in my eye line. A moment before I got cramp in my right thigh. It hurt like nobody's business. I tried not to move.

A moment later I had to do so anyway. Lord bellowed out that I had gone that way. He must have jerked his head to help indicate the direction, because it bounced off the back of Baron's. She cried out in shock and pain.

Keeping quiet didn't matter now. I moved my leg, bent it at the knee and massaged my thigh. Black looked at Kane for orders. Baron had joined in the yelling. I barrel rolled a few yards to my left, got up onto one knee, sighted to the left of Kane and fired the Remington. The bullet skimmed his shoulder and scythed through the bushes behind him. He dropped to the ground and shuffled back into cover again. Black did the same. I fired the last shot in the chamber over his head, threw the gun away and picked up the Winchester. I waited, listening for the slightest movement.

Baron and Lord had stopped yelling. They were grumbling currently. Appeared to have fallen out. They began wriggling about and bouncing up and down. I fired a shot to their right. They stopped immediately.

If Kane and his associate were thinking, they would each make a wide circle to the left and right and get round behind me. From nine o clock I heard rustling again. Then somewhere in the way beyond, the sound of police sirens seeped into the silence. And grew louder and louder. The cavalry had arrived, making enough noise to wake the dead and, in the process, drowning out all the sounds around me. Kane and Black could tap dance up to me with a full orchestra playing and I wouldn't hear them.

Now or never Shepherd...

I picked up the Browning, and with a rifle in each hand, ploughed forwards. Nobody shot at me. I sprinted past Lord and Baron who were yelling stuff I couldn't hear. I dived into the foliage ahead and picked up what I assumed was Kane's track towards the glade. I could retrace his steps back to the vehicles. I was moving now, as fast as the woodland would permit. I stumbled several times and tripped up twice. I was breathing heavily, taking in great gulps of air. I decided to risk calling Harvey. I stopped moving, swung round to look behind me, put the Winchester down and thumbed his mobile number. He answered on the second ring. I told him I was okay, but the sirens were now a mixed blessing.

"Do you want me to call them off?"

"Ask them to leave one running. I can use it as location fix."

"Roger that. Our driver reckons we are six or seven minutes away."

Kane's trail was still clear enough to follow, even moving along at the miles per hour I was managing to generate. I was spending so much time looking down and left and right, I forgot what might be ahead. It came back to me as I stumbled from Kane's track out into the open.

Where Freddie was standing by the Range Rover, pointing an automatic at me for the second time in a little more than twelve hours.

I stood in front of her. My chest heaving, my arms by my sides, a rifle in each hand. She had turned the Range Rover around. It was facing the way we had come. The left side front and rear passenger doors were open.

"Put the rifles on the back seat," she said.

"I don't think so," I said.

"Don't give me the Bruce Willis stuff again. I may need a hostage to get out of here, but I would rather shoot you than waste any more time. Where are my clients?"

"I left Mr Knight with a broken nose and a bullet in his thigh. Ms Baron and Mr Lord were tied up when I last saw them."

"And my associates, where are they?"

"No idea."

"In which case, we'll quit the field." She waved the automatic at the Range Rover. "Do as I say. Rifles onto the back seat, please."

I walked to the car.

"Stop there," she said. "Throw them in, close the door, and step this way."

I did all that.

"You drive," she said. "But get in from this side." She pointed to the front passenger door. I moved towards it. "Slide across."

I climbed in shuffled across the mid-seats console and slid behind the steering wheel. Freddie climbed into the passenger seat. The single siren was still echoing through the woods.

Freddie stayed cool, eyes fixed on me. "Don't dawdle. But be careful."

I switched on the engine, selected drive, pressed the accelerator, and we began to move.

"Turn left up ahead," she ordered. "We're going out the back door."

Another way to get into and out of the estate. I hadn't thought about that.

Fifty yards later, we broke out of the dense woodland onto a dirt track.

"Right," Freddie said. "And speed up a little please."

I swung right. We took another left and another right and then turned onto the best piece of road so far. Dead ahead, a couple of hundred yards or so, was another double gate. Just as substantial as the version at the main entrance. There was a lodge to our right as we approached.

"You'll have to get out to open these gates," Freddie said. "And they open towards us, so leave room."

I pulled up level with the front door of the lodge. Freddie passed me a big key; the sort of engineering they locked Guy Fawkes away with. I got out onto the road, left the driver's door open and walked around it. As I did so, George Hood stepped out of the lodge door and pointed a hefty .38 revolver at Freddie's head.

"This is a far as you go. Please drop the gun on to the floor at your feet."

Freddie did as she was told.

Hood called back over his shoulder. "Get out here, Sherlock." Holmes appeared. "Ms Settle has put her gun down. Go and get it."

Moments later, DC Holmes had all the guns, and Freddie was sitting in handcuffs in the back seat of the Range Rover sandwiched between two uniforms. And I was congratulating Hood on his brilliance.

"Almost didn't happen," he said. "We shot past this gate ten minutes ago, doing over eighty. The Super yelled at the driver to stop. We hadn't thought about another way in or out."

"Neither had I. So congratulations."

Hood grinned. "Glad to see you. Sorry we cocked up yesterday evening."

"How's Bill?"

"In pieces. Finding May dead on the floor, well..."

"Where is he?" I asked.

"In a holding cell at Trinity Road," Hood said.

We both took time to breathe.

"Now what?" I asked.

"I phone the others and tell them to turn that fucking siren off. And then we all assemble in front of the house."

* * *

Ten minutes later, outside the house, another battalion of coppers arrived. The whole Wells swing shift had been called up, complete with loudspeakers and megaphones. The DCI in charge asked me about the fire power in the woods. He was Welsh; a north Somerset version of Windsor Davies.

"One of the hunters is out of action," I said. "The other two are unarmed. Freddie's two associates have a rifle each. They may have hand guns also."

Then I told him about the tracking system they were using.

"Just leave all that to us, Mr Shepherd. We'll get the buggers out of there, don't you worry."

Harvey tapped me on the shoulder.

"Do you want to have any last words with Ms Settle before we take her away?" He nodded to our right. "She's in the patrol car over there."

I walked over to it. The PC standing by the rear door opened it and stepped to one side. I joined Freddie on the seat. She turned her head and looked at me.

"We'll do this again sometime, Jack," she said.

"Probably not," I said. "There's a wide trail back to you and your wrong doing. And it will get wider as your associates start singing."

"So what do you want to say to me?"

"May Marsh was your mother." I stared into her eyes. She stared back, without blinking. "The result of a brief liaison between her and your father. Deals were done. You were handed over. And nobody said anything more about it. Until Bill told me, yesterday."

Her mouth moved and her lips parted, but she had no words to say.

"You took your mother hostage and you killed her," I said.

I got out of the car, nodded at the PC and he closed the passenger door. I walked towards Harvey without looking back. Behind me, I heard the patrol car fire up and pull away.

Another patrol car gave me a lift back to Barton Hill.

Chapter Thirty-Two

The two uniforms in the front seats talked sparingly; keeping the volume fader at minimum and making no effort to include me in any snatches of conversation. I was grateful. I sprawled on the back seat and tried to relax. The adrenalin in my system seeped away. By the time we cruised into the suburbs of south Bristol my chest was no longer thumping and my heartbeat felt as it should.

I was allowed to collect the Healey on the strict understanding I then drove straight to Trinity Road. I unlocked the car and fished my mobile out of the driver's door pocket. No juice in the battery, no way to call Chrissie or Linda. Mercifully. I wasn't ready to re-run the story of my weekend.

I reported to Harvey's office. He began proceedings by telling me that Bill had confessed to the murder of Len Coleman.

"The thing is, we had no reason to suspect him. We would have accused Freddie of ordering the hit, she would have denied the charge, and we would have gone on dancing and weaving."

"I think Bill would have considered it untidy not to confess," I said. "I guess, deep down in his broken heart, he doesn't care what happens now. Can I see him?"

Harvey shook his head. Sadly I thought. "Not right now, Jack."

The truth was, a lot of people's lives would be poorer with Bill and May gone. People on both right and wrong sides of the law.

We talked about Freddie. I asked Harvey if she had revealed what she did with Walter Cobb.

"No," he said. "Not that she's saying much at all at the moment. When asked about him, she said 'Walter who?' She's down in the basement with her brief. And behind George and Sherlock, a long line of detectives from Burglary, Vice and the Special Crimes Unit are queuing up to interrogate her."

I gave Harvey my theory about Cobb's hubris backfiring on him, and Freddie taking umbrage at his body parts freelancing. He seemed to agree with it. I thanked him for rescuing me. He told me to go and find DC Holmes, who would interview me for the record and take my statement. He stood up and stretched his right arm across the desk. I shook his hand; both of us recognising this moment for what it was. A cease fire, in an ongoing bending and stretching of rights and wrongs, albeit with both of us on the same side. Sort of.

* * *

I drove home, bought an *Observer* on the way, parked the Healey outside my front door, went into the house and poured a small brandy. I sipped it slowly.

Half an hour later, showered and shaved, I examined the shoulder wound. It needed a stitch or two, but it was clean and had stopped bleeding. I managed to dress and bandage it again, keeping it in place by winding a length of Elastoplast tape around my arm. I glided down the stairs. The answer light on the phone base in the hall was blinking. In the kitchen I poured a bowlful of *Special K*. Back in the hall I pressed the message play button, and spooned the cereal into my mouth as I listened. There were five calls; three from last night. The first, timed at 7.04, was from Linda. *Where are you, Jack? Call me.* The second message was from Chrissie, at 7.09. *Hi dad. Where are you? Fancy coming over for dinner?* There was another call from Linda, at 8.54. *Jack, are you so busy you can't pick up a phone?* The fourth, was another from Chrissie, who had called again less than an hour ago. *Are you at Linda's? I'll try again later.* And the last call was a message from Linda, left while I was in the shower. *You can be so fucking annoying, Jack. Where the hell are you?*

I rinsed the cereal bowl in the kitchen sink. The clock on the wall said 10.05.

Feeling better and firm of purpose, I de-constructed the cardboard boxes still piled in the hall, flattened them, stowed them in the boot of the Healey, and took them to the Recycling Centre in Sainsbury's car park on Winterstoke Road. On the way home, I parked in front of the office building. I walked into the cavern under the road. There was no one there. The villagers had gone. All evidence of their occupation had been cleared away. The noise from the road above pounded on.

I called Linda. It took some time to get the story told. I managed to parley it into a degree of sympathy. I offered to buy lunch; then rang Chrissie and invited her and Adam too. We drove up into the Cotswolds in Adam's Espace. The afternoon went well and I spent the night in Portishead.

* * *

On Monday, shortly after midday, I drove up to the *High Combe Estate*, intending to call on James Warburton; now back at home, amazed and furious in equal measure. I didn't get beyond the lodge gate. I spoke to him by phone from the Estate Manger's Office.

"I am truly sorry I deceived you, James."

He disconnected the call.

The following day, I traced Molly and Don, now living in a damp and draughty shed at the back of a car breaker's yard in Hengrove.

Irving from the Public Mortuary called two days later, with news of Martin's funeral. I joined Molly and Don at the crematorium. Along with the priest, we were the only people there.

I located the manager's office and asked about Lily. The manager recalled a visit from her sister.

"Mrs Maxted paid for a brick in the Wall of Remembrance," he said. "You'll find it at the end of the Memorial Garden."

The words on it read *Lillian Margaret Barrett. 1973-2015. No Longer Lost.*

Later that afternoon, two and a half miles across the city, Chrissie and I, Adam, Helen, Monica and Harry from the Drop In Centre, George Hood, a host of May's neighbours, and Bill escorted by two police officers, attended May's funeral.

* * *

At 7 o'clock the following morning, Bill was found lying on the floor of his remand cell; blood from his wrists – his own AB negative this time – staining the linoleum; a razor blade a couple of feet away from him. He was pronounced dead at the scene.

THE END

About the Author

Jeff Dowson began his career working in the theatre as an actor and a director specialising in productions of modern British and European playwrights. From there he moved into television as an independent writer/producer/director. Screen credits include arts series, entertainment features, drama documentaries, drama series and TV films. Turning crime novelist, he introduced Bristol private eye Jack Shepherd in *Closing the Distance*. *Changing the Odds* is the second Jack Shepherd thriller. Born in northeast England, he now lives in Bristol. He is a member of BAFTA and the Crime Writers Association.

Visit
www.jeffdowson.co.uk

ALSO BY JEFF DOWSON

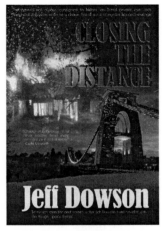

CLOSING THE DISTANCE

Bristol private eye Jack Shepherd has paid a price to become the man he is. The death of his wife, an only recently mended relationship with his daughter and a shooting which resulted in his resignation from the police force.

His new client, Deborah Thorne makes a bizarre request – "Find me". And promptly disappears. A body surfaces in the mud of the Severn estuary; Philip Soames, an uber-expensive shrink, previously a client of Shepherd, and recently his new client's therapist.

Shepherd comes up against a local villain who is also looking for Deborah and punching above his weight as a dog fight promoter and the UK end of a trafficking business run by a pair of ex-pat Serbs. And he slides into conflict with an old friend, the Superintendent in charge of the Soames murder case.

Shepherd battles to stay on the right side of the law, as he struggles to locate his client. In the process, he unearths a story which goes back 12 years to a bloody massacre in a Kosovan village. Finally, all the pieces come together in a series of brutal encounters in the Forest of Dean.